THE LAST ASSET

and Other Stories

by

Jim Lindberg

Breezeway Books

This book is entirely a product of the author's imagination and all incidents, locations, characters, and names are used as fiction. Any similarity to actual events or to people, living or dead, is purely coincidental.

ISBN: 978-1-62550-593-4 (PB)

Library of Congress Control Number: 2008903848

THE LAST ASSET

and Other Stories

This book is for my mom and dad
who never got to read any of my stories.

TABLE OF CONTENTS

Introduction

The tales you are about to experience are all adventures, written just to be fun to read. I'd like to take a few moments to tell you why there is such variety in these stories and then a few moments more to give you a taste of what is yet to come.

You see, I am a really lucky fella because at a young age I got hooked on reading for entertainment. Children's storybooks, comic books, and the work of guys like O. Henry, Zane Gray, or Louis L'Amour. The kind of stories that were a nice contrast to the "study reading" that I had to do to get through school. I have spent many years pursuing different occupations in far corners of our world, in its great cities, small towns, its ranches, and in its desert and mountain wildernesses where I've met a lot of pretty interesting folks. And long ago I found that as enjoyable as reading short stories was, it was even more fun to write them. Now the kinds of stories I like to write are adventures, inspired by unusual people I have met in various nooks and crannies of our planet. I would hear about some peculiar event and think, wow, if that had gone down a little differently look what might have happened!

You see, writing fiction inspired by real life just naturally leads to a lot of variety, like the thirty tales you will find in these pages. Many of these stories are set in our current day like "The Last Asset," the title story for this collection. It tells how, without ever leaving her seat on an airline flight to Germany, a brand new federal agent finds her first assignment to be as short and memorable as any her career could ever offer. Others are Americana, set in the days of the old west, or the era of steam locomotives and newfangled motorcars. And in between are stories about wartime enemies who find that they must cooperate just to survive. There are tales about secrets from deep in someone's past, like one about Montana's Little Big Horn battlefield with its dozens of little white markers; there aren't really any graves there now—are there? Or, if you were a modern businessman buying a tavern from an old barkeep, wouldn't you like to know how the place got its peculiar name?

Within these pages you're going to see how one young boy got a mysterious addition to his coin collection and elsewhere how another suddenly got his chance to become a real newspaper reporter. You will read about a pilot or two facing surreal, unforgettable experiences in the wild blue yonder, and I'll tell you why an old cowboy is desperate to get home. And elsewhere you will find lighthearted humor, a bit of romance, and now and then just a touch of the supernatural.

Now, sit back, relax, and enjoy your ride through these adventures, perhaps with a glass of wine by the fireplace or with peanuts, a cold drink, and a pleasant meal on a long airline flight.

THE LAST ASSET[1]

Sometimes there's only one thing left to do

As the 350 ton Boeing's wheels settled ever so gently onto Munich's 4000 meter long runway 26R Jan's attention was diverted to the fire engines and ambulances that swarmed along side the plane as it slowed. In particular she noticed two jeeps with mounted automatic weapons and several green and white Volkswagen vans marked "*Bayerische Polizei.*"

A few feet away and facing Jan another passenger sat in one of the airliner's few rearward facing seats. With his trim, athletic build and alert blue eyes only gray hair and a weather-beaten complexion betrayed the fact that he was past retirement age.

Across the aisle sat two men in expensive western business suits contrasting with white turbans that marked them as citizens of some Middle Eastern country. In the seat nearest the aisle the younger of the two Arabs sat with his head slumped to one side, his mouth open just enough that one might expect snoring at any time. The other, an older and more muscular Arab, sat wide awake in his seat, his dark eyes never wavering from those of the gray haired man who sat across from Jan, holding a Smith & Wesson revolver in his hand.

"Well, school's over," thought Jan as she glanced outside at the blizzard of flashing emergency lights. Emotionally confused about the coming few minutes she couldn't help thinking of how different her world had seemed when she boarded Euroair Flight 502 just a few hours earlier.

---

[1] Published in *Dan River Anthology*, 2004

9:00 p.m., the Previous Evening

With a glance at her flight coupon to verify her seat assignment Jan slid into 17A, a window seat. She was pleased that there was only one other seat between her and the aircraft's left side aisle. She'd have easy access to the aisle with just one passenger to disturb if she wanted to stretch her legs during the long flight from New York to Germany.

Settling in Jan noticed again the turbaned heads of the two passengers seated across the aisle and a few rows ahead of her. The younger of the two men had smiled pleasantly at Jan and said "hello" as she passed. She was surprised at her reaction to the charisma the man had shown in just that simple greeting. His handsome, dark face, and black eyes had reminded her of the actor Omar Sharif starring in one of his younger roles.

Had Jan already read the afternoon newspaper she had picked up in the terminal she would have known that the man's eyes were anything but those of an actor. Abdul was a legitimate delegate to a recent United Nations meeting and a seriously committed man. And behind those eyes an intelligent mind was concerned with matters far beyond the formal affairs of any international diplomatic body.

Abdul's companion, also with a diplomatic passport, was concerned with more immediate matters. Displaying less charm, his emotionless glance at Jan had been a routine, habitual inspection by an unarmed but very competent bodyguard.

As the stream of boarding passengers dried up it appeared that the single seat next to Jan would stay empty. She hoped so. It would be nice to have the extra space on the long flight.

But at the last moment Jan was disappointed to see one late passenger coming down the aisle toward her. An older fellow with short-cut gray hair that suggested a military man. Something vaguely familiar about the passenger made Jan wonder if she had seen him before. He stopped at the empty seat, shoved a scuffed leather briefcase under the seat just ahead, and sat next to Jan.

By the time the aircraft reached its cruising altitude Jan had finished her perusal of her newspapers. She had read the piece about the handsome Arab diplomat seated not far ahead of her and was idly wondering about the world he must live in. Then, as she laid her paper down, she noticed a photograph that her seatmate was examining beside her.

Jan was startled by the small color photo in the stranger's hand, and for good reason. It was a photo of *her* and was just like the one on her commission card in the badge wallet she carried in her purse! She looked at the man's face and saw that he was smiling pleasantly.

"Relax, Miss. Everything is on the level." As the man spoke he laid the photo on the seat tray in front of Jan and from his jacket pocket produced a wallet of his own. "I'm your immediate supervisor for the next few hours during your assignment to Germany."

Looking at the opened badge wallet Jan saw a commission card much like her own bearing the man's likeness and the title "Chief Field Agent George R. Rearden."

"May I please see your identification, Miss Warran? Then I will explain why we are here."

Jan immediately remembered where she had seen the stranger before. In one of her academy classes George Rearden had given a lecture on "Officer Safety on Foreign Soil." Long ago retired, the man seated next to Jan was a legend among her colleagues, one of the most successful field operatives the agency had ever had.

Fumbling through her purse Jan produced the requested document and couldn't help noticing how new the leather of her wallet seemed, and the obviously mint condition of her silver badge. A stark contrast to the battered leather and worn, gold badge displayed by her seatmate.

Taking her hand holding the wallet in his, George Rearden compared Jan's ID photo to the one lying on the seat back tray, noting, as he expected, that they were identical.

Without taking the wallet from Jan's hand he slowly closed it and held her hand around it.

"This credential can get you a great deal of respect and assistance throughout the free world, Miss Warran. It's a valuable asset that demands honor and responsibility—from you." He let go of her hand and slowly closed his own worn wallet before putting it back inside his jacket. "Please, as a favor to an old man who's seen men die for their country, promise me you will never do anything to dishonor that badge."

"No sir, no, I won't," blurted Jan, embarrassed by such an expression of personal feelings from a near stranger.

"I know that your travel orders say that you are assigned to an office in the American Embassy in Munich for the next six months. They will send you on errands around Germany and other countries. Give you a chance to put some street level polish on your language skills. You studied German and Rumanian, right?"

"Yes sir—"

"Well, those are solid assets, partly why the agency hired you. But, for the next few hours I have a problem to deal with and you are going to help me."

"Yes sir, Chief Rearden. Whatever I can do."

"We're not in the office now, Jan, so call me George. Always a low profile in public, right?"

"Right," said Jan, excited about her chance to work even for a short time with such a well-respected individual.

"Your first trip to Germany?"

"Yes, yes sir, it is."

"Well, you're going to like it."

"I'm looking forward to it, Mr.—ah, George. Will you be briefing me about our assignment?" Jan's curiosity about her first official task as a shiny new agent was growing by the minute.

George smiled at her enthusiastic request for a "briefing."

"Not just yet. All I need for you to do is observe. You are here to be a witness to—and not to participate in—events that will occur soon. Not much of an assignment, but one I guarantee you will never forget. And I want to stress, you will *not* be a participant."

"Yes sir, ah, what —"

"Ah, here comes the beverage cart," said George. Would you like a glass of wine? They'll probably be feeding us soon."

"Just coffee for me," said Jan.

"OK, but let me make a suggestion. We left New York just after sunset, and we are flying east at almost half the speed of the sun's passage, so the night will be short. Sunrise will happen sooner than you think and the stewardess—whoops, "flight attendants" we call them now—they will rattle around feeding people again. So, if you want any sleep you don't need caffeine. A little wine or a beer is a better choice."

Then George smiled at the young woman who was doing her best to be proper in the presence of her boss and said, "Don't worry, you're not on the clock right now."

"OK, sounds good to me," said Jan, relaxing some in the presence of a man most academy students had heard of but never expected to meet. When the flight attendant arrived at their seats Jan asked for white wine.

"You wouldn't happen to have a *Weizenbier* on board, would you?" asked George.

"No sir, we have been resupplied in New York with American brands of beer. But on our flights *out* of Munich it's usually available."

"Yeah, that's what I expected," said George with a smile. "Tell ya what, I'll just have some white wine like the lady here."

"Yes sir," said the flight attendant. "I think you are in luck there. We still have some Mösel left from the flight over." She then set out two small green bottles and two plastic wineglasses.

"You know, sir, I don't quite understand. I've heard that you are retired and yet here you are working on some agency project?"

"Well you see," said George, "there are assets that senior employees have that you younger folks don't. One is that you know enough people so that you can get almost any assignment you want. Even out of retirement if you want it badly enough. For the last two years I have been working on a job that I wanted that badly."

Reaching into his worn leather brief case George removed a manila envelope and handed it to Jan.

"This is a summary of the case I have been working. It's not nice reading but it's real, not an academy exercise. It mentions no names and places are vague, so it's not classified. But the message it conveys about the 'subject' is quite valid. The real case file is back at agency headquarters and is about a foot thick."

Jan noticed a hardening of George's manner that made her uncomfortable so she just laid the envelope on her lap and didn't open it.

After a little more casual conversation Jan nerved up with a question she had been wondering about all evening.

"Sir, I hope you don't mind my asking, but—are you married, do you have children?" As she finished the question a subtle change in George's expression made her wish she hadn't asked.

The solidly built man who almost oozed competence and self-confidence seemed to wilt slightly, then said, "No, I have no family—now. Gwendolyn and I were married for thirty-one of the happiest years a man and woman could ask for. We lived much of it in her native England. Then he swallowed once and continued. "Gwenney's been gone these 26 and a half months. She was all I had."

"I'm sorry to hear that, I shouldn't have—"

"No it's all right," said George. But he turned his head away as he spoke and added "After that wine and one American beer I'm ready for some sleep. You ought to get some too." Then he scrunched into as comfortable a position as he could in the airline style seat, facing away from Jan.

Unable to sleep, Jan sat watching her seat companion. She sensed tiredness about him and just a hint of the vulnerability of a sleeping child. She wondered about the thoughts and memories that must be accumulated in the grayed head resting beside her and wished that she had more time to get to know this man who had seen so much and given so much for his country. Remembering the envelope lying on her lap Jan opened it and found a dozen typed pages with an older document attached at the end.

Twenty minutes later Jan sat staring at the pages in her hands. She felt revulsion, excitement, and a little fear as she thought about the factual record of a man referred to as "the subject." She was impressed with the painstaking detail and risky undercover operation that George Rearden had carried out to gather overwhelming evidence against "the subject." Evidence that would get the man convicted of capital murder in any country that had the death penalty. The subject was an intelligent and charismatic sociopath who had taken up both international politics and terrorism as occupations. Though respected in shadowy parts of the Mid East, the man was as dangerous as a rabid wolf at a Sunday School picnic, and had demonstrated that fact by masterminding the destruction of a British airliner over the Aegean Sea just over two years earlier.

Finally, Jan's attention fell to the older document that had accompanied the case summary she had just read. She saw that it was a copy of an airline manifest, a list of several hundred passengers and their nationalities.

Scanning the list she found a single, circled name. Though she half expected to see it, her heart sank as she read "Gwendolyn E. Rearden, United Kingdom."

Jan didn't get much sleep as the next few hours passed. She watched as George squirmed in his seat, snored a little, and slept with a frown that never went away. Jan felt sorry for this man who had lived with the facts in the summary she had read, lived with the personal agony, danger, and professional frustration that she knew he had endured. Frustration that was there because even though the formal case described in the summary had been presented to authorities in several Western countries including the United States, nothing could be done. The subject always managed to travel under the shield of diplomatic immunity whenever he could be found in public.

Shortly, just as George had said, the sun came up and a flight attendant bringing orange juice woke him from what was a sound sleep. "We'll be serving breakfast in just a few minutes," the young German girl promised.

"Good morning," said Jan, as the senior agent quickly gained his composure.

"Well, a jolly good morning to you, young lady." The old man countenance was gone and Jan was speaking with a well-rested, competent colleague who was in a good mood.

George glanced at his wristwatch and said, "OK, about an hour and a half till landing. Almost time for a few words about what I expect of you. But first, let's enjoy a breakfast. Too bad we're not on the ground. I'd treat you to a "*Bauernfrühstück,*" the Bavarian farmer's breakfast with all the trimmings. I sure could use one."

As the two picked at their typical airline fare George said, "I suppose you read the summary I gave you?"

Jan nodded appropriately.

"Well, would it brighten your day to know that you are riding on a commercial airliner that has several of the world's most vicious international terrorists on board?" George grinned at his remark.

Before Jan could reply he added, "Don't worry, this plane is safe and sound. I just couldn't resist the remark. Few people ever have a chance to make or hear such a statement and walk away from it." Then he added, "I am going to visit the boy's room while you see if you can get us some more coffee, OK?"

Jan noticed that George took his brief case with him.

When the senior agent returned and bent to take his seat his suit jacket swung open slightly, enough for Jan to see a handgun in a shoulder holster.

Aware that Jan had noticed the weapon George smiled and whispered, "Getting a handgun on board a commercial airliner these days, even for a federal officer, is only slightly easier than walking on the moon. But in this business you cultivate assets. And I have enough on both sides of the ocean to get it done." Seeing the apprehension on Jan's face he added, "Don't worry, there's not going to be a gunfight."

"Ah, coffee," said George as he looked up to see a flight attendant arriving with a stainless steel pot wrapped in a white towel.

"What do you want me to do?" said Jan, getting nervous about the unorthodox nature of her first assignment.

"Well, now it's time to give you that briefing you asked for last night. As you have no doubt guessed, the subject in that paper is on board this aircraft." As he spoke he saw Jan's eyes jump to the two turbaned heads seated across the aisle a few rows ahead of them

"Very good, young lady and you are right. Just as both you and I are sitting in seats I specifically requested be assigned to us our subject is in a seat I arranged for him. The farthest one ahead in this section, facing a bulkhead just rearward of the galley. And, if you notice carefully, on our side of the aisle are two seats facing rearward, toward our subject. These seats are normally used during landing and take off by the flight attendants. And they command a great view of our two Arab friends, right? Well, those seats will stay empty until I need them."

Jan listened intently to every word George said, caught up in the demeanor of a trained professional briefing a subordinate on a critical mission. No tired old man now and no boyish vulnerability either.

"Now, Miss Warran, as I said your job is to be a witness to events. You are to remain right here for a time and keep my brief case with you. Later you will see me sit in the rearward-facing seat. When I nod to you, you are to move forward and sit in the window seat facing me. And for damn sure, be very careful around those two Mid-Eastern gentlemen across the aisle from us. Just come forward with my briefcase, take your seat and continue to watch and listen. Got it?"

"Yes sir," said Jan.

"And this is important. I want you to understand that the plan we are following is my responsibility. Is that clear?"

"Yes sir, I understand."

"OK, lets finish breakfast and enjoy our coffee. There's plenty of time."

Then, looking at Jan's untouched hard roll, George added, "Wow, a bagel, no less. Can't blame you for not eating it. *Bauernfrühstück*, that's what we should be having."

Then George brought up a new subject.

"I appreciate your help in this job, Miss Warran. And I hope you learn something valuable from your peculiar first assignment. In particular remember what I said about honoring your badge. And there's another thing for you to think about. It's a little philosophical, but in the spirit of a training officer I want to point it out to you."

Jan nodded, listening intently.

"You have heard me mention assets during our time together. Well, you were hired by the agency because of assets you had acquired by education, by birth, and by initiative. The purpose of your academy training was to give you more, and experience will give you more yet.

"I, at the end of a thirty-four year stretch, have assets that you cannot imagine. I have experience, connections, and access to resources and services that are not yet available to you." George looked aside for a moment and collected his thoughts.

"Now here comes the training philosophy that is my gift to you."

"To have a long and productive career you must keep acquiring assets, by continuous training, of course, but most of all by getting acquainted with people. The world is full of all kinds, good and bad, important and insignificant, but all real. And the more folks you get to know the better. You never know when one of them will turn out to be a valuable asset."

Jan, deep in thought, said nothing.

"And, Miss Warran, there is one last asset that all of us have but rarely ever use. That's because it can only be used once. But it's a beauty of a problem solver."

After a long pause where George seemed to have nothing more to say Jan realized that the lecture was done. She wished again that she had more time to get to know the complex man sitting beside her

"Well, Miss Warren—Jan—this is it. I am going forward now and I will depend on you. And remember, when I nod to you to join me all you are to do is listen and observe. Don't talk to me or get in the way and do not let my brief case out of your control. OK?"

"Yes sir, you can count on me."

George stood up and without looking back walked forward toward the seats occupied by the two Arab men. Approaching the left side of Abdul's seat George became a blur of motion. His right hand delivered a crushing blow to the back of the younger man's neck with sufficient force to partially dislodge the Arab's white turban. It was also sufficient to break Abdul's spinal column, killing him instantly. In almost the same motion George drew his Smith & Wesson revolver and pointed it in a two handed grip at the bodyguard seated next to the dead man. The whole process had taken little more than a second, and Jan was not even sure of what she was seeing as she heard George speak. The old agent's voice was strong and commanding as he spoke to Abdul's bodyguard.

"If you move you will be as dead as your boss."

The husky middle-aged professional killer's eyes showed neither fear nor panic, but he did not move. George was facing an extremely dangerous man and did not look away from the Arab's face even for a second as he spoke to the other passengers nearby.

"All right everyone, just relax. This is not a hijacking and everything is all over. None of you will be inconvenienced in any way. I repeat this is not a hijacking. Just stay in your seats."

Then George spoke again to the bodyguard.

"All right fella, your friend is dead. You can't do anything about that and the world is a better place because of it. You understand?"

The Arab gave no response. He just sat radiating vehement hatred focused on George.

Knowing that he was dealing with a committed fanatic who might well give his life in a dramatic act of vengeance, George spoke again.

"Understand this too, mister. Your friend was a mass murderer who unknowingly included my wife in his activities. I have acted as you yourself might do in similar circumstances. Think about that while you make up your mind about what to do."

Still the Arab did not move or speak.

"While you are thinking let me explain. This revolver is loaded with low velocity cartridges designed to destroy human anatomy with minimum risk to the pressure hull of this aircraft. And if you move I will use all six to make you a live, but useless cripple in a great deal of agony."

Then George backed away toward the empty seat across the aisle where he would have a good view of the bodyguard. Recognizing a resigned attitude in the Arab's countenance, George sat down and nodded to Jan who had been fixated on the whole series of events.

George knew that one of the flight attendants had already notified the flight deck about what she had seen, and that already a hijack alert message would have been transmitted to air traffic control authorities. And as he expected, a uniformed male crewmember soon came down the aisle toward the rear of George's seat.

"Step over to my left where I can see you," ordered George. As the man did so George noticed the three silver stripes on the man's pale blue uniform sleeve indicating that he was the aircraft's copilot.

George, speaking clearly and calmly in excellent German, said, "This is not a hijacking. I have no interest in interfering with your operation of this aircraft in any way. I am a private citizen who has acted without the knowledge or authority of any government. Do you understand me?"

The young, blond pilot nodded and started to speak, but George continued.

"I have just one request. I want you to stop the plane in a safe area, have a mobile stair brought to the door just behind me, and open that door so that I may deplane without being any further inconvenience to you. Understand?"

Again a nod from the copilot.

"Then I suggest you pick up the public address microphone in the galley behind you and calm your passengers. You may tell them that you are completely in control of the aircraft and that there will be no further disturbance."

The copilot watched George for a second, then disappeared into the galley and the announcement George suggested was heard by all passengers, first in German and then again in accented English. Still watching the Arab bodyguard carefully, George spoke to Jan.

"Well, Miss Warran, I'm sorry you had to see all this but I wanted to be sure there was a competent witness to all events and to the conversation you just heard."

Jan said nothing.

"Now, please open my brief case. Inside you will find a letter from me to the agency. Please see that it is delivered to the proper people."

Jan opened the case and took a single sheet of paper out of a plain white envelope. It was a letter of resignation signed by George Rearden, dated a few hours earlier on the previous day. The only other object in the brief case was the worn leather wallet containing George's badge and commission card.

Speaking softly to Jan as he watched the Arab, George said, "I retired from the agency with that badge in my pocket and I expected to die of old age with it as a symbol of my service to the Western world. But, things don't always work out. Please notice, Miss Warran, that my recent actions were those of a private citizen without a badge or commission card to dishonor."

The Boeing completed its descent down the approach glide slope and touched down on the runway. As it rolled to a stop George spoke again to Jan.

"It's a hell of a world we've built, Miss Warran. Here we have a multiple mass murderer who is treated as a diplomat, like royalty, and in spite of the most solid legal proof any court could ask for there is nothing that civilized governments can do about the menace he represents."

There was a slight bump outside the door of the plane that had now come to a stop, and the same copilot George had spoken to earlier opened the passenger door, then stepped back out of George's way.

"Well Jan," said George, "It's been nice working with you and I appreciate your help. Keep a good moral compass and have a good life. Let's hope that you never have to make choices involving the final asset."

As George spoke Jan saw again fleeting images of a tired old man and a vulnerable, idealistic boy in George's solid face.

"Now I have just one thing left to do," said George. "I want to be sure that there is no spectacular trial to embarrass my country."

Then he stood, and motioning toward the Arab guard with the palm of his left hand, he shoved the revolver into his waistband and with his hands on top of his head stepped out the door of the aircraft into a blaze of lights from emergency vehicles.

Against a bulkhead across the aisle Jan could see George's shadow as he began walking down the steps. She shoved her open palms against her eyes and curled into a helpless ball in her seat, waiting for what she hoped would not happen.

But near the bottom of the stairs George lowered his right hand toward his belt. Jan whimpered as she heard a short volley of automatic gunfire, and she knew that Chief Field Agent George Rearden had just paid the price for having used his last asset.

CANDIDO'S BELL

A lighthearted adventure in Mexico's Sierra Madre

March, 1970, El Paso, Texas

With a notebook in his hand Danny Spencer waved as he saw a fellow University of Texas student enter the crowded coffee shop.

"Hey Paulo baby, over here!"

Along with everybody else nearby Paul Martinez noticed Danny and he joined his former roommate at a table where Danny sat eating a beef burrito.

"OK Paulo, you ready to go adventuring again?"

Danny's loud manner of speaking reminded Paul of why he had chosen a different roommate for his last year as an undergraduate engineering student. Paul disliked being noticed in public and with Danny you were always near the center of attention.

"Hey Danny, what's up?" Paul said as he took a seat at the table.

"Well, you remember my chick Lucille, right?"

"Ah, the bubble gum girl." Paul had never cared much for Lucille's constant habit of cracking gum as she chewed, and even blowing small bubbles.

"She had me go with her to a lecture on Mexican history last night—some visiting prof from the University of Chihuahua. Interesting guy, talked a lot about that revolution a hundred years ago."

"You mean when Benito Juarez threw out Emperor Maximilliano, right?."

"Yeah, right. And he talked about how with so much 'revolting' going on towns would hide stuff in churches, in statues and things. And that got me to thinking about what your grandfather—Candy or something you said his name was—said about a gold bell. Is he still around?"

"C'mon Danny, his name was Candido, you know that and he died when I was a little kid. He was named after his own grandfather, the guy who made the bell. And that bell stuff is just an old family story anyway."

"Yeah, well maybe and maybe not. You know what town he was from don't you?"

"Sure. A village called Aguachic down on the Comandaro River. Mostly Indians live there; it's Tarahumara country."

"See, the Comandaro River, that's in the Sierra Madre Mountains, gold mining country, right?"

"Yeah—"

"Well, there you are. We're off in search of the 'Golden Bell,' or at least to check out a few chicks and the local night life," said Danny with a toss of his head that ruffled his wavy blond hair.

Danny's Richard Widmark grin and good-natured excitement made the idea seem attractive to Paul, although he chuckled a bit inside when he thought about what the "night life" would be in a small village back in Mexico's Sierra Madre. But, in spite of Paul's self consciousness riding in the flashy candy-apple red Chevy Blazer Danny's well-to-do parents had paid for, the two had shared some fine trips down into Old Mexico.

"Well, spring break is coming up and—"

"Right on Paulo, just like I said, we're off to go adventuring."

Paul hadn't been much interested in his grandfather's imaginary bell but trips to Mexico with Danny were always fun and it would be nice to see his family's old home town. And what if Grandfather Candido was right after all? Paul sat back in his chair and started thinking about what life might have been like for his great *great* grandfather more than a century earlier in Old Mexico.

Year of 1863,
Village of Aguachic, Mexico

Despite his sixty odd years Candido Martinez Duran labored hard at one of his many trades, that of making adobe bricks. In a pit he used his bare feet to stomp straw, water, and soil into mud of just the right composition and consistency. He would then shovel the mud into wooden forms to shape adobe bricks, each half a meter on a side and as thick as his two fists when placed together. Later, when they were sufficiently hardened, he would carefully dump the bricks out one at a time and stand them on edge where they could air dry into one of the finest wall construction materials known to Northern Mexico. Candido prided himself on his neat rows of drying bricks and on the geometrically perfect adobe walls he could build from them.

Candido's white, cotton clothes made his weather-beaten skin seem as dark as old saddle leather. His ebony eyes peered out from under the broad brim of his straw hat to notice little Manuelito running toward him.

"Señior Martinez, Señior Martinez," called the young boy. "Father Conti wants you."

"Ah, more talk about the revolution," thought Candido as he hopped out of his mud pit and rolled down the legs of his clean *pantalones*.

As Candido walked toward the nearby church people greeted him with extra respect, for Candido had gone to a church school when he was young and could read and write a few words.

Candido stepped into the small adobe chapel and, holding his wide brimmed, sombrero in front of him, stood quietly at the back of the ten rows of wooden benches that served as pews. Father Conti, who had been watching for this village elder, strode toward Candido with a smile.

"Thank you for answering my call so promptly my son." The priest's black vestments made a swishing sound as he moved.

"Of course Padre, I have nothing more important than to answer a servant of God," said Candido. As he spoke he felt uncomfortable being called "my son" by a man who was at least thirty years his junior. And he felt a sense of formality speaking to a stranger who had only recently been assigned by a distant Bishop to minister to Candido's village.

"For these past weeks," began Father Conti, "I have been privileged to care for the spiritual lives of the eighty-seven souls of our village. But once again I find myself seeking your counsel in a more corporeal matter having to do with the earthly welfare of my parishioners."

"I will help you if I can," replied Candido, wishing that the priest would speak more plainly and wondering what the words "corporeal" and "parishioners" meant.

"Let us be seated in the rectory," said Father Conti, waving his black robed arm toward one of two small rooms behind the modest wood altar. "I think it is a little cooler there."

Candido wondered how the priest could be cool anywhere in the Mexican summertime inside his black robes.

The room the two entered was square, barely four meters on a side. In one corner was a simple bed much like one might find in a monastery. Two chairs made from palm fronds woven onto mahogany frames and a four-drawer chest made of the same wood were the only furnishings in the room. As Candido sat in the chair nearest the door Father Conti took a seat right beside the chest.

"I am sure, my son, that you know that Señior Juarez's bandits are becoming more active in this area as they continue their unreasonable defiance of Emperor Maximilliano's government. It is possible that they may visit our village in search of resources, don't you agree?"

Again wrestling with Father Conti's large words, Candido just nodded.

"You know that we have saved a tidy amount from tithing by parishioners on occasions of good fortune in the gold panning business."

There was that word "parishioners" again, but Candido was able to understand what the priest was talking about. It was the the gold dust and nuggets that were stored in the bottom drawer of the chest beside Father Conti.

As a young man long before he came to Aguachic as a carpenter Candido had seen the benefits of education and even now thought of the teaching of reading and writing as the only useful reason for having a church around anyway. Candido and several other townspeople hoped to use the gold to build a schoolhouse and bring in someone to teach the children of their village.

"We surely have enough now to build a tower for our church," continued the priest. "One with a proper bell with which to call God's flock to mass."

"And perhaps there is enough that someone can be brought here to teach our children?" said Candido.

"Well, when we have demonstrated to the Bishop that we are worthy and in need of such things, then God will provide."

As Candido fidgeted in his chair holding his sombrero In his lap, Father Conti opened one drawer of the chest and took out a leather travel case bearing the words "Aguachic Parish" in dark ink on its surface.

"I have your table almost finished," said Candido, embarrassed that the priest had no desk to work from. "I work on it as my bricks dry."

Candido, proud of his skills as a carpenter as well as a brick maker, had volunteered to build a table for use in the rectory.

"Thank you, my son; the church will be that much better for your efforts. But right now I have a greater concern.

"Since the insurrection that I spoke of earlier has reached even our small corner of Mexico I fear that bandits might discover the church's modest treasure."

"Or Maximilliano's soldiers might find it," added Candido.

"Yes, I suppose there is that possibility, but I regard the real hazard to be the Juarista bandits reported to be nearby. I think it is time that precautions be taken to safeguard this church property."

"I think it is the property of the village as well, don't you Father?"

"Yes, of course. In any case I am proposing that you and I, with little knowledge of anyone else, implement a plan I have conceived to hide the gold in the form of a bell."

"A bell? How does one hide gold in a bell?"

"My plan will require prompt action and some small sacrifice on your part, my son. I propose that we let it be known that your considerable skills as a bricklayer are to be used to build a proper bell tower for our church. I know that you have traveled beyond this village and are knowledgeable of city ways. I think you can carry out my plan."

"I do not under—"

"No, my son, I am sure you do not. But here is what I am asking, in the name of your church, for you to do."

With that the priest opened the heavy leather case and removed a calfskin bag closed by a rawhide drawstring. It was heavy enough to be awkward when handled by Father Conti using both hands. Gently pushing Candido's straw hat aside he laid the pouch in the old man's hands as they rested on his lap.

Candido's eyes rounded as he felt the weight of the leather bag, and the burden of responsibility it put on his shoulders and heart as well.

"My son, you are an honest man, and a skilled craftsman. I think that you can take this gold to the foundry in Chihuahua City and have it cast into the form of a church bell. And promptly on your return you can complete a *campanile*, a tower where the bell can be installed and where it is not likely to attract the attention of people whose hearts are more in league with the devil."

"I think such a plan has dangers Father. And I am a busy man. I have bricks to remove from their frames; I have your table to finish I—"

"Sometimes Gods work is inconvenient my son. I ask—I would like to say require—that you prepare to travel soon."

The two spoke more about how a bell could be cast and decided that it should be painted dull green to give it the appearance of an old bronze bell as a precaution during Candido's travels. Candido left the little adobe church carrying the heavy bag at his side covered by his sombrero as he walked home. He had agreed with Father Conti to travel to Chihuahua and get a bell.

That evening Candido talked to his wife, Amilita, about his conversation with Father Conti.

"*Mi Querida*, I have bad feelings about Father Conti. He is new to our village. He is not an *Indio*, he is not even Mexican. He is an *Italiano* from the church in Rome. I know little of such things, but I do not believe that a church so far away can be interested in the children of our little village. But I do believe that it can be interested in gold."

"*Ay mi esposo*," Father Conti is our priest! Do not question such things when he tells you what God wants."

Not at all as sure that churches and God had as much connection as his wife might believe, Candido still felt uncomfortable. As he and Amilita shared a meal of corn tortillas, cheese, and roasted goat meat he thought more about his problem.

"I think that Father Conti trusts the soldiers of Maximilliano too much. I am afraid that even if we hide the gold in a bell our new priest will not be able to keep such a thing secret from the church people in Mexico City, a town that belongs to Maximilliano. And his soldiers are foreigners not of these mountains, like Presedente Juarez's *indios* are."

Deep in thought Candido continued his meal in silence. Finally he stood up and held his wife's face between his own callused hands and spoke to her again.

"*Mi Amilita*, I have decided what must be done. I must get a bell as Father Conti has asked. That I must do. And above all else we must keep the gold of Aguachic safe so that it can be used to bring a teacher for our chidren."

Six days later Candido left the village of Aguachic in a horse drawn wagon on his way to Chihuahua City. Father Conti had wanted him to go much sooner but Candido had insisted on finishing his batch of bricks and the table for Father Conti's rectory, and on building a wooden yoke on which the bell could be mounted on his return and rung for all the town to hear. Candido would then build a bell tower and install the yoke there.

March, 1970,
University Spring Break

Two days of travel took Paul and Danny well into Mexico's Sierra Madre Mountains. Near evening they arrived in the village of Aguachic and found a place to camp under some trees near the Comandaro River which ran through the valley. Leaving the truck with their equipment the pair walked into the little town to find the church. Paul, fascinated with his family's old town, was taking in sights and sounds from all around.

"Ask somebody where the church is," said Danny.

"Oh Danny, that bell stuff was just a story my grandfather used to tease us kids. Let's just find someplace to eat and enjoy the local village life, OK?"

"Hey, where's the church, anyhow," asked Danny of a young boy who was watching the strangers.

Paul repeated the question in Spanish and got just a scrawny outstretched arm for an answer as the boy scurried away. They walked in the indicated direction and came to a tree-lined, grassy area with a raised concrete platform near its center. At the far end of the little plaza was a small adobe building with a Christian cross perhaps two feet tall painted on the stucco over its door.

"That's a church?" said Danny.

"Sure it is," said Paul. "This isn't downtown El Paso, you know. Now, what are you going to do, walk up and ask the padre if they've got any gold bells?"

"No way man, we gotta have a story. We'll tell him we're antique collectors interested in historical artifacts—you know, old church stuff.

We want to buy their old bell or maybe trade a new, better one for it. What do ya think?"

"It's nearly dark now," said Paul. Let's fix something to eat then come back in the morning, OK?"

Year of 1863,
Village of Aguachic, Mexico

With a heavy heart Candido Martinez Duran stood beside the yolk he had built to let his fellow villagers hear the ring of the new church bell he had brought from Chihuahua City. But the bell had produced a poor sound and had even cracked on the third attempt to ring it loudly. This had surprised Candido. He didn't know that bells had to be cast of a special alloy if they were to have a proper sound, and this bell was definitely not cast of the proper metal. No, not at all. Candido knew that his fellow villagers had expected better work from him.

Using his horse drawn wagon Candido moved the bell to a corner of the storage room next to the rectory. Father Conti, not at all concerned with the bell's poor performance, nodded pleasantly as he watched Candido work. "Please, my son, come to my rectory when you are finished," he said.

After piling some other stored items around the bell to keep it out of sight, Candido stepped into the rectory where he found Father Conti sitting at the square, wood table that Candido had finished before his trip to Chihuahua City.

"Ah, there you are, my son," said the priest. "I think we have done what we can to protect our treasure, don't you agree?"

Again, standing as before with his sombrero held in both hands in front of his snow-white, cotton clothing Candido felt odd being called "son."

"Yes Father, I agree. The gold of Aguachic is now as safe as it can be. When better times come then It can be used to build a school."

Father Conti thanked Candido for his efforts and Candido politely took his leave to go home to his Amilita and the dinner she would be preparing. And perhaps she would allow him just a small cup of *mescal* after their meal.

Aguachic, Mexico, 1970

"Hey, up and at 'em," yelled Danny as he woke Paul from a comfortable sleep in the back of Danny's Chevy Blazer. "We got things to do, man."

It was the morning after their arrival in Aguachic and all Paul wanted was to see if anyone remembered his grandfather Candido, maybe even old great *great* grandfather Candido.

But Danny had other things on his mind. "I want to find the priest and see if they have any bells in that majestic cathedral we saw yesterday."

"C'mon Danny. Don't make fun of the church. It's small because the town is small, but it is a church and it's just as real as any other one."

"Oops, sorry, Paulo, I keep forgetting this is your old home town!"

Half an hour later the two students had found the village's only priest, a frail fellow with pure white hair named Father Holguin. Paul, speaking Spanish, had introduced himself and Danny to the elderly gentleman. The three sat in the rectory in simple mahogany and leather chairs around an old table made from hand-hewn lumber. The priest had indeed heard of Paul's ancestor and mentioned several local people who were Paul's distant relatives.

Finally, getting impatient with the meaningless Spanish conversation, Danny asked if Father Holguin spoke English.

"Yes I do, my son."

"Hey, great. You see, I'm interested in church artifacts, bells and stuff like that. We're down here trying to find an old church bell that we could take back home for my fraternity's dining hall. It would be cool to have a genuine antique bell to call the guys to dinner."

Paul sat back in his chair with a frown, embarrassed at Danny's somewhat "Ugly American" behavior.

With a smile for Paul, Father Holguin said, "Our church is too small for a bell of any kind, let alone a belfry to put one in. I think to find such 'antiques,' as you call them, you would have to go to a market in a large city, perhaps even to Mexico City itself."

Danny sat back from the old table, disappointed. Paul turned the conversation again to the village's history, and he and Father Holguin resumed their use of Spanish.

A few minutes later Paul had thanked Father Holguin for his help and the two boys started toward the door of the small church."

"Oh just a moment my sons," called Father Holguin. "Talking to you about your ancestor—the gentleman named Candido—reminded me of some words I came across in records left by one of my predecessors. Perhaps we do have something that you might like to see. It is in our store room just over here."

Father Holguin opened the door to the building's only other room and said, "I think there is an old bell in here somewhere. But not a real one."

"Hey, cool!" Danny quickly joined the priest, excited by what the room might hold.

After moving some dusty boxes Father Holguin pointed toward one corner. About a foot tall, crudely cast and a little lopsided, sat a dull green bell-shaped object.

"It is not a proper church bell at all and as you can see it is cracked. My predecessor at the time it was made recorded that it was not usable. Give me a moment to look into the records; perhaps I can learn more."

Father Holguin then returned to the rectory where he opened a drawer on the same ancient wood cabinet that Father Conti had used to hold the village gold long ago.

While the priest was gone Danny used his pocketknife to scratch an inconspicuous place on the lip of the bell. What he found was bright, yellow metal under the dirty-green painted surface.

"Woo-eee, look at that Paulo old buddy."

Paul did indeed look, and had to admit that maybe his grandfather's story was true after all.

Both boys straightened up from their examination of the bell as they heard Father Holguin returning from the rectory.

Smiling at Paul and holding a dark, leather-bound book the priest said, "We are in luck. I found something more about your ancestor."

"It appears, from personal notes made by Father Conti in the year of 1863, that a gentleman named Candido Martinez Duran did much construction work for the church and throughout the village. He even built the modest furniture that we find today in my rectory." Looking at Paul, he added, "Señior Martinez was a well-respected citizen of the village of Aguachic."

"It was Señior Martinez who was sent to Chihuahua City to purchase a bell for this church. It was to have been installed in a bell tower that he was planning to build. It seems, however, that other than a large pile of adobe bricks that he stacked at the rear of the church to be used in the bell tower he accomplished very little. The bell that he brought from Chihuahua was tested in the plaza and found to be unusable, having cracked badly."

"Well," said Paul. "That's probably the bell—"

Danny interrupted Paul with an inconspicuous elbow to the ribs.

"There is more," said Father Holguin, raising his hand to adjust the spectacles he had also brought from the rectory.

"It seems, Paulito, that your ancestor fell upon hard times. Father Conti notes that not long after testing the bell Señior Martinez suffered a stroke and thus spent his remaining days with much diminished mental capacity. He did little more than wander about the village telling people that 'It is in the stump.' No one knew what he meant."

"In the stump. A tree stump?" asked Paul. "What was in the stump?"

"Ah, that is not clear. Father Conti wrote that a modest quantity of gold had been entrusted to Señior Martinez, who was after all a respected village elder, for purposes of purchasing a bell. Father Conti suggests further that Señior Martinez was either robbed or deceived in his purchase in Chihuahua City and lost the gold, or perhaps stole it himself."

"Sadly, it is written that during his last few months of life Señior Martinez was scorned by the citizens as a fool who lost or stole the village treasure. When pressed for information about the matter all the old gentleman could do was mutter something about a secret being 'in the stump'."

"Hey-hey," said Danny. "Seems we've got a genuine treasure tale right here in beautiful downtown Aguachic! Somebody scammed the church collection plate money and hid it in a tree."

"Danny, knock it off, church records are not a joke. You should—"

"No no, my son, your friend is right. Many people tried in vain to find whatever small treasure there might be by digging up stumps or dead trees all around the village. I know this because the village has an old rumor about a lost treasure hidden in a tree. I have always thought of it as just a story for old men to tell in the plaza."

"Did anyone find anything?" asked Danny.

"I doubt it," laughed Father Holguin. "At least the church records offer nothing more on the matter."

The three chatted more about the old bell they were looking at, with Danny trying to hide his excitement about the yellow color he had found earlier when he scratched the old relic.

"Father, I am still interested in this old junk bell, just as an antique. Would you consider selling it?" asked Danny.

"I doubt it is worth selling; it cannot be worth more than scrap metal and I am not authorized to sell church property without 'going through channels' as you Americans might say."

"Gee, we sure would like to have it Mr.—ah Father Hoguin. See, it would be a sentimental thing for Paulo here, what with it being part of his family history and—"

"Oh Danny, leave it alone; It belongs here in the church," said Paul with a sheepish glance at Father Holguin.

"Hey I've got an idea," continued Danny. "How about a trade? We'll go back to the States and get you guys a first rate bell and trade for this junk one. We'll get one that works and sounds fine," said Danny.

"Hmm," muttered the old priest. "Perhaps a trade like that could be done. But it seems like a lot of trouble for you over a piece of 'junk' as you call it."

"Scrap metal with a personal story to it," said Danny. "A cool thing in our fraternity house and all."

"Well, I have some parishioners to visit yet this afternoon and it is already midday. I will think about your idea and we will talk of it again in the morning."

Half an hour later the boys were back at their campsite beside Danny's truck, talking about what they had learned.

"That bell's gotta be the gold; that's why nobody ever found it," said Danny. And that's why the thing didn't ring right. Made of gold it's bound to sound off-key or something."

"Maybe we should just tell Father Holguin what my grandfather Candido said and—"

"No way, man. I can buy these guys all the bells they want. We gotta get that green thing; it could be worth a fortune and the Catholic Church has all the billions it needs. They won't miss one old bell."

"Maybe you're right. It would make a great story and all," said Paul sitting with his chin on his knees, his back against one of the Chevy's wheels.

"Sure, and we'll hang it up in our frat house for awhile, for kicks, OK?"

"Your fraternity house man. I live in the dorm, remember?"

"Yeah, OK. Anyway, it would be our bell, you and me together old buddy. You just gotta help me get that old guy to agree to trade."

"Father Holguin is an ordained priest. Don't call him an 'old guy.' You could show a little more respect if you want to get that bell."

"OK, OK. But the bell's what we came here for, right?"

"Yeah I guess," said Paul. "Tomorrow we'll see what Father Holguin wants to do. I want to go see him for confession anyway."

"Confession? You're going to confession down here? Jesus, I didn't know you were such a dedicated 'mackerel snapper,' man."

"Knock of the cool dude crap Danny. I'm gonna take a walk; I have relatives down here you know!" Then Paul stomped off in the direction of town.

In the little adobe church Father Holguin sat at the wood table examining the records left by Father Conti more than a hundred years earlier. He was thinking about old Candido Martinez Duran who had built furniture for the church, probably even the very table Father Holguin was sitting at. Stretching out his arms, he put one hand on either side of the thick, mahogany tabletop and held it as he thought about the man who made it. According to the records the old fellow also made a pile of adobe bricks for construction of a bell tower.

Father Holguin sat back for a moment then stood up and walked outside and around behind the church where he found a mound of dirt against the back wall of the building. Since the structure was built on flat ground the little hill, perhaps three feet above the surrounding land and maybe 20 feet long, seemed out of place.

Smiling, with his hands clasped behind his back, Father Holguin went back inside the church and looking through the rectory door he saw again Candido's old table. This time he noticed something that he had not given any thought to the hundreds of other times he had seen that table. The top was a slab of thick, wood boards, hewn by hand. But the stand itself was an evenly sawn section of a tree trunk. It had been cut from a large tree, one larger than any around the village now.

A section of a tree trunk, thought Father Holguin. Sitting on end to hold the tabletop, it was almost a tree stump. With a smile the old priest thought of a demented old man's words about a secret that was "In the stump."

It took Father Holguin a few minutes to find a rusty pipe wrench that he could use to remove the four iron screws that held the tabletop to the section of the old tree. That evening he sought out two villagers who he knew were experienced prospectors. He told Manolo and Enrique that the church had a special job for them.

Five Weeks Later in Aguachic, Mexico

Having almost completed their second visit to Aguachic, Danny and Paul were ready to head back to El Paso. In the back of Danny's Blazer was the old, green bell that Candido Martinez had hauled by wagon from Chihuahua so long ago. Father Holguin had been happy to trade the old bell for the one the boys had brought with them. The new bell, cast of bronze and polished to a brilliant finish, would no doubt produce a proper tone. Though it was expensive, Danny had paid for the bell himself.

"Time for celebration old buddy; we really scored on that one!" Then, noticing that Paul was quieter than usual, Danny added, "Don't be such a downer, man."

"I think I'm gonna walk around the town a little, kind of say good-by." Then Paul ambled up the village road leaving Danny with two young boys who were fascinated with the bright red paint and shiny chrome of Danny's Chevy.

Remembering that he had not gone to confession as he had planned last time he was there Paul decided to visit Father Holguin one more time.

Since there was no confessional booth Paul just sat with Father Holguin in the rectory. As Paul spoke the real reason for visiting Aguachic just bubbled out. Father Holguin listened patiently as the troubled young man even suggested that perhaps they should put the old bell back where it had been for so many years.

When Paul finished he just sat quietly, looking at Father Holguin who sat with a nondescript expression. The priest let Paul squirm in silence for a time, then smiled.

"My son, your words have pleased me very much and have taken a disappointment from my shoulders."

"What—"

"No no, let me finish. Let me show you an interesting old document that I was not aware of during your previous visit. Here, help an old man lift this table top if you will."

Paul had not noticed that the four iron bolts were gone from the old table, and all the two needed to do was lift the heavy mahogany top off.

"There," said Father Holguin with a sweep of his hand. "There you have the 'stump' that your great great grandfather spoke of during his last days." Then he reached into the hollow center part of the old tree section and removed a large folded paper, yellowed with age, and handed it to Paul.

Paul carefully unfolded the paper and saw writing in faint letters. Looking up he indicated that the note was beyond his ability to read the handwritten Spanish.

"You need not read it, my son. I will tell you its message. It was written by Señior Martinez in the days just before he traveled to Chihuahua to obtain a bell, as Father Conti had instructed him to do.

"You see, your ancestor did not trust the church of his time and wanted to protect the 'village treasure' as he calls it, from both Juarista rebels and Maximilliano's soldiers. So he did not follow the plan conceived by Father Conti. He did not take the gold to Chihuahua, and he did not steal it.

"When you were here before perhaps you noticed—no, probably not, it was behind the church. Anyway, Señior Martinez hid the treasure—gold dust and small nuggets— by mixing it into the adobe bricks he made, supposedly for use in constructing a bell tower. I believe that he spent his remaining days accused of theft and trying to explain to anyone who would listen, but God had sealed his lips."

Father Holguin then patted his hand against the solid adobe wall just to the right of his chair.

"Just behind this wall was a mound of dirt, the weathered remains of Señior Martinez's pile of bricks. Recently it has received the attention of trusted villagers, and the gold has been recovered."

"My God," muttered Paul, and then blushed at his words.

"What was my grandfather going to do with the gold?"

"From Señor Martinez's note it is clear that he had one purpose all along. He wanted the gold to be used to build a school for the village children, so they could learn to read as he had done."

"How much gold was there?"

"I think by American standards it is modest, but from our local point of view it is adequate to build the school Señor Martinez wanted and to provide for a small bell tower for our church as well, one that will hold the fine bronze bell you and your friend Daniel have delivered to us."

"But what about the old bell?"

Father Holguin laughed and answered, "Take it home with you with my blessing. Indeed, your friend Daniel will be disappointed to find that its yellow metal is brass and other scrap metal, but it can be used to call fellows at meal time as he suggested. He should find that to be 'cool' is that not so?"

"As I mentioned, Paulito, I am pleased that you were not so quick to practice deceit as was your friend Danny. I had hoped you would talk to me. Next spring we will have completed construction of our schoolhouse and bell tower and I think you and Daniel should come here to hear your bell ring. And at that time I will show you the name Candido Martinez Duran engraved on it."

Half an hour later Paul told Danny about the bell they were hauling home.

"Aw what the heck," said Danny. "It is an antique with a pretty nifty story and we did have another adventure, hey Paulo?"

"Sure did, and we can stop off for a little of that 'night life' in Chihuahua City on the way back," said Paul, glad that Danny's natural good nature had prevailed over his disappointment.

As they drove away from the village of Aguachic Father Holguin's last words, "*Vaya con Dios, mis hijos,*" kept running through Paul's mind.

THE ADVENTURERS

Bilbo Baggins would know about such things

Jason lay still, listening to the waves of the English Channel lapping at the sides of his rubber raft. It had been four hours since the brilliant beam, like a burst of sunlight, had suddenly shattered the nighttime darkness. A searchlight had illuminated his Royal Navy patrol boat for mere seconds before a crashing explosion from a German submarine's deck gun destroyed the craft. Jason had heard voices from his fellow crewmen in another life raft, but they were too far away to make contact in the dark. Since that time he had been drifting alone, miles away from land.

Jason was thankful for two things. One was that the summertime weather was unseasonably warm and calm, almost guaranteeing a quick rescue—by someone. The other was that the dark of night was melting away into the dawn of a new day.

Somewhere to the northeast Jason heard the sound of an aircraft engine. He grabbed a flare pistol from its stowed location in the raft, but then put it away when he made out the ungainly shape of a Fieseler Storch, a German light observation plane. The pilot continued on course toward the southwest, apparently uninterested in the yellow raft that must have been visible against the gray water even though the sun was not fully up yet.

Jason was having serious doubts about his decision to leave home to help England in its fight against the aggression of Hitler's Germany. What had been an exciting idea was now looking foolhardy. Still, with the optimism of a 19-year-old, he was sure some surface vessel would pick him up soon.

About an hour later Jason heard the engine sounds again, coming from the southwest. Staring in that direction he saw the same aircraft returning along its original rout. Helplessly exposed in the now brilliant sunshine, Jason waited and watched.

Then he noticed just a faint trail of smoke coming from the plane. Suddenly the smoke trail became heavy and dark and the pilot made a descending turn toward the little raft. Jason watched in awe as the plane crashed into the water a few hundred meters away.

It took Jason half an hour to row his raft to the crash site. What he found was little more than one of the plane's landing floats and the smell of gasoline in the air. And a leather-jacketed arm draped over the aluminum float.

Jason paddled to the other side of the float, where he found the semiconscious pilot bobbing in the water like any other piece of wreckage. Only his inflated life jacket was keeping him from drowning. With great difficulty Jason hauled the pilot into the raft and left him in a heap at one end. Fortunately the German was not a large man.

Seconds later the fellow coughed up more water and opened his eyes. When he saw Jason's British uniform his right hand went toward a shoulder holster under his left arm. When he realized the holster was empty the half drowned pilot slumped back and glared at Jason who held the man's pistol in his hand.

"Do you speak English? If so, I think you should thank me for pulling you out of the water."

After a long silence and more coughing, the German mumbled, "Thank you," and sat up in a more comfortable position, clearly uninjured.

"Hey, stay put or I'll shoot."

The German sat back, put his hands out to the sides in a cooperative gesture, and said, "I am *Feldwebel* Karl-Heinz Lindt of the Deutsche Luftwaffe. May I ask who you are?"

"I am just a lowly recruit in the Royal Navy. I think you are a German officer."

"No, I am *Feldwebel.* You would call me sergeant."

"You're just a young kid, like me," said Jason. "How come you're a pilot anyway?"

"I have 22 years and have been flying for six of them."

Sensing skepticism in Jason's expression, Karl added, "Until this year I flew only gliders. I think you call them sailplanes, yes?"

"Now Hitler has made a regular airplane pilot out of you," said Jason.

"Herr Hitler has not made anything of me! I joined the Luftwaffe to fly with motors and to do new things."

"Hey, OK, I didn't mean to upset you."

"You are as you say, 'upsetting' me very much with my pistol. Do you expect me to attack you?"

Jason looked at the Walther P-38 in his hand, still pointed menacingly at Karl, and then shoved the weapon into his overcoat pocket.

"No, I don't; I guess we're gonna share this raft for awhile. You just stay in your end, OK?"

"*Ja*," said Karl. "But can you tell me your name? I think you are American, not so?"

"No! I'm Canadian; name's Jason Emory. I came here to help get rid of your 'Mister Hitler' before he makes too much more trouble."

"You sound like an *Amerikaner* just the same."

"Yeah, well, I come from Vancouver, Western Canada. It's close to the border with the states but I speak genuine Canadian, don't make any mistake about that!"

Karl laughed with a little cough. He leaned over the side and spit out some more salt water and smiled at the man who seemed less dangerous by the minute. Then he said, "I think Canadians and Americans are similar, like Germans and Austrians, not so? You must be one to know the difference."

Smiling at the remark, Jason said, "Yeah, maybe you're right."

Both men sat for a time in silence listening to water lapping against the raft.

"You speak English real good. Hell, with your Limey accent you sound more British than I do."

"Limey? Ah yes, you call the British 'Limeys' and they call you 'Yanks,' I think. And those are good names, not so?"

"Yeah, they're OK," said Jason, but 'Yank' means American. "How did you learn such good English, anyway?"

"I studied in school at home and then worked one year in Manchester before the war to learn new things."

"You seem to like 'new things' a lot," said Jason. "So do I."

"And you have come here from Canada to make a grand adventure, yes?"

"Adventure?" Jason thought about the word and said, "Yeah, maybe that has something to do with it. But I don't fly airplanes around the ocean at night."

"Ah yes, I think we are both adventurers," said Karl.

For a time the two young men slouched in their respective places, again just listening to the saltwater lapping pleasantly against the raft's inflated rubber sides. Then Karl spoke.

"We are supposed to be enemies, not so?"

"Yeah, I guess so."

"I think we are only two adventurers who have come together on an ocean," said Karl.

"Yeah, well, maybe, but I still have your gun." Jason had a fleeting thought about returning it, but knew better. Instead he took it from his pocket and as a gesture of good will dropped it over the side into the water.

"*Ach, Dummkopf!*" uttered Karl, rising to a kneeling position. "That was mine!"

"Hey, hey, this ain't no place for a war," Said Jason. "I got rid of that thing to keep us OK till we get picked up. Besides, you've already lost quite a bit of Mister Hitler's stuff this morning," said Jason.

Startled by the German's behavior, Jason thought of the flare pistol stowed by his left leg.

"*Ja,* the Storch belonged to the Fatherland. But that pistol belonged to *me!*"

"Ooch! I didn't know that. But you would have lost it anyhow when we get picked up."

"That would be decided by who picks us up, not so?"

A silence ensued, each young man aware that they were in waters heavily trafficked by boats and airplanes at war.

Finally Jason broke the silence. "What happened to you anyway? What were you doing out here at night?"

"That is not the business of a British sailor like you!"

After another long, awkward silence, Karl spoke again.

"I was to drop a message container to a German ship far to the southwest. I flew as ordered and found a ship. Unfortunately, the wrong ship. It was British; it shot the motor of my Storch."

"Jesus, now who's the dummy," said Jason.

Karl glared at Jason, who was about to laugh. His own scowl gave way to a smile.

"*Ja*, perhaps I myself was the business of British sailors, not so?" Then Karl smiled at Jason.

"An adventure," said Jason. "One that Bilbo Baggins would have said might make you late for dinner!"

"Ah, you know of Mister Tolkien. You have read his books?"

"Just 'The Hobbit.' I read it after I came to England."

"You must read more. Mister Tolkien has written many fine things."

After a few quiet minutes Karl, who had noticed the raft's chest of emergency supplies, said, "This raft has some drinking water, not so?"

"Yeah, there's water and other stuff here," said Jason as he put one foot on top of an orange colored waterproof compartment.

Karl pointed to a large pocket on his uniform leg. "I have chocolate. I would like to drink water that is not from the ocean. We can make a good exchange, yes?"

Both men relaxed a little more as they shared chocolate, water, some biscuits and canned beef from the raft's supplies.

As he finished his can of water, Karl said, "I think that life should have many adventures. The world is big and there are many things to do."

"Yeah, me too," said Jason. Then after a moment's pause he added, "But some people's adventures can be too big, like Hitler's—we gotta get rid of him."

Karl sat up straighter and said, "What happens to *Der Fuhrer* is yet to be seen. Germany's place on the continent is not just an adventure."

"Yeah, well, we'll see."

The two young men sat quietly, each with his own thoughts.

"Hey, there's a ship!" said Jason, pointing toward the north.

"*Ja*, I have been watching it," said Karl. "It has altered course toward us."

"She sees us! Is she British or German?" blurted out Jason.

"Ach, I have already proven this morning that I do not recognize the nationality of ships well. But you are a sailor. What do you think?"

"Can't tell. It's not a big vessel. We'll know soon enough." Then Jason added, "I guess one of us will start another adventure today."

"Yes," said Karl. "I think that one of us will be late for dinner."

Jason reached out to Karl, offering his hand, and said, "Good luck man."

Karl took Jason's hand and said, "*Ja, Glück auf mein Freund.*"

The waves lapped gently against the side of the raft as two young men quietly watched the approaching boat, each with his own thoughts about life's next adventure.

MEXICAN SUNSET[2]

The sky can tell it all when you live close to the land

The little Chevy truck made its way out of the canyon from the west. Paco and his five-year-old daughter, Palomacita, had been traveling for more than an hour since leaving their home in the Mexican town of Acension. Progress was slow as the battered truck, much older than its driver, met the challenges of the rough road. Paco was afraid that his little girl didn't have much time left.

Ahead to the east Paco could see the vast expanse called Lago de Guzman, the 40 kilometers of flat, white, dry lake the travelers must cross to reach the road that would take them to the city of Juarez and its hospital.

As the road dropped down toward the dry lake Paco noticed the puffy clouds overhead. Brilliant white billows in sharp contrast to the blue of the clear Chihuahuan sky. Even the mountains to the east seemed close enough to touch.

But today Paco was not in a mood to appreciate the beauty of his native Mexico. He watched his daughter as he drove carefully along the rough road and he tried to avoid the worst of the bumps that he could see produced flickers of pain on the trusting little face beside him. Still, like any good farmer, Paco noticed the sky. He knew that its clouds could tell him something about what was to come.

When the tired old truck had reached the dry lake Paco was pleased by its faster progress across the smooth dry lakebed. And he had noticed that behind him the clouds were thicker, a layer almost on the western horizon with an uneven, almost bumpy look.

---

[2] Published in *The Healing Inn*, Issue 3, 2000

Borregitos, or "sheep clouds" Paco called them. They meant that the weather would be different tomorrow. A hint of yellow at their bases suggested a pleasant sunset to come.

Then, with a lurch to one side the truck's right front tire let go. Not a good thing on this day, but flat tires are part of the business of living.

"*Ay, mi hijita*," said Paco to his daughter. "We have to stop now. How do you feel?"

"It hurts, Papa."

Palomacita tried to smile, but Paco could see the pain in her dark eyes. He regretted the whole day he'd used to sell two goats. But selling the goats had been necessary to get money for gas for his truck.

With a tightness in his chest at the thought of the extra time they must now lose because of the tire Paco reached over to touch his daughter's face. Two soft little hands reached up to hold his coarse, callused one, for it was as comforting as any could ever be.

"I will fix the tire and I will open the door on your side so you can help me."

Paco got out of the truck and dug some tools from behind the seat. As he did so he noticed that the clouds looked even whiter in the late afternoon sunlight and that the blue of the eastern sky was getting deeper. The *borregitos* to the west had turned to gold.

As he had done before Paco used an old jack to remove the truck's wheel and then took the tire from the rim. He examined the rubber inner tube and found the problem. A puncture caused by a mesquite stump.

While getting his patches and rubber cement from behind the truck's seat Paco thought of the mule that had kicked little Palomacita. He felt nothing about the mule. Mules kick and if you are in the way, well, you get hurt. That is also part of life. But Paco's eyes became misty as he thought of his child's ribs, broken by the animal's hoof, and of the pain in her eyes. It was his pain too.

Paco added one more patch to those already present on the old tube. "She's so tiny and frail," thought Paco as he looked at Palomacita on the seat of their truck. Palomacita smiled a little when she noticed him looking at her.

As Paco put the tire back on its rim he glanced again at the sky. The sunset was now bright orange and even the fluffy clouds overhead were taking on color.

Since sundown was near Paco knew that they would have to wait till morning to continue their trip. The old truck had no lights; there could be no driving in the dark. Paco had planned to spend the night somewhere because the journey was too much for one day. But he had hoped to be closer to the doctors who would help his Palomacita.

Paco began pumping air into the tire with his hand pump. A slow process, but the old pump had always worked before and would have to work now.

"Papa."

Paco heard the voice of his little helper who had been watching from the seat of the truck and he thought of the dark bruise he knew had spread across her chest.

"Papa, I'm thirsty."

Leaving his task unfinished Paco gave Palomacita some water from their plastic jug and realized it was time to eat, too. He brought out a paper wrapped package that he knew contained several tortillas and some boiled goat meat. He shared this meal with his daughter who, in spite of her pain, seemed happy to have this time alone with Papa. Alone on the great white desert with the beautiful blue and orange sky overhead.

"*Que lindo*," said Palomacita. She had been watching the sunset and even though she was not old enough to have seen many she knew that this one was unusually beautiful, something special.

Sitting for a moment with his arm around his daughter's shoulders Paco watched the sunset and he too knew it was unusual. As he ate he thought of his wife who had prepared their meal and had added some asadero cheese as an extra treat. He thought of her warmth as she had hugged and kissed them both, and told them she would pray for them as they traveled. He knew that at this moment she would be thinking of nothing other than her youngest child and of her husband who would keep her little girl safe.

The lengthening shadows of mountains to the north made Paco think again about the coming night. With a blanket he made a bed for the child on the seat. Then he went back to the chore of pumping the tire and mounting it on the truck. As he worked he prayed for help in getting his little girl to the clinic in Juarez.

After the work was finished Paco went to the bed he had fixed for Palomacita.

"Papa, see the sky," said Palomacita. "Our sky, it's so pretty!"

Overhead was a vast dome, blue-green in the west changing to sapphire blue in the east, set throughout with flaming billows of orange. The still, clean air made the colorful clouds on the horizon seem almost close enough to touch.

"*Ay Dios*," said Paco. Walking a few feet from the truck, he turned in a circle watching the sky. In all directions, even to the eastern horizon, islands of orange hung in an azure sea above the brilliant white of the dry lakebed. Paco stood with outstretched arms as he watched the red-orange sun slide behind the horizon.

In the special solitude that comes at sundown Paco let himself be swallowed by the sky and land around him. As the calm air cooled it became less dry and took on the special softness that is evening in the desert. The scent of greasewood and tiny spring flowers added to the wonder of being alive. In the distance the silhouette of a red-tailed hawk circled in silence.

"Our sky," his daughter had called it, and Paco knew just what she meant. All the world was nothing more than the two travelers, the brilliant white salt flat, and "their" sky. The dazzling orange jewels set in the deep blue dome above overwhelmed Paco. In the calm evening air he could see, feel, and almost hear the sunset that filled all creation.

The father and child sat for several minutes in a silence broken only by the faint sounds of birds and insects. For a time the pain was forgotten. Paco knew that these moments were like nothing he had ever known before, that this was something he was not likely to experience again.

Then the farmer who had spent his life paying attention to what the sky had to say, understood. He realized that the sky was telling the father, the child, and the mother back home that all was well, that the pain would go away. As the evening light faded, Paco fell asleep with his little girl cradled in his arms.

THE PASSENGER[3]

Sometimes a pilot or other fool needs a helping hand

As the taxi pulled into the parking area of the small airport the driver looked at his customer in the rear view mirror and muttered, "What the hell we doin' out here anyway? In another hour this place ain't gonna be nothin' but wind and water."

"We're out here because I'm paying you fifty bucks to get me here," came the impatient reply.

In the back seat Jed Sanderson was thinking of the approaching hurricane, the eighty miles of water between the island and the mainland, and of his nine-year-old daughter. In critical condition with pneumonia, the frightened child was asking for her father.

"Jesus, don't ya know there ain't no planes gonna leave from here now," continued the driver. Then, with a touch of sarcasm, "In case you ain't heard, there's a hurricane comin'."

Jed shoved three twenty-dollar bills at the driver and ran toward the small terminal building. The driver shrugged his shoulders, turned his taxi around, and headed for the island's high ground and shelter. As Jed reached the terminal he met a young woman who was obviously leaving, carrying a box of papers.

"Hey, what are you doing here?" she asked. "You ought to be heading for shelter. You can come with me if you need a ride."

"No, I've got to get to the mainland before the storm hits," said Jed. "I've been told there's a guy out here who has an old 'T-6 and is about to fly it inland. You know where I can find him?"

---

[3] Published in *Dan River Anthology*, 2002

"Oh, yeah. Steve Kendall. He's down at his hangar about to go. If you're riding with him you better hurry. All the other planes have left." She pointed toward a wooden hangar about a hundred yards away.

Yelling "thanks" over his shoulder Jed ran toward the designated building.

As he reached the hangar's open doors Jed saw a bright yellow American made AT-6, a two seat World War II fighter-trainer aircraft. This particular one had been built for use by Great Britain and, complete with Royal Air Force markings, was what the British called a "Harvard."

Inside the hangar a man wearing an orange colored flight suit was busily lacing his boots. Gray, crew cut hair, and an ample belly suggested that he was well past middle aged.

"Steve Kendall?"

"Yeah, that's me."

"Hey, great," said Jed, relieved. "A mutual friend, Stan Roberts, told me that you would be taking your 'T-6 to the mainland. I gotta get a ride."

Steve removed a well chewed but unlit cigar from his mouth and looked at the flustered newcomer.

"If you're trying to catch a ride with me you're out of luck. You better get to high ground. Storm's damn near here."

Then Steve noticed Jed looking at the nearby airplane, and said "Yeah, I've got this Harvard here all right. It's worth about forty thousand bucks. But look over there." Steve pointed at another plane sitting in front of the hangar, one Jed hadn't yet noticed. A P-51 Mustang, another World War II fighter.

"That Mustang is worth ten times as much, so I guess you know which one I'm flying out of here," said Steve. "Since it's a single-seater I can't take any passengers. You got to head for shelter. Suzie, the gal that runs the office here, she can give you a ride."

Though Jed hadn't noticed, the young lady was still waiting to see if the stranger would need a ride.

"Mr. Kendall," pleaded Jed. "I have a child over in Centerville that may be dying. I don't have time to waste in a shelter. I gotta get inland, now!"

The older man realized that he knew of this visitor through the previously mentioned mutual friend. "Your name Anderson or somethin'? he asked.

"Sanderson, Jed Sanderson."

"Yeah. Well, maybe we can help each other. You're a pilot. You got any tail wheel time? Can you fly that thing?" asked Steve, nodding toward the bright yellow Harvard.

"Yeah, I've got a lot of time in tail draggers. But not any as big as that," replied Jed.

"Well, when that damn storm hits it's gonna wreck this hangar and everything in sight. Since I'm self-insured, I'm gonna be out one pretty yellow airplane. You're welcome to fly it out of here if you think you're up to it."

Jed looked at the Harvard's big radial engine and thought about the plane's reputation for killing pilots by spinning easily when carelessly handled.

"Yeah, I can do it," replied Jed. "Just give me a quick briefing on the thing and let me flip through the flight manual for a minute or two."

"She's full of fuel. Let's roll 'er out," said Steve. The two men pushed the big Harvard out onto the ramp beside the even bigger Mustang.

With Jed in the front cockpit Steve, standing on the wing, ran through the world's shortest briefing on how to fly an AT-6 and helped Jed get the radial engine started.

"Wait a minute," said Steve as he jumped to the tarmac, ran back into the hangar and returned carrying a brown, accordion folder and an aviator's helmet. "If you do get this thing out of here in one piece we ought to save the paperwork too. This plane's been around some, so the logbooks add a lot to its value. You ever heard of Douglas Bader?"

Jed had indeed heard of the man, a decorated British fighter pilot who became an Ace during World War II even though he was a double amputee fitted with artificial legs.

"Bader served as an instructor pilot using this Harvard," continued Steve. If you had time to look at the logs you'd see a lot of entries where he gave instrument flying instruction to Limy student pilots in this airplane. This old helmet here has some faded initials on it. The first is a "D" sure enough, but ya can't read the second. Might have belonged to the old boy, but who knows."

With that comment Steve tossed the folder and the aged canvass and leather headgear into the rear cockpit.

Steve handed Jed his business card and said, "If you and this airplane aren't a rolled up ball of scrap aluminum by tomorrow, give me a call. You'll be the new half owner. With a friendly smile Steve patted Jed on the back, wished him luck, jumped off the wing of the Harvard, and ran toward the waiting Mustang.

Jed sat in the cockpit and, checking all the instruments, verified that the engine was running exactly as it should. Then he read the takeoff, landing, and "emergency go around" procedures. He was pleased to find a modern navigation-communication radio, and knew he would have no trouble finding the Centerville airport. That is, if he could fly the beast.

As Jed was studying the situation he saw the huge, four bladed propeller on the Mustang slowly begin to turn and heard the fine, old Merlin engine rise into a mellow, twelve-cylinder roar. Seeing the Mustang taxitoward the runway Jed focused on his own problems.

Jed looked over at the girl standing by her car. Suzie, that was her name. He looked at the darkening sky and at the windsock. The wind was picking up and the visibility was dropping. If he was going to fly he had better do it now.

The poor visibility was no problem for the airplane but like many private pilots Jed had no instrument rating. He knew that if he tried to fly on instruments he would almost certainly lose control of the aircraft. He wouldn't just wreck the plane on landing like his new friend had hinted. If Jed lost it in the clouds the plane would spin and turn into a smoking crater in the ground.

Suzie stood waiting as a light rain started to fall on her secure looking passenger car. Just a thousand feet up were the cold, lead-gray clouds. Hearing and feeling the rumble of the Harvard's six hundred horsepower engine, Jed knew he had no business being where he was. But thinking of his daughter who might be near death an hour and a half away, Jed made his decision. He waved to Suzie, closed the canopy, slowly eased the throttle open, and began taxiing to the runway.

Lining up on the runway Jed noticed a distinct left crosswind, so with the stick all the way back and all the way to the left he began smoothly opening the throttle. Quickly speed built up and after a couple of swerves Jed got the machine under control. When the plane seemed ready he eased the stick forward some to pick up the tail, and eased off on the left aileron.

After building up more speed, the aircraft seemed to want to fly. So, with the throttle full open, Jed eased the stick back more and the Harvard lifted off smoothly as though it too was happy to be escaping the approaching storm. A few minutes later Jed had the craft trimmed out straight and level at an altitude of eight hundred feet and pointed toward his daughter's hospital bed.

As he flew over the white capped waves Jed soon saw the coastline. He had been able to climb a bit higher as the ceiling raised somewhat. But inland conditions were worse.

Thinking of his lack of instrument flying skills Jed began to regret leaving the security of the island's hurricane shelters. But now he could do nothing but "press on," as many of the Harvard's earlier pilots might have said. So, still tense from the surges of adrenaline he had experienced during the take-off and climb, Jed continued toward his destination.

After some minutes Jed became a little more comfortable. He had been trying to learn to scan the aircraft's artificial horizon, air speed indicator, and turn coordinator repetitively, hoping he might be able to keep some degree of control if he flew into clouds. But, concentrating on the instruments, Jed failed to notice that features on the ground were becoming indistinct. The ceiling was descending and suddenly the visibility dropped to nearly zero.

With adrenalin surging through his system and his stomach in a mess, Jed realized he had lost visual reference to the ground. He knew he would soon quite literally not know up from down.

Concentrating hard on his feeble attempt at instrument flying, Jed thought of his options. He should try to make a 180-degree turn and fly back out of the clouds, perhaps descending, and find a place to make an emergency landing. But the frightened pilot knew that his chances of managing a 180 turn without losing control were slim, so he chose to maintain straight and level flight, hoping to run into clear air.

Then Jed felt the unmistakable tremble of turbulent air over the Harvard's wing and at the same time saw that his air speed was dropping. The Harvard was about to stall and would likely spin. But Jed was a good pilot, at least in planes he was familiar with, and he instinctively eased the stick forward to pick up speed.

But too much! The air speed was building too fast! So he brought the stick back, but then the air speed became too low, approaching a stall again. Pilot induced oscillations it is called. Jed knew that he was just about finished as a self-taught instrument pilot.

Jed fought to get things stable as he sat inside his lonely aluminum box hurling through the rain and fog at 220 miles per hour. He felt the tingling sensation all over his body from too much adrenaline and knew he was about to lose control of his stomach too. If he didn't get his air speed and angle of attack under control he was just seconds away from impact with the ground.

Then, as the terrified pilot tried desperately to regain control of the airplane, he felt the control stick move sharply in his hand. Not just from air turbulence. Three distinct, quick jerks on the stick. The unmistakable signal a student pilot who has really loused up a maneuver might receive from an instructor in the aft cockpit. The signal that says, "I've got the airplane."

But Jed was alone. He continued trying to fly the Harvard.

Then again, three sharp bumps on the stick. At this point, without actually letting go of the stick, Jed gave up. He tipped his head back and screamed at the cold, wet, grayness outside his canopy.

As his lungs were exhausted Jed regained a little self-control and noticed that something had changed. The vertical speed indicator was reading zero, the air speed was at its proper cruise value, and the craft was in a gentle turn toward Jed's originally chosen directional heading. The Harvard was under control.

Slowly regaining his composure and realizing that he still had his hand on the stick, the frightened pilot placed his feet back on the rudder pedals and started to take control. But as he did so he felt again the same three distinct jerks, and he backed off.

With his heart thumping Jed turned around as best he could and looked into the rear cockpit, trying to see the seat that normally would have been occupied by a flight instructor.

It was dark in the clouds and from his restricted position Jed couldn't see much, but he knew he was not alone. Just a shadow of a figure, but someone was there in the instructor's seat. Jed turned back forward and closed his eyes.

Opening his eyes again, Jed looked at the control stick. It was moving slightly from time to time, just as it should. His stick and rudder pedals were clearly following the control inputs from whoever, or whatever, was flying the plane.

Out of the confused muddle his mind had become Jed remembered the words of one of his own instructors from long ago. Words telling him to "calm down Laddie, just relax." Jed did as he was told and became just a passenger riding through the gray murk.

Jed began to wonder about his thoughts. No instructor had ever called him "Lad, or Laddie." But he sure wasn't going to look into that rear cockpit again. Not right now, anyway.

Jed had lost all track of time when he noticed that the gray outside was getting lighter. The visibility was improving and the airplane was descending into clear air. Before he could turn to the rear cockpit Jed felt again that he was recalling words from long ago when he had been taking dual instruction.

"All right Laddie, you're in the circuit. You've got the airplane; mind the undercart." Jed felt the thoughts were his, memories from past days of instruction. But the choice of words was definitely *not* his.

Taking control of the stick and rudder pedals, Jed was back in control of the airplane. As he looked forward out of the cockpit he saw not only clear air but that he was lined up on a final approach for his destination airport, safely out of the hurricane's path.

Jed got out the checklist and prepared for his landing. He did not forget the "undercart," and after verifying three green lights indicating safe landing gear, he came over the airport boundary at ninety miles per hour, just like the manual said, and set the yellow Harvard down gently on the broad runway.

After taxiing to the parking ramp and shutting down the engine Jed sat for a few minutes totally exhausted, listening to the crack and tinkle sounds of the cooling engine. Then he opened the canopy, stood up, and looked into the rear cockpit. The aircraft document file was stowed neatly to one side of the seat. Noticing this Jed remembered how Steve Kendall had carelessly left it lying loose on the seat and how he had thrown the old flier's helmet there as well.

But the helmet was not on the seat either. Spotted with rain, the old canvass and leather headgear was hanging neatly over the control stick, right where any pilot might put it after use.

"Well," said Jed to the beautiful yellow machine, "you're half mine now." As he picked up the helmet and looked again at the faded initials he felt sure he knew whose they were. He carefully folded the old leather and put it inside his jacket. Then, with a rubbery feeling in his legs, Jed hopped off the wing and went inside to phone the hospital, confident that he would soon hear that his daughter was doing just fine.

RIDE COWBOY, RIDE[4]

Sometimes all that matters is getting home

Frank Piersall sat easy in his saddle as his little sorrel came down off a mesquite-covered ridge. He was hazing four skittish calves toward the Lazy A Bar ranch corral two miles ahead. Sixty-two years as a working cowboy had taken their toll on his lanky frame and he squirmed a little to accommodate his arthritis to the business of staying mounted. A single rider was coming toward him at an easy lope.

The rider was Jess Maxwell, foreman of the Lazy A, and he spoke to Frank as he reined in his mount.

"Hey Piersall, this came for ya off the stage in town. Says 'Urgent'."

A minute later Frank had finished reading the letter and had shoved it inside his shirt.

"Lordy, Mr. Maxwell, I gotta go, now!"

"Sure, Frank, Sure. I can have your wages ready for ya first thing in the morning."

"Won't do; there's still good light left. I gotta go—"

"OK Frank. You been a good hand here—deserve a break." The foreman admired the old man, a sure enough "brush popper" who never shirked at the prospect of working a stray steer out of tangled manzanita and cactus no matter how rough the country.

"I'll take these animals in for ya; you get your gear together. We'll send your wages down home, with a little extra."

"Thanks boss. I just gotta go!"

With both arms resting on his saddle horn Jess watched Frank head for the bunkhouse. In the modern Arizona of 1890 old time cowboys like

---

[4] Published in *Dan River Anthology*, 2005

Frank were a disappearing breed. The foreman knew that all the old fella had to show for his lifetime on the range was just a small farm down near Tucson, and like many of his kind Frank had to work for a few weeks now and then for one of the big ranches to make ends meet back home. With a shake of his head Jess turned his attention to the four strays that were already spreading out too much to suit any good cowhand.

The next day Frank was making progress southward, toward home. Holding the reins in his left hand as was his habit, he reached inside his shirt for the letter. Shaking it out with his right hand and shielding it as best he could from the wind, he read the message again. It had been written on Monday. "Three, maybe four days ago", thought Frank, unsure of just what day of the week today was. With almost ninety miles to go Frank wanted to dig in his heels and pick up the sorrel's pace, but he knew better. He'd have to settle for the slow lope that the man and animal had settled into.

Having ridden through much of the night Frank was half asleep as he vaguely noticed the Wickenberg Stage coming along the road in his direction.

George Middleton eased back on the stage's reins, slowing the vehicle some to share the narrow road with the rider he saw approaching. Then he spoke to the man riding on the seat to his right.

"Hey Arnie, ain't that old man Piersall?"

"Believe it is. Looks to be in a hurry."

Both men waved as the rider and stage met and passed. But Frank kept his head down, oblivious to the greeting, riding like the stage wasn't even there.

"Jesus, he's been ridin' hard," said Arnie, referring to the lathered up cinch on the horse and the flecks of white foam flying from the animal's mouth.

"Yeah, I never knowed of Frank to push a mount like that!"

"Old buzzard hadn't oughta be doin' that," muttered Arnie. Gonna wreck his self or that sorrel, one or the other."

After sunset Frank walked the tired sorrel into a grove of trees where there was grass and water. Because of a pain that was developing in his left shoulder he had shifted the reins to his right hand with his left lying on his leg.

Frank unsaddled and hobbled the mare, gave her a short rubdown, then let her graze. For a moment the sad condition of the loyal little cutting horse made Frank feel a tinge of guilt. But thoughts of his Sarah and their little two-room house eighty miles away made the horse seem unimportant.

Frank spread out his worn bedroll, pulled off his boots and arranged both with his saddle to serve as a makeshift pillow. Curled on his right side because of his arthritis, the old cowboy slept.

The next morning found Frank alternately walking and loping the sorrel along the main Tucson road. The cantle of his saddle was bare now with no bedroll in place. Several hours before daybreak Frank had just pulled on his boots, saddled up, and taken his seat. He was riding home.

Ahead he saw the stage-line's remount station and knew he could stop for water and maybe a little grain for the sorrel. Sam Lewis and his wife Martha would be there. And now Frank was just thirty-eight miles from Sarah and the little home they had shared for more years than he could remember.

Sam was standing near the water trough as Frank rode up, stepped off of the sorrel and handed the reins to Sam.

"Help me out some, will ya Sam? Water her, and maybe a little grain. Loose the cinch awhile too. I gotta' use your outhouse, then get ridin'."

Sam was shocked by the condition of the horse his friend had handed him. "Jesus Frank. This animal ain't got no ride left in her."

"Please, Sam. Do what ya can. . . ."

Frank headed toward the simple wooden outhouse and nodded to Martha as she came out of the station's door.

Sam and Martha looked at the horse, at Frank's retreating back, and each other.

Minutes later Martha shoved two bean and cheese burritos and Frank's refilled canteen at the tired cowboy. With a faint but grateful wave of thanks Frank took the food and water and chanced to look toward the horse corral where he saw his sorrel munching on hay that Sam had spread for the exhausted animal.

"Sam, get her saddled up! I gotta ride, damn it!" Annoyed at the delay, Frank had shouted at his friend.

"Easy, Frank, easy," said Sam, waving his hand over toward a hitching ring set in concrete near the water trough.

"Your saddle's on my black Morgan over there. He'll get ya wherever you're goin' just fine. So get your butt on his back and God be with ya!"

Frank looked at the fresh and powerful Morgan, big enough to hint at some European draft blood in its ancestry, and knew that he couldn't ask for a faster way home.

"Oh Lordy, Sam. Thank you—tell Martha thanks too." And then the cowboy rode.

An hour before sunset Frank topped a little ridge and could see his adobe hut in the cotton wood trees near a grassy spring. His spring, his home. And his Sarah. Minutes later Frank galloped into the yard where he was met by Lalo, a fifteen-year-old neighbor boy who helped out around the place when Frank was away.

Frank's left arm was numb now, and nearly useless. With his right hand on the horn he left the saddle and slid to the ground before the Morgan had come to a complete stop.

"Inside Señor Pancho, inside!" shouted Lalo, using the Mexican equivalent of Frank's name as he always did. Lalo waved toward the open door as he caught the bridle of the big Morgan.

As he entered the front room Frank found Doc Ambrose standing near the door to the tiny bedroom at the rear of the adobe.

"It's the typhoid, Frank, she's done. She's been fighting the miseries every minute just waiting for you. Anybody else would have given up days ago."

Saying nothing Frank stepped to Sarah's bedside. He sat gently on the bed and put his callused hand on the frail woman's cheek and saw her eyes slowly open. And then they filled with light of recognition, and the old cowboy saw his wife's smile at its very best. At that moment Frank gazed into the most beautiful face he had ever known.

"You come home Frank. I knew ya would; now we'll be all right," said Sarah, her voice frail like a handful of dry leaves. But in the dim light the gray haired lady in the sweat soaked bedclothes beamed with the happiness of being with her husband one more time.

"Hold me Frank, just hold me."

With his chest tight with pain and his left arm hanging uselessly at his side, frank used his right arm to pull Sarah's frail body against his own. Sarah's right hand slowly reached up to her man's face. And for a few precious minutes the two held each other without speaking in the fading light of the windowless adobe room. Their room, their home.

Twenty minutes later Doc Ambrose stepped up to the bed. No one had answered when he knocked on the wood doorjamb as he entered. Seeing no motion, he struck a match to push away some of the darkness. Sarah's open, but unseeing eyes answered his question. Then he pushed lightly on Frank's shoulder and getting no response put his fingers on the old cowboy's neck.

Lalo was sitting on the porch, his white straw hat in his hands, not sure what he should be doing when Doc Ambrose came out of the adobe house. With a glance at the western sky where the sun had just settled behind the hills Frank had ridden in across, the old man sat down beside the boy.

Busying himself with getting out his pipe and stuffing it with tobacco, he spoke to Lalo.

"They're both gone son. They've gone together."

Then the two sat side by side in that special solitude of the waining desert sunset, each aware of how good it is to be alive.

GOLD IS HOW YOU FIND IT

There's more to gold than meets the eye and more than one way to find it

I eased the rented Ford Taurus along the narrow road with the windows open, enjoying the musky smell of northern rain forest mixed with ocean air. To my right breakers crashed against rocks and sand with the pleasant sounds one finds on ocean beaches anywhere in the world.

I carefully checked coastal details against the topographic map on the seat beside me. Things had changed a lot in this special part of the Pacific Northwest. A road had been built and summer cottages were scattered all around. It was hard to believe that this was where I made my discovery so long ago.

A streambed running through the forest toward the beach had to be the place. Still, it was hard to be sure. Not far away was a new cottage with a tidy driveway leading out to the road.

"Not at all like the old man's shack," I thought.

I got out of the car and collected my gear, disappointed that my planned hike of several miles was turning out to be a walk of just a few hundred feet. Still, with the pleasant excitement of visiting a place that is an old friend, I started down the stream toward the beach. In a few minutes I would confirm that this was indeed where I had found gold long ago.

I had been hiking for several days as I came up the coast from the south on that rainy, winter afternoon more than fifty years earlier. I was thinking of my little Chevy parked a few miles up ahead and how warm and dry it would be on my way back to Seattle.

After hiking for hours along beaches and over rough headlands that jutted into the ocean I was thirsty in spite of the cold mist so I walked up a little stream to drink. Afterward I sat for a while immersed in the solitude of the undisturbed old growth rain forest. Then I took a steel gold pan from my pack and put it to use.

I pulled moss from the downstream side of rocks that were situated just right in the little creek and washed the sand from the roots into my pan. With the pan partly submerged, I sloshed the contents carefully, splashing out the lighter material and leaving the heavier stuff.

Then I saw it. In the quarter teaspoon of black sand that I had isolated was the unmistakable glint of gold. A single flake about the size of a pinhead.

Later, with more flakes and two tiny nuggets stored in a glass vial in my shirt pocket I sat by my pack on a distinctive, long, flat outcropping of rock and thought about what I had found. I knew that I was in a national forest where no mining would be allowed. But I was only an interested outdoorsman. The discovery would be just a pleasant secret for me.

I decided to try one more pan of root debris and gravel. As I sat bent over in the uncomfortable crouch gold paners must suffer, working with my hands in the cold water below my feet, I stopped for a moment to stretch my back.

A man who is alone in the outdoors gets sensitive to what's going on around him and in this quiet time I heard a faint noise that I knew was out of place. Something was emerging from the timber behind me.

It was a man, the first I had seen in days, and an uncommon man he was. The dismal gray light showed a mound of rough clothes topped by a beat up felt hat over two eyes peering out from a bushy mass of hair and beard. In his right hand was an old Enfield rifle.

This apparition from the dark forest looked like something from dim history to me. The rifle, pointed in my direction, may not have been a deliberate intimidation but it did cause me to think of the revolver that was strapped to my own right hip. No doubt the old guy had noticed it.

"Hello," I said, turning to face the man.

"You findin' anything?" came a gruff reply after a distinct silence.

"Yeah," I answered in what I hoped was a pleasant voice. "A little color. There seems to be some gold around here."

"Yep. There's gold here, sure is," said the face full of whiskers. "That's why I put a claim on the place."

"Eh, uh huh," I muttered.

I knew he could not have filed a legal claim on this parkland. But, caught there with a gold pan in my hand and standing on what an old man with a rifle said was his claim made land use regulations seem a bit academic. I thought about the rules of etiquette for a fella caught claim jumping and considered my options.

"Sorry about that," I said. "I didn't know there were claims around here. Didn't even know there was gold here till a few minutes ago."

I soaked in my awkwardness a little longer and then the bushy face smiled with a flash of white teeth between gaps where others had once been. Transferring the Enfield to his left hand, he stepped forward and offered his right to me.

His name was Luke and I told him mine. After a minute to get comfortable we started to become friends.

"I didn't know there were claims here," I ventured again, still curious.

"Well, there's one," said Luke. "Mine. Actually, we ain't really on it just here. Boundary's over there." He pointed down the little creek toward the beach.

When he saw my puzzled look he explained.

"You can't do no minin' up here 'cause it's gov'ment land. But their boundary's down there, at the high tide line. A minin' claim goes down t' the low tide mark. So, I got mine laid out between the high and low tides."

"Hey, that's new to me. Kind of tough to work though isn't it?"

"Yep. Ever' day I gotta start over movin' the sand off' a where the little streams cross the beach goin' to the ocean. Once I get enough color saved up I'm goin' to bring a Cat in here t' really get things goin'."

This old man on a bright yellow Caterpillar tractor fighting to get his gold from the sand the tide would bring in each day. That would be a sight to see.

We talked a little more that day, then I hunkered under my pack and headed toward town. But I came back several times in the next few months to use the solitude of that Pacific coastline. Each time I did I spent some time with Luke.

He showed me how to use mercury to soak up fine gold dust from the black sand in a pan and how to distill the mercury out of the resulting amalgam to leave spongy, almost pure gold. He used half a raw potato to catch the mercury vapor and condense it for re-use. Luke cautioned me about the used potato. He almost lost a dog once when "The pooch got awful sick after eating one of them spuds."

In those days I was used to the rough life of men alone in the mountains. But still, Luke's cooking was a bit tough for me. The first morning he offered pancakes I said "sure." He produced some things that sort of looked right, and served them up on a flat utensil that may have been a plate in an earlier life. I contemplated eating.

"Y'want some syrup?"

"Sure, I said again," already in over my head.

Luke handed me a glass jar of dark fluid with the inevitable rusty lid. I dumped some of the contents onto the pancakes and wondered about the lumps that came with the syrup.

"Never mind them bumps," said Luke. "That used to be a peanut butter jar."

So we shared a hearty breakfast. In spite of appearances Luke was a pretty good cook.

We talked of mountains and streams Luke had known. Of other gold, of silver, and of a beryllium deposit in Alaska trapped on government land where Luke couldn't mine it.

Late one evening as I decided to go outside the shack Luke had a word of caution.

"Mind where ya step, son!"

It seems that a skunk lived near the shack, taking advantage of scraps. According to Luke, "One night I stepped on his tail and he squeaked some. I 'pologized, and he didn't fire at me."

Luke claimed he and the skunk had been friends ever since. Probably so. Plenty of other animals and birds would drop by his shack, sometimes passing in one side and out the other.

We talked of northern winters, of timber cutting, salmon spawning, and the great bears of Alaska. I told him of the single flake of platinum I had once found in my pan. Luke showed me how to find the glass balls that would wash up on the beach. Japanese fishnet floats that had made solo trips across the North Pacific drifting with the ocean currents.

Luke had spent a lifetime wandering the mountains of the Northwest. Trips of months at a time alone in the wilderness of Western Canada.

"Don't you ever worry about getting sick back there alone when you can't get to town for help," I once naively asked.

"Only times I been sick 's when I got too close to some town."

At the time we were sharing a morning pot of coffee. We must have been a little too close to town just then, because Luke had a sore throat. He was curing it by putting "just a touch" of kerosene in the coffee he was sipping.

On one summer night when the sky was solidly overcast I commented on how bright the moon must be to make it so light outside so late at night. Luke laughed and I knew I'd said something dumb. There wasn't any moon that night.

"C'mon son, there's somethin' you gotta see."

"Sure," I said and pulled on my boots and poncho to face the misty wet rain forest one more time.

To my surprise there was enough light outside to make walking easy even though it was almost midnight. As we reached the beach I saw what Luke had to show me. As each breaker came crashing in its foam had a blue-white glow. That soft phosphorescent light reflected from the low overcast sky was lighting up the forest.

We walked to a quiet lagoon where the water was still and several feet deep. No glow there. At least not until Luke threw a rock in. The stone left a trail of glowing bubbles all the way to the bottom. Other flashes along the bottom marked where a small crab had scurried out of the way. Wherever the ocean was disturbed it glowed with the contributions of billions of fluorescent plankton in the water. The tiny creatures near the bottom of any ocean's food chain.

Luke and I sat on the beach in silence that night, each with his own thoughts. He chewed on the stem of his pipe, but never lit it. I sat with my arms across my knees in the cold mist and thought of the unspoken wonders I knew were stored in that old man's mind, collected through a long, good life. And I wondered too about the adventures that must lay ahead for me. On that overcast night in a wet rain forest beside a softly glowing ocean two friends, each with his own thoughts, sat together near opposite ends of their lifetimes.

The next morning Luke asked me for a ride back to Port Angeles. He packed up his gear, along with his Enfield rifle and several rusty-capped glass Alka-Seltzer bottles crammed full of gold dust, nuggets, and lumps of gold amalgam. As we headed off to town I wondered if there was enough to buy a tractor.

I never saw Luke again. My work took me far away from the Pacific Northwest and he was pretty old. Maybe he came back to his claim, maybe he stayed in town but I don't believe anyone ever worked that claim with a tractor. In the fifty years that have since passed that beach has been for me a place where I really found gold.

After leaving the rented Ford Taurus I walked down the stream bed and took a gold pan out of my day pack. A modern plastic pan, smaller and lighter than the beat up steel one that had doubled as a cooking pot half a century earlier.

Feeling conspicuous in a place that felt more like residential area than the forest I remembered, I scrunched down beside the stream and panned some more moss just as I had done before. A little work with the pan and I had two yellow specks glinting in the sun. I had found the right stream.

Nearby was the familiar rock outcrop where Luke and I had sorted things out about whose claim was where. Then I walked down to the beach and imagined one more time a bushy-faced old man on a bright yellow tractor fighting the tide to get his gold. Another man's dream, both man and dream long gone now.

Looking out toward the breakers with their foam gleaming in the sunlight I thought of a time when I had seen them glowing in the dark. And I thought too of the occasional gold nugget that would be lying just below the sand at my feet.

As I turned to go back to my rented car I noticed a lady standing on a lawn not far away, watching me. I had forgotten about the houses and for just a few minutes the beach, with its familiar sounds and smells, had become the remote, uninhabited land I had once known it to be.

I walked over and said "hello." Once again I had intruded on someone else's domain in this place.

"Hi," she said.

Just then her husband stepped out of the back door, having just arrived home. He waved at me and walked over to kiss his wife.

"Name's Andy," he said. "This is my wife Sue."

Andy's white shoes were new and clean, and his tanned skin and athletic build presented the image of vigorous youth.

Wiping away perspiration with a towel, he added, "I've been playing tennis next door."

Having ducked inside the house Sue came back with two cold bottles of Rainer beer and another of mineral water, and we talked.

I found it hard to imagine a tennis court around there. Last time I'd seen the place Luke's crude shack was the only human mark on the countryside for miles in any direction.

We three talked of places and things, but of new ones different from those of Luke's world of long ago. Sue was an investment banker, Andy an engineer for Boeing in Seattle. We had all seen some of the world, and we talked of jet aircraft, the stock market, of London and Rome. I had once owned and flown a Boeing airplane, an antique Stearman. Andy had sat at the controls of a 757 in flight. I told them about the Indians in the Sierra Madre of Mexico, the Eskimos of Greenland, and the jungles of Brazil. Sue had seen Egypt's Valley of the Kings.

As the sun slanted toward the ocean we shared an evening meal on their back lawn enjoying fine conversation just as Luke and I had done long ago. Occasionally I would look toward the rock outcropping fading into the dusk not far away. A place where an old man with a rifle had startled a young man with a revolver, a gold pan, and a silly look on his face. I didn't mention the gold to my hosts. It was Luke's gold anyway.

The sun sank low enough so that a layer of clouds over the ocean lit up with yellow-orange color. "The sky often lookes like that. We picked this spot because of the view," Sue said. "Sometimes there's gold all over the sky!" As she spoke she held her husband's hand as they sat side by side, enjoying their place on the Pacific Ocean coastline. Thinking of Sue's comment, I wondered if these folks knew about the gold that was at their feet as well. They didn't, of course.

Old Luke had found gold on this beach. The kind that puts bread in your belly and adventure in your heart. I had found my gold there too, a kind that a man carries in his mind. Now these two people had found theirs in this same place just by holding hands as the sun goes down.

I could tell that it was their custom to share the evening light into the dark so I finished my glass of wine, thanked my hosts, and walked back to my rented car. I put my daypack in the trunk and felt in my shirt pocket for the little glass vial with its two flakes of gold. I would put them together with several more and a few nuggets I had found long ago.

"There's no doubt about it," I thought as I started back to Seattle, "Gold is *how* you find it."

THE HANGMAN

Every family has its darker secrets

Two days after they buried his father in the little Mexican cemetery high on a hill overlooking the Rio Sabinas River young Billy MacRay sat at the farm's kitchen table across from a slight built man, not much over five feet in height. The boy was still morose about his father's not unexpected death from a long bout with consumption. Billy was now an orphan at the age of sixteen since his mother had died two years earlier.

"Well Billy, there ain't nobody left now but me and you to run this place, so that makes us partners. What d'ya think?" said Billy's Uncle Jeb.

"I wish they hadn't called him that," muttered Billy, referring to a name the local Mexican folks used for his father. "My dad never stole nothin' and he sure ain't never killed nobody."

"Heh, you mean *Bandido Gringo?* Folks meant it good-natured Billy. They all liked your pa, and they believed him when he used to joke around and say they was a killer in the family," replied Jeb.

"But they say he was a bandit? Way back? People say they seen the posters—"

"Yeah, well, my brother-in-law, old Dave MacRay, he wasn't quite the ripsnorter the local folks here like to make out he was. Maybe now's he's gone I oughta tell ya a little more about your own pa."

"But he said lots of times he wasn't the man-killer in the family. There's only the four of us, me, ma, and—and you. What did he mean, anyhow?"

"Well, my sis' and your pa used to kid around about that because of my past. They liked to up my reputation in suspicious minds hereabouts," said Jeb with a chuckle. "Even made me more interestin' to the lady folk a time back."

"Anyhow let me tell ya about your pa and the Cattlemen's Association. But first I got somethin' to give ya." Jeb handed a small brass key to Billy.

"You just put that in yer pocket. It used to belong to your ma. Later on you might want it."

With his eyes tearing up a little Billy did as he was told, more interested in what Uncle Jeb had to say than the key.

Eighteen Years Earlier

A single rider came into the dusty South Texas town of Yucca Flats. No one would have paid any attention at all except that the frail looking stranger was dressed entirely in black clothes and sitting a black saddle on a jet black gelding. The black stovepipe hat scrunched on the rider's head added an almost comical effect. No one in town knew the newcomer, but everyone knew what the visit meant. The stranger never said a word; just clip-clopped down the street, a mule with a packsaddle in tow, and stopped at the local hotel.

The stranger walked into the hotel, hesitating for a moment to look at a tattered wanted poster near the door. In a hoarse voice like someone with a bad cough and using just a word or two the stranger took a room for the night and made no further offer of conversation. That suited the desk clerk just fine anyway.

Next, after stabling the horse and mule, the stranger walked to the newly constructed gallows in front of the courthouse. After climbing the few steps to the gallows floor and studying the structure, which had been built according to specifications, the slightly built stranger walked up the fancy marble steps of the court house and sought out the sheriff's office.

At the office entrance was another wanted poster, just like the one at the hotel. "Dave MacRay," said the poster in big letters just above a hand drawn picture of a man's face. "Wanted by the Yucca County Cattlemen's Association for various misdeeds perpetrated on its property and for murder," continued the message just below the sketch. This time the hangman pulled the paper off its nail, folded it, stuffed it in an inside pocket of a black four button suit coat and entered the office.

Again using just a word now and then and coughing some like someone with consumption or something worse, the visitor expressed the need to know the weight and height of the condemned man for whom "professional services" had been arranged. The deputy took the visitor to Dave's cell and left the two alone together, glad to stay away from the condemned man and the unpleasant stranger with the bad cough.

Early the next morning with the help of a local handyman the hangman spent about an hour installing a trap door release mechanism that had been taken from the pack saddle of the mule tied to the structure just below. Next the rope with its noose, wrapped with the traditional thirteen loops, was inspected and placed in position.

With a glance the hangman made sure the jet black horse was tied to the base of the gallows right beside the pack mule. According to habit the hangman wanted to leave the town and its gallows immediately after the job was done, which is why the mule was almost completely packed and ready to go.

Across the street Johnny Muldoon, who had been sleeping off a drunk on the sidewalk in front of the town's only bar, watched the events at the gallows. With the expert eye of a working cowhand Johnny noted the hangman's horse, a fine Morgan gelding that was well suited for more than just standing around.

"Hell of a waste of good horseflesh on a fella that just leads a mule around from one hanging' t' the other," muttered Johnny as he came to a sitting position on the board sidewalk, wondering where he'd left his own mount the previous night.

That afternoon found Dave MacRay on the gallows trap beside the hangman who stood with one hand resting near the gallows release lever. With his hands tied behind him Dave was watching the deputy who had escorted him from his cell walk down the short flight of steps to stand beside the sheriff and a local magistrate at the base of the gallows.

Convicted of murder by several witnesses, all in the employ of the Cattlemen's Association, Dave MacRay was about to meet his maker. Because of the early hour that had been requested by the association, hardly anyone was around to watch the proceedings.

The local minister climbed the stairs, spent a few moments with Dave, and departed. Like most people in town he wanted as little as possible to do with the hated Cattlemen's Association and any of its activities.

The hangman placed a black hood over Dave's head and slipped the noose around his neck. Suddenly the condemned man began a series of violent contortions right on the gallows trap door and to everyone's surprise freed his hands. The onlookers saw Dave MacRay appear to plunge his right fist into the hangman's midsection, doubling the frail figure over. As the deputy started toward the wooden steps Dave grabbed for the hood over his head.

Straightening back up the hangman lunged for the release lever and pulled it just as the condemned man got his hands on the noose. With a clunk the trap door opened and Dave fell, but not before he had gotten the noose off his neck. Dave hit the ground on his feet. Moments later he and the hangman's fine Morgan were on their way out of town in view of astonished onlookers who watched the two disappear around the corner of the red brick First Mercantile Bank building.

The MacRay Farm on the Rio Sabinas, Mexico

"Wow," said Billy. "My pa, he done that? He escaped right off a gallows?"

"Yep, he sure did, replied uncle Jeb. And when he did he took the hangman's reputation right with him. The hangman just dumped everything off the pack mule, climbed aboard, and rode out of town without bein' paid or nothing. Folks say that nobody ever heard of that hangman again."

"Woo-ee, that makes pa an escaped murderer. No wonder he never would leave Mexico. He sure couldn't go back to Texas," said Billy, not sure what to think.

"Now hold on nephew. Your pa told you he wasn't a man-killer, and he never lied to nobody. So don't you go accusing him now."

"But the poster, and you—"

"Your pa had a bone to pick with the Cattlemen's Association over a good spring on a 160 acre homestead they took from him. I never knew much about the details, but yer pa made a habit of bustin' up association offices from time to time tryin' to get even. Kinda dumb thing to do, but he did get back most of the cash he figgered they owed him for stealin' his place. That's how he got his start down here in Mexico."

"But the murder, what happened?"

"Billy, that association bunch was as crooked as a dog's hind leg, and they needed to explain a murder of a rancher over t' Marrion County. What with your pa bein' such a well know nuisance in their offices they just natural pinned it on him. Wasn't hard to do; they owned the judge in those days."

"Wow," said Billy, still digesting what he had heard. "But what pa kept saying about him not being the killer in the family. That was just a joke, right?"

Then Billy thought a little more and his expression changed as he said, "Uncle Jeb, where were you when all this happened? Did pa mean that you—"

"Now nephew, before you get to thinkin' too far down that road I suggest you go use that key I give you a while back."

"It's the key to Ma's old trunk in the attic, right?" said Billy as he retrieved the forgotten key from his pocket.

"Yep, sure is. I think you oughta see what's there so you can make up your own mind about your old uncle's past."

In the crude storage space above one of the rooms in the adobe house Billy had shared with his mom, dad, and uncle all of his life the boy looked at the open trunk. Inside he found folded clothing that all belonged to his mother. Slowly he took each item out and laid it beside the trunk, including the simple white dress his mother had been married in.

At the bottom Billy found the dainty black boots, slim black pants, black four-button jacket and the crushed stovepipe hat. And underneath the garments he found the simple wanted poster with its coarse sketch of a man that looked a lot like his pa.

Getting Acquainted

The distinction between friend and enemy is not always clear

Northern Africa, November, 1942

L ieutenant Harry Nelson lay on his back, eyes closed, wondering what happened. He felt as if he had been flying just minutes ago, and as the fuzziness cleared somewhat from his aching head he realized that he had passed out. But he knew that he sure wasn't flying now. He was in a bed. Somebody's bed, somewhere.

Confused and apprehensive, Harry kept his eyes shut and without moving listened for sounds around him. Hearing nothing for some time he cautiously opened his eyes to find that he was alone in a hospital room. He could see an intravenous needle in his left wrist with a tube attached to a bottle on a metal stand. After moving a little he found that his rump hurt and was bandaged. Harry realized that he was being treated for a wound, but by whom?

Nothing in the room gave any hint. He couldn't see anything written except the label on the intravenous fluid bottle that was feeding his arm. But the label was far enough out of his line of sight so that he couldn't read it. For another twenty minutes the American pilot lay in the bed wondering whether he had reached an Allied hospital or was a prisoner in the hands of the Germans.

Suddenly the door opened and a nurse entered. In the moment before he closed his eyes to feign unconsciousness Harry had the impression of a buxom, middle-aged blond woman. Some nearby equipment was adjusted and he felt the woman hold his right wrist, checking his pulse.

The Previous Day

Lieutenant Nelson stood beside the abandoned hangar and looked out at the weed-covered dirt landing strip and at his damaged P-40 fighter plane. It was a typical North African summer day with a light breeze and nothing of significance in sight for miles in any direction except the remains of an abandoned emergency airfield, one that had been built by either the British or Germans as the fortunes of war shifted back and forth in North Africa. Exhausted from lack of sleep, Harry was vaguely aware of the tiny dot in the blue sky off to the Northeast.

For the past few days the twenty-year-old Arizona cowboy, turned pilot by the war, had been living off his dwindling emergency rations and a few dates he had found on the ground in a nearby grove of palm trees. Fortunately the trees marked a small oasis. Just a big puddle, but enough water to keep the downed airman from dying of thirst. But despair at his plight and realization that he was as likely to be rescued by German as he was by Allied forces had taken their toll. Harry was reaching the end of his endurance.

As the minutes passed the faint sound of an aircraft engine rousted Harry from his trance-like state and he focused more intently on the tiny dot that was growing bigger in the distance. "American, please American, or British; God, don't let it be a German." The wretched pilot looked around for somewhere to hide in case the approaching aircraft saw his downed fighter plane and landed on the little dirt strip to check things out.

The American pilot's pulse raced as he saw that the single engine aircraft was not even going to circle the field to take a look. It was making a direct approach for the little landing strip and would soon be on the ground. Harry knew that its landing roll would cause it to come to a stop not far from his own disabled P-40. Since Harry's view of the approaching aircraft was head-on he couldn't see nationality markings and the silhouette was not one that he recognized.

Harry made his decision. He ran to his helpless aircraft and hid as well as he could behind the machine. Perhaps the new arrivals would look into the old wooden hangar first, and this might give Harry a chance to surprise them from behind. The American felt some comfort from the .45 automatic strapped to his sweat stained flight suit, right over his heart.

The gray and tan colored aircraft reached the end of its landing roll and as it made a slight turn off the dirt strip it revealed its markings to Harry. The well-trained American had already recognized the ME-108 for what it was, a side-by-side two-seat aircraft manufactured by Messerschmitt AG to teach German pilots the art of flying. The new arrival was a little brother to Germany's fearsome ME-109 fighter planes, one of which was responsible for the plight Harry now found himself in. In an earlier air battle Harry had lost a dogfight to a German adversary who caused enough damage to Harry's engine to leave him a helpless airborne cripple. Harry had been lucky to escape the scene alive and limp away to a forced landing just a few miles south of the Libyan shore of the Mediterranean Sea.

Cowering beside the oil and smoke stained bulk of his own wrecked engine and with his heart in his throat Harry waited to see what his visitors would do. As the seconds ticked by he wondered what such an unarmed German airplane was doing in a war zone.

Hauptmann Klaus Eberhardt and *Feldwebel* Dieter Kröner sat side by side in the cockpit of the ME-108, glad to be alive and on the ground. Though Harry had been too excited to notice, the propeller of the German plane had just been windmilling as the craft glided for the last half mile under the careful hand of its pilot. Its engine had quit from fuel starvation. Both men were lucky that they had not been forced to make a landing in the waters of the Mediterranean Sea.

Minutes later the two German airmen stood beside their aircraft. Klaus held a 7.62 mm Luger pistol in his right hand; Dieter left his own Walther P-38 in its shoulder holster. Both men checked all their surroundings as they approached the abandoned hangar, the strip's only building.

"*Das Flugzeug,*" said Klaus, indicating with his pistol barrel that Dieter should look over the damaged American plane. So much for Harry's feeble plan to get the drop on the two Germans.

Seeing the two enemy airmen split up, Harry realized that his chances of surviving had gotten a lot worse. He knew his best bet was to kill the enemy soldier who was approaching his hiding place and then deal with whatever situation remained with the other man. The twenty-year-old American had never seen a German soldier before and the thought of deliberately shooting a total stranger, a man he could actually see or talk to, gave him butterflies in the stomach. But this was a German, and Germans were what Harry was in the business of killing.

As Dieter approached the American airplane, now holding the 9mm Walther in his hand, he saw a brief movement beneath the left wing. The German fired a single shot, then dived behind a stack of empty wooden crates, the only available cover. Dieter's single shot was good enough to tear part of the heel off of Harry's right boot. It also served as a warning to Klaus, inside the old hangar, that there was trouble outside.

Harry, realizing that the empty wooden crates concealing Dieter from view would not stop a .45 slug, fired two quick rounds at where he thought the German was hiding. After waiting for about a minute, he was about to fire again when he heard a voice from behind him.

"Do not do that more, *Amerikaner*, and you must give me your weapon." The English words were spoken with a thick German accent.

The frightened American pilot turned around and saw the Luger pistol in the hand of a large, blond man with the bluest eyes Harry had ever seen. Carefully he handed his .45 to the German. As he did so the second German, uninjured by the shooting, walked up and stood beside his comrade as both men inspected the helpless American pilot.

With his hands in the air Harry leaned against the cowling of his airplane's damaged engine and listened to the incomprehensible German conversation between his two captors. He took fleeting comfort in the American made aluminum structure, warm in the midday sun, as it pressed against his back. Finally, waving the muzzle of the Luger, Klaus motioned for Harry to walk towards the shade offered by the wooden building about fifty yards away.

As the little group reached the shaded area Harry was startled to hear the command to "stop," and "turn around," spoken by one of the Germans in clear English. He did as ordered and stood facing his captors.

"What are you called and what unit are you?" asked Klaus, with his thick accent.

"I am Harry Nelson, a Second Lieutenant in the United States Army Air Corps." Harry followed that statement with his serial number.

"You do not answer! You must speak what unit you are. You must speak what you make—what you do here!" Klaus's broken English was barely understandable to the frightened American who did not respond further. Klaus started to raise his pistol as if to strike Harry across the side of his head, but Dieter stopped him.

"Lieutenant Nelson, my colleague, the captain, has asked you what unit you are from. A simple question, don't you agree?" Dieter's command of the English language was far better than Klaus's and Harry was somewhat disarmed by the friendly tone and clear words.

"Huh, I ah, I only have to tell you my name, rank, and serial number."

"Yes, and you have already done that. But the captain and I would like to know where your base is. As you can imagine, we want to know if there are more Americans nearby."

As Dieter spoke Harry was standing with his back toward the small hangar, with the two Germans facing him, all three men taking advantage of the shade the building offered. Harry, whose attention had been fixated on the menacing Luger in Klaus's right hand, glanced over the man's shoulder toward the low hills behind the two Germans. Thus he was the first to notice that the three men were far from being alone.

"Oh Lordy," muttered Harry, "there's more. . ." Harry just pointed over Klaus's shoulder, and seeing the expression on the American's face was enough to make the two Germans turn around to learn what had caught their prisoner's attention. What they saw was a group of horsemen at full gallop coming straight at them. Several had some sort of long barreled rifles and the others were waving broad, curved-bladed swords.

The mounted horsemen began firing at Harry and his German captors so all three men took cover behind the same wooden crates that had suffered two rounds of fire from Harry's .45 automatic. In the confusion the American found himself behind the two Germans who were both firing back at the horsemen. Unfortunately, one horseman got lucky enough to put a rifle bullet right into Klaus's head, killing the German captain instantly.

Harry grabbed Klaus's shoulder, jerked him over onto his back and, with a glance at the terrifying Luger now lying in the sand, grabbed his own .45 automatic from the German's waistband. In seconds Harry found himself side by side with Dieter, trying to survive the attack from the screaming Arab horsemen.

The German and American soldiers, with the cover of the wooden crates, managed to discourage the attack and the remaining Arabs turned and rode back past the bodies of three of their fellow attackers. Soon the shooting stopped with dead or dying Arabs littering the scene in front of Harry and Dieter.

Simultaneously the two enemy airmen, on their knees in the sand behind the crate, turned toward each other. For a tense second each man stared into the other's eyes, not knowing what to do other than hold his weapon pointed at the other man's midsection.

"He's very dead," said Harry, indicating the lifeless German captain lying beside him.

"Yes, I would say so," responded Dieter.

Before either man could act both heard a hideous scream as a dismounted and wounded horseman appeared just behind Dieter and raised a gleaming scimitar in an obvious attempt to remove the German's head. Without thinking and still pumped up from the battle, Harry fired a single round from his .45 into the chest of the attacking Arab. The man collapsed, dead, on top of Dieter who squirmed out of the way. Again the two men made eye contact over pistol barrels. Harry, with a two handed grip on his .45, felt that his thumping heart would explode his chest as he considered his next move.

"Thank you old chap," said Dieter. "I think we need to cooperate for awhile longer, yes?" All the while Dieter's Walther pistol never wavered, and both men knew that the slightest wrong move would leave both of them as dead as several of their attackers.

"I think we better find out who else is still alive out there, yes?" Dieter slowly pointed his pistol away from Harry who responded similarly.

Both men then looked over their flimsy wooden shelter and saw that just one of the bodies littering the landscape showed any sign of life. Together, and looking in all directions at once, the two uneasy partners approached the wounded man. Dieter kicked the man's rifle farther away as Harry checked the severity of the Arab's wounds.

"He's shot through the stomach, won't last long," said Harry. Let's drag him over to the shade, make his dying more comfortable for all of us."

As they moved the dying Arab, the man regained enough consciousness to begin speaking words that were incomprehensible to Harry, and from somewhere in his white robes the man produced a knife in a feeble effort to continue fighting. As Harry took the knife away he was surprised to hear Dieter utter a quick series of words in the same language the Arab had used. Words that ordered the Arab to stop resisting, and the surprised man did just that. A lengthy conversation ensued as Harry watched, astounded that the German could talk to the wild-eyed Bedouin.

"What the hell was all that?" demanded Harry, knowing that as an American Soldier he should just shoot the German, not carry on a conversation. But the man sounded just like the Limy soldiers at the field near Manchester where he had recently been stationed, and moments earlier the two had fought for their lives, side by side. Harry clenched his .45 automatic, his nerves tighter than a banjo string.

Smiling at Harry and enjoying the American's obvious confusion, Dieter replied. "It seems that this group of Bedouins, or more likely bandits, came here for water. That spring is their property, as they say. They cannot tolerate 'infidels' using their water supply."

"All this fuss over a puddle of filthy water? Jesus, we coud'a shared; they didn't have to start shooting."

"Ah, I see you have not been here long, Yank. A 'filthy puddle' to be sure. But here any source of water that can be used by a man, horse or camel is valuable. It is politically, economically, and even religiously important. Your first lesson about life in North Africa."

Harry said nothing, but noticing that Dieter had retuned his Walther to its holster, Harry did the same with his .45. "Well, what happens now?"

"We have quite a bit more on our plate than you are aware of my American friend. It seems that we have killed the leader of this pack of rabble. And that is unfortunate because according to this gentleman, who by the by seems to have expired, those who ran away will come back with the leader's brother and many, many colleagues."

"Oh shit, that's just swell," muttered Harry, as he looked down at the Arab and saw that he sure enough looked dead. "I'm gonna get the hell out of here."

"Bloody good idea, old chap. But how do you plan to do that? Use your airplane?"

Both men looked toward Harry's shot up aircraft and Harry muttered "My engine ain't going nowhere. But there's your plane." As he spoke and not sure how the German would react, the American pilot thought again about the .45 automatic at the ready in his shoulder holster.

"That too would be a good idea were it not for a severe shortage of petrol in my craft's tanks," replied Dieter, with a pleasant smile. "My deceased colleague and I did not drop by this lovely spot just for a drink of 'filthy water' as you call it."

"You ran out of fuel? Completely out?"

"Yes indeed, and it was 'good to the last drop' as you Yanks are fond of saying. We chose to detour around an air battle; not a good plan it would seem."

"Jesus, you got a perfectly good plane with empty tanks and I've got one with a wrecked engine—"

"But perhaps with a spot or two of petrol, right Yank?"

"Yeah, I've been thinking about that. There's more than an hour's worth for my engine, enough to run that pipsqueek plane of yours all afternoon."

"Pipsqueek? An American word I think, right old chap?"

"Yeah. Let's get busy and haul gas from the '47 to your crate."

Harry and Dieter both began searching for old cans or whatever else might be useful. A short time later both men were huddled under a wing of the P-40 draining gasoline into a metal bucket they had been using to carry fuel from Harry's plane to the ME-108.

"I think that is all that we are going to get," said Dieter as he handed Harry the half-filled bucket.

"How much does that crate of yours hold?" asked Harry.

"I have been calculating. I think the Messerschmitt will now fly about 300 kilometers."

At this point the big question about a destination was in the minds of both men, but neither had mentioned the subject yet. After an uncomfortable silence Harry brought up another subject that had been on his mind.

"I gotta ask, just who the fuck are you anyway? You talk English like a Limey, and Arabic too for Christ's sake. Are you even really German?"

"I am pleased to inform you, Yank, that I an indeed a genuine born in Stuttgart German citizen. I am the son of a German diplomat who was posted to several foreign assignments during my formative years. My modest attempts to use the Queen's English are the result of attending schools for three years in London. My familiarity with Arabic comes from the streets of Alexandria, here in Africa, where my father was posted for much longer. I have been told that I have a talent for languages."

"What else do you speak, for Christ's sake?" said Harry, not anxious to approach the destination problem that was in both their minds.

"French actually. Something I picked up, along with a wife, in Paris before the war—"

"Oh shit, looky there!" Harry pointed past the front of the P-40 to a hillside about 300 yards away. A group of several dozen horsemen, all dressed in white or light blue burnooses and turbans, were watching the activity near the airplanes.

"Well, it appears that we have dallied here a bit too long. Those gentlemen have come to claim their 'filthy water,' wouldn't you say?"

"Jesus. Look at 'em, just waiting there in a mob."

"Yes, I think we taught them earlier today that charging right in is not the best course of action."

"Let's make a break for your plane," said Harry, "and—"

"I think guns in your aircraft are electrically operated, not so?"

"Hey, yeah they are, and those clowns are sitting right in front of the thing! If we can move the tail a little to aim it we can raise holy hell on that sand dune!"

Harry scooted from the shade under the wing back to the tail assembly, and Dieter followed.

"See, we can't do much about the elevation of these guns, but when I get in the cockpit and start shooting, you can shove the tail around some and spray slugs all over the place, OK?"

Dieter nodded his understanding and as Harry ran forward he was glad he had left the canopy open after his forced landing. He hopped into the cockpit of his familiar airplane. After flipping a few switches Harry knew his guns were active and he mashed the firing button.

The roar of three wing-mounted .50 caliber machine guns almost deafened Dieter, but the German paid attention only to the area on the distant hillside that was being churned into a miniature sandstorm by the steel cored bullets from Harry's plane. Shoving on the tail assembly, Dieter could indeed aim the guns and soon terrified Arabs were scattering as they saw several horses and their fellow attackers go down from direct hits or from ricocheting slugs. Soon no one except the dead and dying was in sight in front of the aircraft. Dieter stared in amazement at the piles of gleaming brass cartridge cases under the fighter plane's wings. The German soldier had never seen machine guns in real action before.

After the shooting Harry sat in the cockpit, thinking again about the problem that he and Dieter must now settle. They could agree on getting the hell out of there all right, but to where?

Harry jumped to the ground to find Dieter standing by the plane's left wing. The two men looked at each other for a moment and in unison ran for the Messerschmitt. Dieter arrived first and climbed onto the plane's right wing with his Walther pistol in his hand. As Harry skidded to a halt he saw the menacing handgun and got a choking sensation in his throat. Without thinking he grabbed Dieter's feet and pulled him off the wing, both men falling toward the ground. As they hit in a jumble of arms and legs there was the sound of a single 9mm pistol shot and the scream of an injured man.

"Jesus Christ, you Kraut bastard! You shot me; you shot me right in the ass!" yelled Harry as he grabbed for his .45 and hauled it out. Trying to point the gun at Dieter, Harry saw that the German was just standing there with an amazed expression, looking at the Walther in his hand. Dieter's pistol was clearly not pointed at Harry. Overcome by the pain in his rear end, and realizing that he had been shot by accident, the American dropped the .45 to the ground and grabbed his left buttock with both hands in an effort to ease the pain.

Dieter jumped to the Messerschmitt's cockpit and opened a first aid kit. Then he cut open Harry's uniform pants, jabbed a morphine injector into the American's thigh, and tied a compress bandage onto the wound. Then, again with the Walther in his hand, the German waited for the morphine to calm Harry some, all the while watching for returning Arabs. And as he waited he scurried to the hangar and took a sky blue burnoose and turban from one of the Arabs who had died in the earlier attack, taking care to get one that was not too bloody. Returning to the airplane, he stuffed the clothing behind the seats of the two-place ME-108.

"How could I have been dumb enough to trust a German," muttered Harry as the morphine reduced his pain enough to make him coherent. "You fucking Kraut sonofabitch!"

"We both know that was an accident for which I am responsible. I would apologize and discuss the event further, but time is decidedly lacking. You must get into the cockpit immediately and fly us out of here."

"Fly yourself out of here, damn it! I've had enough screwing around with you."

"I . . .I can't," said Dieter.

"Eh, what did you say? You can't? You flew the fucking thing in here, you—"

"No, it was the captain who was assigned yesterday to transport me. I am not a pilot."

"You said—"

"Perhaps I misled you a little."

After a few seconds of silence, Harry broke into a grin in spite of his injury and said, "So, you can't get out of here without me, right, 'old chap' or whatever the expression is?"

"That is correct. We must leave now, and since I am the one holding a pistol, I will choose which compass course we take when we get airborne. I am not pilot enough to take off or land, but I can steer an airplane in the sky, and I am an excellent navigator. Now get your bloody arse into the left seat, now!"

Both men smiled at Dieter's use of the profane British word 'bloody" and its obvious double meaning. Harry reached out his hand and Dieter helped the wounded American pilot into the cockpit of the German training plane.

The instruments and controls were familiar to Harry, and as Dieter read him labels on some switches, the two got the Messerschmitt's engine running and in a matter of seconds they were airborne. As Harry banked the plane to the left to see the little field they had just departed, both men could see behind the hill they had shot up so thoroughly with Harry's damaged P-40. There, in a smaller group than they had been earlier, were several Arabian horsemen, undoubtedly trying to decide how to exact vengeance and free their water hole from the clutches of the evil infidels.

Once airborne Harry put the ME-108 on an easterly heading and began thinking about how he was going to approach some British or Egyptian airfield in an airplane with clear German markings when he had no knowledge of local radio frequencies and codes. As he flew his thoughts were interrupted by Dieter who tapped the magnetic compass with the muzzle of his pistol.

"I think, old chap, that we should leave the navigation to me. I suggest a turn of about 180 degrees in the direction of Bengasi. I am overdue at my new posting. We must not disappoint Herr *Feldmarschall* Rommel, right old boy?"

"Screw you. I'm heading for Tobruk or Egypt."

Dieter gently tapped the muzzle of the Walther on the right side of Harry's head, and said, "You seem to have forgotten who is driving the surrey just now."

His shoulders dropping in resignation, Harry made the ordered turn. "What the hell is your job anyway? You may be German alright, but what were you doing here in this unarmed airplane—or is that a military secret?"

"Isn't it obvious, old sot? I am an interpreter, sent to help the General ah— 'talk things over' with captured local Arabs who have been quite a nuisance with their sabotage here and there."

"Fuck you, fuck it all," yelled Harry, frustrated by his feeling of helplessness, the prospect of becoming a prisoner of war or worse, and nauseated from the pain in his rump in spite of the morphine.

"You ain't gonna make it to your buddies today," said Harry as he slammed the stick to the left with some left rudder and then hauled back on the control yoke. The ME-108 rolled onto its back, then dived for the ground in an inverted turn and leveled out again right side up. Harry had executed a reasonably good split-S maneuver in spite of his unfamiliarity with the aerobatic characteristics of the German airplane and the excruciating pain in his rump. They were back again on a heading toward Egypt.

Surprised by the violent maneuver, Dieter dropped the Walther in a reflex effort to hang on to whatever he could in the cramped cockpit.

"You got a choice, Kraut. Either you come with me and become a guest of the British Army, or we are both gonna be a smoking hole in the desert." British chow ain't much . . . in a prison camp, but . . . make up your mind."

Dieter, recognizing from Harry's slurred speech that his captive American pilot was passing out, gingerly took the controls and eased the plane back toward Field Marshall Rommel's army. With a frightened, but cool-headed non-pilot at the controls the Messerschmitt droned westward.

One Day Later

Lying in his hospital bed Harry realized the futility of keeping his consciousness a secret. So, he opened his eyes and saw that a blue-eyed blond nurse, clipboard in hand, was watching him. The woman had to be German. Harry felt a surge of adrenaline as he waited for her to speak, sure that he was a prisoner of war.

"Coming around now are we Ducks? Your pulse is just fine too."

Harry felt a wave of relief at the nurse's clear cockney accent. "You—You're British!" he stammered.

"Well, that's what me mum told me when I was just a wee lass."

"Hey, great! I gotta notify my unit, I . . . who—"

"Not now love, you just keep resting. I'll let the doctor know you're awake."

"But where am I? What—"

"Other laddies need tending." With a gentle pat on Harry's shoulder the charismatic lady disappeared out the door.

Harry did as he was told, relaxed, and slept a little. Later, awakened by a disturbance in the room, he opened his eyes again to see a man in a U.S. Army uniform sitting in a chair opposite him. Harry noticed that the captain did not have medical corps insignia on his lapels.

"Hey, an American. Who are you?"

"I'm Captain Harvey Maxwell, a liaison officer officially, an intelligence officer more precisely. And now I would like you to tell me why some surly looking Arab drug you to our doorstep claming he found you in a wrecked airplane. And, in particular, why your arrival aircraft seems to be of German manufacture."

Harry did his best to explain his circumstances, hoping to be believed. At the end of his story he pleaded, "You can contact my unit; they'll tell you who I am."

"Oh we will Lieutenant, we will. And if things check out as you say we'll get you back where you belong in a few days."

Relieved, Harry lay back in the bed.

"One more thing," added the captain as he handed Harry a folded sheet of paper, a handwritten note. "We found this stuck inside your tunic. There were no other papers in your aircraft."

Unfolding the letter, Harry asked, "I suppose you guys have read this?"

"Of course, Lieutenant, no secrets from an intelligence officer, right?"

Slowly, Harry read to himself.

"Having just shot the man who saved me from decapitation by an obnoxious Arab I find myself with a spot of guilt. Not a good way to say thank you, to be sure. I also realized that I would likely maim us both in an amateur attempt at landing "our" airplane. So, I nobly chose to fly eastward and do my crashing somewhere near medical aid for damaged American pilots. With more luck than that of a drunken Irishman, I managed to get us both onto terra firma with only minor bumps and thumps.

"You see, I have also reasoned that with a bullet hole in your bum you would make a poor prisoner of war, whereas I might fare much better, particularly if I was to don some stray clothing I have purloined and pass the remainder of this unpleasantness as an Egyptian.

"Best of luck old chap. Perhaps, God willing, we will meet again after all this is sorted out. After all, you did give me your name, rank, and serial number. *Auf Wiedersehen*, Dieter."

Harry lowered his hand holding the long note and made eye contact with the captain.

"We intelligence types would like you to explain that note, Lieutenant. The man who rescued you from the plane crash claimed to know no English."

"I presume Sir that the 'surly Arab' as you called him was the man who put the bullet hole in my butt, like I told you. If so, I think that along with who knows what else, he speaks English better than me. He sure uses fancier words, anyhow."

"I think you need to tell us who and where he is, Lieutenant. We'd really like to talk to him."

" Sir, I don't even know his last name, let alone rank or serial number. We were pretty busy. And I'd sure like to talk to him again some day too.

SUITCASES[5]

Cleverness and sophistication can carry one to a deserved station in life

Sipping a much better quality after dinner brandy than he was used to Dick listened dreamily as his wife discussed business with their host. Though Jane was not letting it show, she too was basking in the luxury of Carlos's Bogotá home, one of the finest anywhere in Colombia.

"You realize that this business has its problems," said Carlos.

"Oh you mean those little government people with their paperwork, taxes, import regulations and all that," said Jane. "They just don't realize how sophisticated modern international business has become."

Carlos laughed and said, "Yes, 'little government people' as you call them. And you two are 'sophisticated' enough for the work?"

"Sir, as you know I have a degree in business from—"

"Yes, yes, of course," said Carlos with a pleasant smile.

The well-dressed gentleman then set down his nearly untouched glass of bourbon and ice and said, "It seems that we have reached a potentially profitable accord. And now that our business is concluded I would like to show you both my city at night."

This is a story about Dick and Jane, two entrepreneurs. They bought merchandise overseas to retail in the United States.

Earlier Dick had spent some time in South America with the Peace Corps. Having a charismatic personality and gregarious nature he had made a lot of friends. One of these friends was Carlos who was now well established in a major industry with production facilities in Colombia and business offices in Peru.

———————————

Jane was a graduate of UCLA where she had met and married Dick. With a degree in business administration she felt that she knew a lot about the world and was determined to get right out there and grab her part of it. Dick, however, had found class work boring and quit school to work as a technician for a communications company. He was good at his trade.

Jane realized that Dick's income, though adequate to get her through the university, was not enough to really get hold of the life style that was proper for her. So, utilizing her professional education and considering their mutual talents, she formulated a business plan.

At Jane's suggestion Dick made contact with his old friend Carlos. Happy to hear from Dick and interested in Jane's business plan, Carlos invited the couple to his home in Bogotá where they were treated to a taste of the life style that was more appropriate for Jane. Dick liked it too, and Carlos liked Jane's business plan. He invited the couple to work with his organization as independent contractors helping him export his product.

The details of Jane's business plan were simple. The profit potential for Carlos's product was so great that production and transportation costs were almost inconsequential. So, Jane suggested that every few weeks Carlos deliver a quantity of his product to her at his distribution center in Lima, Peru, in four small packages. She and Dick would then deliver three of the packages to Carlos's office in Houston and keep one package as payment for their services. Carlos and the couple could then market their shares of the product independently wherever they chose. A very efficient business since no bookkeeping or paperwork would be necessary.

So Dick and Jane became contractually responsible for importing Carlos's product into the United States. This would not be difficult except for one thing. The United States Government was not very sophisticated about Carlos's product. Jane knew that those bureaucrats had erected some trade barriers that the couple would have to contend with—red tape that was impossible to handle in any practical way. So, Jane chose to conduct business by just leaving the little government people out of the picture as much as possible.

Now in this area Dick was able to make a real contribution to Jane's business plan. Like Jane, he too was more clever than those mundane government workers. He simply bought two identical new pink women's suitcases and with his skills as a technician built an almost undetectable false bottom into one of them.

When Dick showed Jane his handy work she was quite impressed. "But why the second suitcase?" she asked.

"Aha," said Dick. "It's additional security for you, my love."

When he explained Jane was impressed with both her husband's ingenuity and his consideration for her well-being.

Having completed their preparations the entrepreneurs set out for Peru with the two pink suitcases containing Jane's personal clothing and emergency equipment, and another older one for Dick's things. They arrived in Lima light hearted and optimistic about their business future. It would afford them a life style that was proper for people as clever and sophisticated as they.

The next day Dick placed four packages of Carlos's product in the suitcase with the false bottom along with Jane's emergency equipment. Jane's clothing and personal items were placed in the second, unmodified pink suitcase. The couple then headed to the airport in Lima. Alone, Jane checked in for her flight to Houston and checked the single suitcase containing Carlos's product as baggage. At a different counter Dick checked in for the same flight and was assigned a seat in a different part of the aircraft. He checked in his own old suitcase and the unmodified pink suitcase containing Jane's things.

After arriving in Houston, Jane collected the suitcase containing Carlos's merchandise and proceeded to the customs inspection station. Dick picked up his own single piece of luggage and watched inconspicuously. After seeing Jane pass through customs successfully he then retrieved the second pink suitcase containing Jane's clothing and passed through customs inspection himself.

That evening the two entrepreneurs celebrated the success of their first business transaction. This involved a bottle of Italian spumanti and a large pizza. In the morning they would put a single package of Carlos's product into their own safe deposit box and deliver the other three to Carlos's office in a Houston suburb. Each went to sleep that night with pleasant thoughts about the growth of their inventory in the bank.

Dick and Jane made several trips to Lima, conducting their contractual duties for Carlos just as they had done the first time. Each time they used two new suitcases that would always look just alike. The work was a little monotonous and not very challenging for people as clever as they, but their inventory was building nicely. Soon they would be able to move to another part of the country and begin their own retail operations. The planned move was a professional courtesy to avoid direct competition with Carlos in Houston.

Part of their success in passing customs inspections was due to the large volume of passengers using the Houston airport each day. Inspectors seldom actually looked inside suitcases. They relied on their own judgment about people, and watched for nervous body language. No problem for cool types like Dick and Jane.

Occasionally, however, just at random an inspector would actually examine the contents of a bag. It was this last eventuality for which Dick had contrived Jane's emergency system.

Once Dick's old suitcase and the pink one he was carrying had been subjected to such a random search. When asked about the women's clothing and cosmetics, Dick just told the inspector that the case belonged to his wife who had missed the flight and would be along on a later one.

Twice Jane had been asked to open her single pink suitcase, and the inspector had examined her emergency equipment without realizing what he was seeing. The false bottom, crafted with great skill by her husband, was not noticed.

That is, not until their eleventh trip when Dick was shocked as he watched Jane's attempt to pass through customs inspection. Instead of the casual banter between a courteous inspector and an attractive woman, Dick saw the agent call a more senior inspector over to help him. The second inspector, a middle aged woman, approached the inspection station and asked the other travelers waiting for Jane's processing to be completed to please go to some other line. Then the two officers opened the false bottom.

Dick knew that Jane's only hope now was to take advantage of her emergency equipment. He glanced at the baggage carousel and saw that, as it should be, the new pink case containing Jane's personal articles was waiting along with a few other bags.

"Wait! That's not my stuff," said Jane to the older agent whose nameplate said "M. Bascomb. She then picked up a bra and shook it out by one strap for all to see. "This is not my size at all!"

Clearly, the bra was much too large for Jane's modest figure.

"And these panties with little cupids and hearts," continued Jane. "Black net stockings, and my god, that yellow skirt. I wouldn't be caught dead wearing this stuff!" Jane seemed sincerely indignant about the contents of the case.

Agent Bascomb watched Jane for a few seconds, then reached for a small cosmetic case lying among the other articles. She opened it and took out a bottle of perfume and noted that it was a relatively cheap scent, not at all like the Red Door that she recognized on Jane. Next she opened a lipstick and found a bright red hue. A color completely inconsistent with the subdued, but tastefull colors of the clothing and lipstick that Jane was wearing.

"I've picked up the wrong bag," pleaded Jane.

As she spoke Jane looked toward the carousel and then pointed. "Hey, there it is! That must be my bag over there!"

The two customs officers looked toward the carousel.

"OK ma'am, please step over here with me," said Agent Bascomb, motioning toward a nearby office. "And Frank, gather up this stuff and bring it to the office along with that other bag."

Dick, according to their plan for such an occasion, passed unobtrusively through a different inspection line and walked out to their car in the long-term parking lot.

Reaching the office, Agent Bascomb offered Jane a chair and took a seat herself behind a desk. Frank brought Jane's pink suitcase into the office, placed it on the desk, and left.

Agent Bascomb proceeded to examine Jane's passport and asked about name, date, place of birth, and other details about the document. Jane confirmed that everything was indeed correct. She then asked Jane questions about her trip. How long had she been gone? What hotels had she used? Did she enjoy Peru?. Jane felt more relaxed as she answered each question honestly and politely. The conversation took several minutes.

Then Frank returned with a pink suitcase.

"Oh, that's mine, from the carousel," said Jane.

"Ah, thanks Frank," said Agent Bascomb. "Just set it here on the desk with the first one."

Frank did so and Agent Bascomb noted out loud that indeed both items of luggage were brand new and appeared identical. Not an unreasonable coincidence since hundreds of such items are sold each month.

"Now Ma'am, you say that this is actually your suitcase?"

"Oh Yes, it must be."

"OK, then, would you please open it for us?"

Jane did so.

Agent Bascomb then examined the contents, noting with just a glance at Frank, that two bras appeared to be of a more appropriate size. There was a small container of Red Door, the perfume that Agent Bascomb had noticed that Jane was wearing. Although neither of two tubes of lipstick matched the shade Jane was wearing, they were consistent with Jane's apparent taste in clothing as were all the other items in the case.

"There is no lipstick here that matches the shade you are wearing," said Agent Bascomb, looking at Jane.

"No, I have it in my purse."

"Ah yes, of course. It does look like you've picked up the wrong luggage as you say. You should be more careful."

"I sure will," said Jane, realizing that her ordeal was over.

"Well, in any case, I hope we haven't unduly inconvenienced you. Please accept my apologies and, incidentally, welcome home."

"Oh, no trouble at all," said Jane, relieved.

Frank then picked up the first case, containing Carlos's product, and left the room. Agent Bascomb shook hands with Jane and indicated that Jane was free to leave with the suitcase containing her proper personal effects.

"Oh my God, that was close!" Jane said to Dick as she got into their parked car.

"Is everything OK?" blurted out Dick.

"Yes. Just fine. Those government people, just doing their little thing. They didn't have any idea what was really going on."

"Great." said Dick.

Then, genuinely proud of the emergency system her husband had invented, Jane smiled at Dick and said, "Worked just like you planned. Thanks lover." Then the couple drove home.

Carlos would have to be notified, of course, but he had agreed that once in awhile a shipment would be lost. He was prepared to accept that with no hard feelings. After all, with his experience he knew that international transportation systems were not perfect.

Jane and Dick didn't celebrate with bubbly wine that evening since they hadn't made any profit on the trip. But, realizing that not all business deals work out as planned, they were not too disappointed.

That evening while emptying her suitcase Jane made a discovery. Looking closely at the case she suspected that it might have a false bottom. But that was not possible. The one with the false bottom containing Carlos's product had been kept by Agent Bascomb.

"Honey, look at this!" said Jane.

Dick did and found that there was indeed a false bottom, but not like the kind he built. With a screwdriver he pried it open. Inside he found some batteries and some other items that with his technical skills he recognized to be an antenna, a transmitter, a microphone, and an electronic homing device. It was then that Dick and Jane realized that those little government people could also buy new pink suitcases and build false bottoms. As the couple pondered their discoveries they heard a knock on the door, which they answered.

"Good evening folks," said one of a pair of men who introduced themselves as government employees. Agents Cortez and Jamisson, respectively.

During the next few days the pair of entrepreneurs discovered that the government red tape and their bureaucratic problems were much more complicated than they had thought, and were likely to get worse. In fact, they found that they were actually going out of business and would have to forfeit their inventory to the government.

However, their business venture was not a complete failure. It did make Dick and Jane financially independent. As a result of their activities they are both living in all expenses paid facilities provided for them by the United States government. And they even have a guarantee that they will be able to stay there for the next seven to fifteen years.

On his yacht off the coast of Mexico Carlos read in a Houston newspaper about his contractor's problems. Since he needed the services they so ably performed he was disappointed, but only slightly so. He knew he could easily find other independent contractors who believed themselves to be more sophisticated than those little government people.

THE LONELY GRAVE

Monuments and markers don't always tell the story

J ust as I finished stomping the snow off my boots on the porch the door opened and the lights of the kitchen along with suppertime smells pushed the cold Montana night away behind me. I stepped in and got a big hug from Sarah. My glasses promptly fogged up so all I could see was a blurred shape as Sam's big voice said, "Mike, ya been gone too long!" It was good to be back visiting old friends but I sure wasn't prepared for what that evening held in store.

Old Sam had been a merchant seaman during the Depression years and had spent World War II in Europe, part of it as a prisoner of war. By the time I met him he and Sarah had raised a family while he worked as a peace officer and got himself elected to public office. Sam had seen a lot of life that I knew about. Just how much more I was about to find out.

After supper Sarah and I cleaned up the dishes. Then Sam and I sat by the pot-bellied stove in the living room. A little blackberry brandy and the smell of wood smoke made a fine defense against the harsh winter just outside. All seemed well, but Sam just stared at the fire through the little mica windows in that old stove.

Finally Sam looked up and said, "D' you think—ah hell, neither do I," then went back to staring at the fire as he rolled his glass between the palms of both hands.

Concerned about my friend who was getting along in years, I said, "Think what? Are you folks OK?"

"Oh sure, we're fine," said Sam, gathering his thoughts. "Y' see, I need to talk about something from way back. I never told anybody about it 'cause they'd think I was crazy, or drunk."

Sam was not much of a drinking man and I knew he had been about the most respected sheriff the county had ever had.

"I've never told anybody, but now I'm telling you for a couple of reasons. First, 'cause you're a writer and such things ought to be got down on paper." Sam's voice trailed off.

"You said a couple of reasons," I replied to get things going again.

"Yeah, well, I gotta tell about this 'cause I figure Curly would want me to."

"Who's Curly?" I asked.

"I'm comin' to that," said Sam after a sip of brandy. "Y' see, something happened back when I was a shiny new deputy, my third week on the force. We had this '46 Ford patrol car then. It was winter and late one night I was coming north up the highway along the Little Big Horn, right near the park there at Custer's battlefield.

"Anyhow, that old two lane road was slick with frost and I was drivin' a little too frisky. I spun that Ford right off the pavement. There I was, stuck in a ditch. I fooled around awhile provin' t' myself that I wasn't gonna get unstuck, and figured out that this new deputy wasn't doin' much to 'serve and protect' as the saying goes.

"Didn't have radios in our cars in those days and it was about two in the morning. Nobody was likely to come along the road for a while so I figured I'd get some help from my brother-in-law. He lived a couple miles away across the Little Big Horn. Knowing it'd be frozen that time of year, I decided to take a short cut.

"Y' know, it just wasn't my night. I tore my new uniform pants goin' through the barbwire fence gettin' down to the creek. Four dollars those pants cost me.

"Anyhow, I went down into a bunch of trees near the creek and found that there was still some snow left in the shady places. The next dumb thing I did was t' slip on a rock, fall down and bung up my ankle. After tellin' the world in general what I thought about that, I just sat there in the mud and snow. Me in my shiny new tore up policeman suit with my ankle hurtin' like hell."

At this point Sam quit talking and looked hard at me. He had noticed that I was developing a pretty good chuckle as I listened to his story.

"Mike," he said, and almost laughed a little himself, "though I can see as how it might seem like it, what I'm telling' you ain't funny."

I sobered up and Sam continued.

"Now, like I said, I sat there talkin' to myself about what a swell job I had done so far that night, and then I tried to walk some. My ankle hurt so I sat down on a log. I figured by then some thinkin' might be a good idea.

"Y' know, for winter it wasn't a bad night. Cold, but no wind, almost a full moon. I was in a lonely but pleasant bunch of trees. Lookin' up to the north I could see right up the draw to Custer's Ridge. The moon was so bright I could just about see the spot where the old boy turned in his badge back when he pissed off the Sioux and Cheyenne like he did.

"Now that draw was all winter-dead grass and mud, except for all the little white markers the government put up where Custer's boys each had died. In the middle of the night with things bein' quiet as a snowflake, those markers made me feel, y' know, a little funny, lookin' like gravestones like they do.

"Now I knew they weren't really graves. The Army had collected all the bodies long ago and buried 'em somewhere else. And the Indians didn't handle their dead by usin' graves anyhow. So, as I stood up t' try my ankle again I muttered somethin' out loud about how 'There's no graves around here.'"

Sam paused at that point, his face a little pale.

"That's when it happened," said Sam, shaking his head a little and avoiding my gaze.

"A big boomin' voice, right under my feet or maybe in my head or somewhere said to me, clear as hell it said, 'Yer wrong, son, they's one, and it's mine!' Now that startled me so bad I damn near sprained the other foot when I hopped a step and fell back down in the mud. Lookin' around I couldn't see anything that could of been that god awful voice. Then out in front of me, just out of the moonlight by a tree, there was a thing. An' it sure as hell wasn't where the voice had come from."

"Jesus, Sam," I muttered, almost interrupting his story again.

"About then I grabbed my service revolver, scared round eyed, and wished I knew where the hell my flashlight was. Then that thing, that figure, moved more into the moonlight. It was wearing a blanket and some leggings made of animal skin, had some chunk of fir wrapped around its head. Looked like a man, an Indian, like the pictures of the ones the soldiers fought, except he was older'n Methuselah and had one real stove up leg. He hobbled right up to me usin' some old stick for a crutch and looked down at me sittin' there on my butt' in the wet snow.

"His eyes. God, those eyes. He was lookin' at me, but his eyes were both dead. Y' know, like a blind old dog. But it felt like what was behind those eyes could see right down my spine. Damn near peed my pants."

Sam swallowed like his throat was dry and poured a little more brandy into his empty glass. After a sip and some more staring at the stove he went on with his story.

"Well, I had my revolver pointed up at the old guy, holdin' it with both hands t' stop the shakin' and I asked who the hell was he. He didn't say anythin' at all, just pointed up toward Custer's hill, he did, usin' his crutch t' point with.

"Then the old guy talked. Not the same voice I'd heard earlier, just an old man's wheeze. 'Look there, *washichu*, there!' He was still pointin' with his crutch. 'Look hard, see good,' he said.

"Called me *washichu*, the old Sioux word for white man. I knew then for sure this guy was an Indian, but a lot older'n any old buck I'd ever seen."

Looking down at his glass Sam collected his thoughts, then spoke again.

"Mike, you've known me a long time. You know I'm no screwball or any such thing."

I nodded appropriate reassurance of my opinion of Sam's sanity record.

"Yeah, well, maybe in a minute you might think different, 'cause what happened next is crazy. I mean, I was there, but even now I sometimes don't believe it. But it wasn't a dream. In the other room I got proof. I'll show ya. Every once in a while I think back and figure I must'of been nuts. Then I get that thing out and look at it, to see it's real."

"Jesus, Sam," I said. "What thing—"

"I'm comin' to that; show ya when I'm done.

"Y' see, there I was, sittin' in the mud with my hands in my lap and my revolver pointed at my own foot, helpless as a baby. Needed a diaper like a baby too 'cause I'd definitely peed my pants by then.

"Then I looked off t' where that crutch was pointin'. What I should've seen was mud and dead grass in that draw that runs up to Custer's Ridge, and those little markers bein' white in the moonlight. But what I saw wasn't like that. No markers at all, no dead grass, no moon, *no night.*

"What I did see was broad daylight, and green grass in that draw and a clear blue sky. Well, mostly blue. There was lots of dust and smoke along the top of the ridge, and about a million soldiers, horses, and Indians hollerin' and screamin' everywhere, goin' all directions."

Sam's eyes were a little moist as he swallowed hard and said, "Mike, there I am; I'm in old Custer's battle, I truly am."

"About then that old Indian taps me on the head with his crutch, then points off to one side. I can tell the old guy wants me to look at somthin' special goin' on just up the draw.

"There's this wagon comin' down a hill and it spills over on its side with pots an' pans scatterin' all over. The driver is a big guy, probably a cook or somethin'. He jumps off the wagon neat as ya please and stands on the ground in the middle of a hell of a mess. There's some Indians and maybe three or four soldiers shootin', bashin' and stabbin' at each other.

"I see two bucks come at the wagon guy, the cook or whatever he was, and they're screamin' like banshees. But that cook, he has an iron skillet in his hand and he slams those bucks both along side the head and puts 'em on the ground. Just as he does that I hear one of the soldiers yell at him, 'Curly, over here!'

"Well, that big fella, he must've been six-six or so, he scoops up a rifle that had fallen off the wagon and runs toward those soldiers that were just being finished off by the Indians. His hat starts to come off, and just before he jams it back on his head I see why they called him Curly. That fella is bald as a billiard ball. Sure looked funny there for a second with the sun shinin' off his dome.

"Anyhow, he fires the rifle at one Indian as he's runnin' to the fight. He can't save his buddies; they're goners. But old Curly wades in swingin' his empty rifle in one hand and that damn skillet in the other. When he's done there's busted up Indians everywhere with him the only man left standin'.

"Now Curly looks around some and just then from out of nowhere he catches a bullet right in the head and drops like a poleaxed cow.

"About then that old Indian standin' over me taps me on the head again with his crutch, then points over to where there's this other Indian who'd been watchin' the whole fight. He's a real young kid, standin' there with nothin' but a bow and some arrows. Looks nervous, probably his first scrap.

"The kid walks over to where Curly is layin'. Turns out though, Curly ain't dead. He's just been knocked senseless for awhile by a slug that tore his scalp open and made his head bloodier'n hell, like scalp wounds usually do.

"Anyhow, about then Curly comes to and sees that kid gettin' an arrow into his bow. Now Curly, he was big, but he was even quicker than he was big. Usin' both his hind legs he grabs and kicks that kid's leg and busts the knee all to hell, real bad. In a second the kid was down, Curly on top of him, gettin' that bow.

"Next thing another Indian carryin' a long battle lance comes ridin' up on a sorrel pony. Curly manages to get an arrow squared away in the kid's bow, and lets it go at the new fella.

"Apparently Curly's no expert at shootin' arrows, and he misses the rider, but hits that sorrel right in the butt. Now the horse takes a dim view of that and rears up on its hind legs real quick. This dumps the Indian off on his own backside, right on his lance, bustin' the shaft clean in two.

"Now it seems Curly's head wound, gleamin' red in the sunshine, is still botherin' him 'cause right about now he decides to faint dead away, right on the other side of the sorrel from the pissed off Indian.

"With a knife in his hand the Indian comes chargin' around the equally annoyed horse only to find Curly lyin' on the ground lookin' real dead and with his bloody bald head lookin' like he's already been scalped!

"Now this warrior looks around and sees the kid with the busted leg who has been sittin' on the ground watching the action unfold. He ignores the kid and notices Curly's dead buddies and goes over t' where he starts collectin' scalps."

Sam stopped his story and choked up, his face pale again.

"Y' know Mike, I was a cop for twenty-eight years and I've seen a lotta crap, what with what folks will do to each other and with automobile wrecks and such. But I never seen anythin' like that buck doin' his scalpin'."

Sam looked at me with tears down his cheeks and said, "Mike I'm not crazy. I really was there." Then he coughed a little, kind of embarrassed. Out of courtesy I looked away and reached for my forgotten glass. "Jesus, Sam, I—"

"No. Lemme finish, I gotta get this done."

Sam collected himself and went on.

"Y' see, Curly isn't quite done yet. He comes to and looks up and sees that Indian carvin' on a soldier's head. Some poor bastard with corporal's stripes; I can see things that clear. So Curly comes to his feet with his own bloody head shinin' red in the sun and with a roar that could stop a grizzly he charges that Indian. Gets his hands around that buck's neck and when the fella quits kickin', then he lets go.

"Curly sits there for a few seconds, then picks up the scalp that Indian had just taken off the corporal. He stands up, walks off a ways, then sort of sits down, holdin' the scalp in his hands.

"Now y' see, one more Indian has come up on horseback just in time t' see Curly come off the ground and choke the guy that did the scalpin'. This new fella rides up t' where Curly is at and sits there on his horse. He looks down at Curly's bloody bare head, him sittin' there holdin' the corporal's hair in both hands.

"About then the kid, usin' the busted lance for support, hobbles over to the new guy. While the kid just stands there Curly just sort of slumps over on his side, this time gone for good.

"I'd almost forgotten where I was, till that damned old Indian with the crutch taps me on the head another time. I look up at those dead eyes, and he says, *Washichu!* Look hard. Hear hard, now!

"Well, I do just that. I look back at the rider on his bay mare talkin' to the kid and I listen hard, like I been told.

"Now I can see that rider real clear. So help me God I don't know how I can tell, but he's old Crazy Horse his own self! I hear him too, talkin' to the kid. He says, 'This white man has come from the dead to take back his own hair.' So help me, that's what Crazy Horse said. Then he straightens up on that bay and says to the kid with the busted leg, 'He has seen more on this day than any man should. He will be taken to a good place and buried in the white man's way. You will do this for him.' Then Crazy Horse just rides off up the draw."

Sam paused, shook his head a little, and continued.

"Well anyhow, about then I felt a cold chill, and everything got dark again. There I was, just sittin' in the snow lookin' at those little white markers all lit up in the moonlight, everything quiet as a mouse. I looked around and I was alone in that bunch of trees.

"Y' know, it was a good place all right, peaceful, kinda hidden, with the starry sky and all. But when I looked around to where I thought I heard that first voice I knew it was a lonely place, even for a grave."

I couldn't help interrupting Sam again and said, "Jesus, Sam, you sure you weren't—"

"Y' see, I thought you'd say somethin' like that. But there's proof. Just lemme finish.

"Now there I was, sittin' in the snow messed up bad—I'd even barfed on my shirt when I saw that scalpin' thing, thus humiliatin' my uniform some more. I was gettin' cold and figured I better try walkin' again. So I picked up my revolver that had slid out of my hand into the snow, wiped it off some and put it away. I knew I needed somethin' to lean on, so I looked around, and there was that old fella's crutch. A long stick lyin' right in front of me. I used it to hobble back to my patrol car and start the engine so's to get warm.

"I sat there in that Ford for about two hours till a truck driver gave me a ride to town. I sent a wrecker out to get the thing unstuck and gave my boss a story about bein' run off the road by another car in the dark. I sure as hell wasn't goin' to say what *really* happened. Not hardly."

Sam sat there for a while and relaxed, done with his story.

"Sam, that's weird—"

Sam raised his hand, palm toward me, and stood up.

"Wait a minute, I told you there's proof." He went into a bedroom, then came back and handed me a wooden pole.

"This is the old man's crutch, the stick I used t' get back to my car."

The stick was hardwood, worn smooth with use, with some carvings and an old rawhide wrapping near one end.

"Y' see those marks on it? I've had folks up at the University check it over," said Sam. That old man's crutch, it's a busted off part of a Sioux battle lance!"

As I sat there holding that stick and thinking about the voice in that lonely bunch of trees I knew Sam was right. Curly did want his story told.

HOMECOMING

First order of business when you've been away from home

Montana, 1925

Wilson Moraty sat in the back of the courtroom annoyed, like everyone else, that the overhead fans weren't working. Perspiration from Will's forehead made his gray beard tickle, but not enough to cause him to let his gaze deviate from the events playing out at the other end of the room.

As the jury began filing back in Judge Amos Brown banged his gavel twice and demanded quiet in the court. As the crowd took a few seconds to obey, the jurors took their seats. Like the silence that comes when a buzzing insect finally lands, tranquility filled the room.

"Alright you folks, I've been told you have us a verdict. Ezra, you're the foreman, you tell us what you decided."

"Sure Amos . . . ah, Your Honor. We spent the morning talking it over and we decided it was just an accident."

"Sam, you gotta say is this defendant guilty or not guilty of manslaughter. That's the law."

"OK Your Honor, sure. We say he's not guilty."

Immediately the crowd burst into a babble of voices. *He knew what he was doing. . . jurors are scared of his pa. . .* Bits and pieces of opinions filled the courtroom until Judge Amos Brown again slammed his gavel on the bench, three times.

In the back of the room Wilson Moraty rose to his feet, his attention focused on the proceedings of the court.

"Order in the court! Right now, damn it!" Glaring at the uniformed police officer standing by the bench, Judge Amos Brown added, "Bailiff. Anybody opens his mouth, you haul 'im out of here, got it?" Knowing the judge's no nonsense attitude toward any disruption in his court, the crowd of townspeople settled down.

"Now, you, the accused," said Judge Amos Brown, speaking to a young man dressed in an expensively tailored business suit. "You better thank that lawyer of yours for doing a fine job of confusing this jury. You are free to get out of my court room!" Then, with a disgusted look at the jury he added, "Y'all are free to go too, with no thanks from this court!" Several jurors were already scurrying out of the room.

"Hold on just one minute, Your Honor." Like that of a drill sergeant calling his troops to order, the commanding voice from the back of the room grabbed everyone's attention as Wilson Moraty walked toward the judge's bench. Worn riding boots, faded denim Levis and a sheepskin vest made one think the man was a local rancher, and that was true. But the star of a Deputy United States Marshal on his blue shirt made it clear that he was more than just an interested visitor in court.

"Marshal Moraty," I didn't know you were with us today, said Judge Brown. "This proceeding's over. You got something to add, it's too late now."

"Yes I have Amos, yes I have," said Wilson Moraty as he strode toward the bench.

The twenty-three year old defendant and his attorneys stood together near the bench. All impeccably dressed, they looked like a shiny new pennies in a mud hole amid the crowd of local farmers and working folks.

The room became quiet again—even without Judge Amos Brown's gavel—as nearby onlookers saw the facial expression and purposeful stride of the deputy marshal. Then the silence was broken forever by the explosion of a Colt .44-40 revolver as Deputy Marshal Wilson Moraty walked up to the defendant and shot him right between the eyes.

"*Now* the proceeding is over," said the deputy as he turned the Colt butt first and handed it to the uniformed bailiff whose jaw dropped open, speechless, as he accepted the firearm.

The next day Sam Moraty sat on a steel bench in Wilson Moraty's jail cell. Sam had his head in his hands and elbows on his knees in despair as he talked to his older brother. Wilson Moraty just sat, his face an expressionless blank.

"Jesus, Will. I still can't believe you did what you did. Jesus!"

"The bastard was guilty, everybody knows that."

"Yeah, but my God, Will. You've been a marshal for twenty-four years; You know sometimes the courts don't work right, you—"

"I know the law is a pile of crap, Sam. I've seen little guys go to the pen for a lot less than what that guy did. And I've seen more than one murderer get off 'cause he had money enough to buy the right lawyer, or scare some jurors, or—"

"You should have quit bein' a lawman long ago, Will. You spent too much of your life seein' the rotten side of the law and—"

"Time's up fellas," said a jail guard. "Judge said I could only give you fifteen minutes."

Reluctantly Sam Moraty stood up and said, "Anyhow, we're getting the best lawyer we can for your trial. And everybody knows you and what you've done for us all these years. It'll be OK."

Wilson Moraty stood up and shook his brother's hand as he said, "I know how the law's gonna work out this time. I'm gonna be gone for awhile for sure. Sam, you gotta take care of Martha for me; God, I just want to be with her . . . ."

"Sure I will; you know how I feel about Martha. Hell, I'd of married her myself if you hadn't found her first!"

Two weeks later Sam Moraty sat again in the same jail cell talking with his brother more about the past than about the bleak future that was facing Will.

"You could have done better tryin' to defend yourself," said Sam. "You clamed up too much; you should have let the jury see that you care, that you cared about people, all your time as a marshal, and that—"

"All I care about is family. Martha, you, and the old folks."

"Well, we got the appeal, said Sam." "And we're getting another lawyer for that. With a—"

"Wish I could just go up to the high pasture, with Martha. We'd have a picnic, like we used to do so much."

"Jesus, Will, they're gonna haul you off to the state penitentiary and all you think about is having a picnic!" muttered Sam, frustrated with his older brother's calm disregard for the whole situation. Sam was beginning to realize that Will was not the same man since the shooting. Morose and matter-of-fact about everything, Will didn't seem much interested in his own future, one that was not looking good anyway.

"Jesus, Will, I know being away will be tough. You two have been holdin' hands through life long as I can remember, but you gotta pay attention to reality now and help us with the appeal. It could take months, but we'll—"

"There's blue lupine blooming up there in the white oaks at the head of the valley this time of year," mumbled Will. "Martha loves blue lupine. They were blooming all over the place, near three foot tall, on the day I asked her to marry me. . . ."

Two Years Later

Wilson Moraty sat in his cell at the state prison, excited about the news he had gotten just a few hours earlier.

"Hey, old buddy, tomorrow I'm going home," Will said to his cellmate. "First thing there's gonna be a picnic right up the valley in the white oak trees, just me and Martha. She loves it there; it's our favorite spot."

Will walked back and forth across the cell clasping his hands together, and then spoke again.

"And ya know what, Ralph? The best part is I'm going home at just the right time of year. The lupines will be out! The blue flowers, the green grass, and those big old white oaks, it's gonna be fine. A picnic again, for me and Martha. Sam, he's been takin' care of Martha for me. I'm goin' home tomorrow."

Just then a guard tapped on the bars of the cell to get Wilson's attention. "Lights out Will. You OK?"

"Sure, you bet Lewis, lights out. And I'm just fine, too. Goin' home tomorrow and—hey Lewis!"

The guard, who had started to walk away, turned again to Will

'Yeah, Will. Somthin' you need?"

"Yep, there sure is. When I leave tomorrow will you keep an eye on Ralph here for me? His time's not up yet, and since he can't talk he has a hard time letting anybody know when he needs some company."

State prison guard Lewis MacPherson looked at Will for a few seconds and at the stark cell with its single bunk, then shook his head and said, "C'mon Will. Like I been tryin' to tell you for weeks Ralph's just a mouse damn it! He can take care of his own self."

Three days later Sam Moraty and a neighbor, Ed Benson, sat in a horse drawn wagon just pulling away from the concrete platform of the small town's railroad station.

"Sure am sorry the appeal didn't work out, Sam. Sure would have been a better thing if Will had got a life sentence for what he done. And that damn governor, he could've stopped the execution; he should have thought more about what Will did for all us folks, his bein' the marshal and all."

Sam Moraty said nothing as he and Ed drove the team up the valley road out of town. Just a few miles away was the head of the little valley where the white oaks grew on the Moraty cattle spread.

Glancing back to make sure the state issue pine box coffin was riding all right, Ed noticed another object in the wagon.

"Hey Sam, I been meanin' to ask. What's that you got under that cloth back there anyway?"

Sam Moraty didn't answer, and Ed just shrugged his shoulders and kept quiet, knowing that his friend needed quiet time of his own.

Finally, the two reached their goal in the high country of the Moraty Ranch. Ahead they could see another wagon, a few saddle horses, the local preacher's surrey and a group of friends and neighbors standing in a green meadow under a magnificent white oak tree. Blue lupines were blooming like an ocean of color mirroring the deep blue of the high country sky. But in spite of the beauty of the early summer day the mood was somber. For at the feet of the gathered visitors were two graves, with one headstone, bearing two names. "Martha Gilbert Moraty, born December 5, 1874, died March 13, 1925" and "Wilson Delbert Moraty, born August 14, 1870, died May 26, 1927."

The grave on the left was freshly dug, and ready to receive the coffin Sam Moraty had brought from the railroad station.

After the little funeral was over and most of the visitors and the minister had gone, two cowhands, one who had come by horseback and another who had driven up the work wagon, finished filling in the new grave and expressed their regrets to Sam. One cowhand headed for the work wagon as the other went to fetch his saddle horse.

As Ed climbed onto the freight wagon, Sam asked, "Ed, would you mind taking the wagon back by yourself? I'd like a little time alone up here with my brother."

"Sure Sam, sure."

"Hey boss, I'll leave you my mount," said one cowhand. "I'll ride back with Ed." The cowboy then stepped out of the saddle and handed the reins to Sam.

As Sam walked away, Ed muttered to his passenger, "Too bad Will had to die to get justice. Will's shootin' that guy was too good for the bastard."

"Yeah, hope he rots in hell," said the cowboy. "Gettin' drunked up, running over Martha with one of them new motor cars, then his old man threatin' the jurors . . .," mumbled Ed as the wagon continued down the valley.

A few minutes later Sam Moraty took the object that had caught Ed's attention in the wagon on the way up the valley over to the freshly turned dark soil where he then took off the white cover cloth and spread it between the two graves. Then he set down the basket, stocked with fried chicken, deviled eggs, two apples, and one bottle of white wine.

"Great day for a picnic," said Sam as he gazed around at the fine Montana sky. "Hope you two like the wine; we grew it here on the ranch just for you." Then Sam took to the saddle and with a touch of the fingers of one hand to his hat, turned the mare around and headed down the valley.

Never Turn Your Back on a Veterinarian

Advice from Monty McPooch

Y'know, these last few months have been really something for me. Last winter I was part of a family, but a really dysfunctional one. My littermates and I, well, let's just say we were abused, and me being low pup on the totem pole, I decided to run away from home. In some ways a dumb move, what with it being a cold West Texas winter and all, and I never reckoned with those damn coyotes either.

Y'see, I'm a Mexican immigrant, well of Mexican descent anyhow, from Chihuahua. Yep, I'm five pounds of genuine Chihuahua (I try to keep a low profile 'cause I don't have a green card!) Anyhow, even though it's desert here east of El Paso, the place can be colder'n all get out in December. That's when I decided to run off. I had to; that big gringo where I was livin' kicked me once too often.

So, there I was wandering around the edge of El Paso, but way out in the greasewood and cactus that covers most of the land. I had a few bad days there let me tell you. Hungry! Wow, I was ready to eat anything that moved, or had ever moved, for that matter. Y"see, us Chihuahuas, we're naturally pack animals. Back in the Old Country south of the Rio Grande we'd hunt in packs, and whatever there was we'd all get at least a little to eat. But being one little five pounder out there alone, well, I got real hungry.

Anyhow, late one evening I was hainging around a house, hoping for some scraps, when the owners came home. Boy those headlights scared me, and I scrambled up on a porch chair, trying to keep out of the way. They saw me, figured me for some stray, ignored me, and went inside. Next day a guy there, I'll call him Jim, felt sorry for me and gave me a few scraps of turkey left over from some big dinner. Wow that hit the spot. Then Jim cut a hole in an old cardboard box and put a blanket inside, then left me there on the front porch with a bowl of water. He was makin' points fast, that guy Jim.

Well, you know us Chihuahuas; scrunching up inside some secure feeling box is a good deal, so I hung around some. I sucked up all I could, tryin' to get more sympathy, (and more turkey) and put myself on my very best behavior. No barking or yapping, and lots of soft, black eyes looking as lovable as I could.

Apparently this started to pay off 'cause Jim's lady, name of Angie, she let me in the house! Well now, there I was in a new home, and boy first thing I did was to put up some little signs to let all dogdome know that it was *my* house. You know, hike up a leg and put a little squirt here and another there, no big deal, but important, that's for sure. Well, this didn't go over too well and I got thrown out on the porch again.

So, back with the charm, soft black eyes, waggly tail, and all. I was really trying hard, but I didn't often get back into the house. I didn't think I was making much progress toward survival, but it turns out I was doin' better than I thought.

Y'see Angie and her mother whose home it was decided to keep me permanently and got into their car and headed for town. They were going off to buy some nice things for me. Chew toys, a carrier, some dog chow—stuff like that. Boy, without knowin' it I was home free. But then I really blew it.

What I did was panic when I saw them drive off to town. I ran after them hard as I could for a long ways, but I couldn't keep up with that SUV. (Us Chihuahuas, our little legs aren't any good for chasin' cars. You hardly ever see us goin' after tires 'cept maybe on some small bicycle now and then.) Then what was really bad was, I got lost. I ran so far I couldn't get back to the house. Later I found out later that Angie and her ma were really sad when they got back from town with all the goodies they got for me and I was gone. After a couple of days they figured I was gone for good.

Those two days were tough for me too, let me tell you. All I could do was wander around the West Texas desert tryin' hard not to be breakfast for some coyote or such and things were looking real bad. But, way out in the desert there was a little house and some folks there took me in. They knew I was lost, so they put up a notice down at the local dog pound. I shudder when I even mention that place, but it paid off.

You remember the fella Jim, the guy who gave me some turkey? Well, he had sense enough to go to the pound and read lost dog notices, and by golly he found out where I was! The folks who found me lived four miles of open desert from where Angie's mother lived, but the gals came and got me. Wow was I glad to see them. And then I discovered that I had a bunch of genuine possessions (*pertenencias*, we call 'em back in the old country) of my very own. A big sack of kibbles, a plastic dish, and a nifty carrier with a fine, warm blanket. And especially the two gushy ladies and Jim; they all seemed to really like me. As you might guess, I was back on my best behavior, soft black eyes and all.

Well, there I was, back indoors again, and I thought I had it made. But for some reason those folks still got upset about the little signs I left here and there around the house. You know, just little claim markers. Heck, man, a guy's got to look out for what's his.

But the squirts seemed to upset everybody, so at night they put me in a little bathroom with tile floors and I just had to deal with that. It wasn't good, that's for sure.

Well, Angie and Jim, they took me off to some place way far away, their place as it turned out. And I heard them talking about taking me somewhere to get me computerized and some other stuff. They had a big back yard with a rock wall and all, and put me out there regularly enough to handle my personal business, in a manner of speaking.

But they were still touchy about my putting up little signs here and there indoors to mark this new turf. And I remember somehow this got mixed in with some talk about me getting shot, a veterinarian we had to visit, and that computer. That didn't sound good to me. Especially the getting shot part.

Well, there was a lot more to that visit to this veterinarian lady than I could have ever expected. A heck of a lot more. Y'see, that lady was a bit of a thief.

Oh she talked a good story. She put me on a table and Angie and the turkey guy Jim, they all talked about me and poked and prodded a lot. Seemed like nice folks, real concerned about me. Then Angie and Jim, they went away and left me there!

Well, the next day, that was a doozy, to say the least. This veterinarian lady picked me up the next morning and put me back on her table. She seemed really nice, petting and soothing and all. But then she got behind me and whooee, she shoved something up my own personal butt! Boy, was that a sensation. I still don't know what she took out of there or what she did with it, but whatever it was she called my "temperature." Then there was some talk about some computer chip they were gonna poke in me. Where, I didn't know, they'd already used up the obvious places.

And then this fella who was one of her henchmen, he poked me in my arm with some kind of pin and then I got to feeling strange. Kind of good, then sort of sleepy, and bingo even scared as I was, I just went to sleep! Can ya imagine? With all that goin' on I just zonked out.

Anyhow, later on I sort of woke up, feelin' ok, but a little woozy. Finally I got awake enough to realize that I was a little sore back where my transmission is, and on the back of my shoulders too. Still bein' sort of out of it I just dozed some more till Jim came and got me.

"Good doggy, everything's OK," Jim says.

Yeah sure. "Everything's ok," he says. Well, what the heck does he know? He's not the one whose crotch hurts like the dickens and who has a big band aid on his front arm where they stabbed me with a pin. And he isn't out two parts from his inventory! "Everything is OK." Ha! He probably doesn't even know about that little lump they put right between my shoulder blades. Lick hard as I can I can't get rid of the dang thing.

Well, Jim took me home, and he and Angie treated me real good. I got some kibbles, some extra chicken jerky strips, and, along with all my other stuff, a brand-new leather chew toy.

I figure I've managed to survive that visit to that veterinarian lady OK, but I sure wouldn't want to do it again. All in all, I was home in a nice place, good chow, fine bunk, and that lady Angie, well, she's the greatest. She's the alpha dog in my world; she was then and she is now too. The turkey guy Jim, he's a good guy too, but definitely the beta in my pack.

But you remember I told you that that veterinarian lady was a bit of a thief? Well, here's what happened. Y'see, next morning I was tending to a little personal hygiene as we dogs do. I was licking up a storm and that's when I noticed that something was missing at my back end. And that place was sore as all get out. A couple of things back there were just gone. I figure that veterinarian lady got 'em when she was shoving that damn thermometer up my tailpipe.

When I licked up my shoulders, well, right away I found that little thing she stuck under my hide there. I can feel it and it won't lick away, not at all. My Angie says it's a "computer chip," whatever that is. Jesus.

Me, a natural born chihuahua and now I've been bugged. It's sure no compensation for what that lady took off me when she was back there. Let me tell you, never turn your back on a veterinarian! There's no tellin' what can happen.

Now I gotta admit, as nice a guy as Jim, my beta pack member, is, I have one complaint. As I mentioned earlier, we have a great back yard all surrounded by a rock wall. Jim, he lets me out there to handle my personal business from time to time, and that works out fine, usually. But dang it, just when I build up a nice collection of my little prizes I like to leave here and there, well, here comes Jim and grabs 'em all! Can ya imagine that? I can barely put together one or two nice pieces in any one day, and then, just when the collection is getting some real character to it, well, here he comes. With his dang paper sack he walks all over and picks everything up. Ruins some of my best work, he does! Then I gotta start over building a collection. Anyhow, I do get to put up my little squirts back there in the yard; Jim can't get those! Kinda funny though, putting up my signs just doesn't seem as important now as it was before that veterinarian lady messed around back there behind me.

I think I understand though. My Angie was talking to her sister one day and I think she said that taking a couple of things out of my "little purse" as they called it has something to do with my interest in puttin' up little signs. They may be right. My pouch was what that veterinarian lady stole things out of all right, and I kind of think it was on purpose. One day I hope my Angie will maybe get me a couple of silicone implants to make things at least *look* like they should back there.

Well, that's my story. All in all I'm in good shape now. My alpha and beta are good folks, even though Jim sometimes tells folks that I'm a perfect socialist, whatever that means. He says I suck up a lot and expect to have all my room, board, and medical expenses paid by somebody else while I do no useful work of any kind. Well shoot, isn't that what being a good doggy is all about? It beats chasin' lizards around the desert down in the old country, that's for sure.

GOING HOME[6]

Even the best pilot occasionally takes a chance

Awakened by the late night phone call Steve sat on the edge of his bed in the darkened hotel room thinking about an automobile wreck and his injured son. Timmy was alive, but in an intensive care ward in a Key West hospital! And Steve's wife Sue had been so hysterical on the phone someone else had helped complete the call for her.

"Got to get home—now!" thought Steve.

As a corporate pilot for a wealthy businessman vacationing in the Caribbean Steve knew the fastest way home. A fully fueled twin-engine airplane was sitting ready at the island's airfield. He could have that Cessna back in Florida in less than four hours. But first he'd have to deal with his new boss.

Mr. R. H. Monahan took his visits to the island's nightlife seriously. This man who affected the lives of several thousand employees did not have a reputation for being overly concerned for the well being of any of them. How would the guy, probably hung over, respond to a newly hired pilot's plea to go home immediately?

If old Monahan would just cut his vacation short that would save trouble in the long run because one way or the other Steve intended to take the plane home—now.

Suddenly the phone rang again right under Steve's hand which he had not yet removed from the receiver. He sat more upright on the edge of the bed.

After mumbling "hello," Steve heard his boss's voice on the line.

_____

[6] Published in *Words of Wisdom*, June, 1999

"Grab your socks and hit the deck, son. I gotta be in the office before the first rattle of business. How soon can you get that clunk of mine in the air?"

"Immediately, sir," blundered Steve. Then he added, "Well, I need to check the weather and preflight the aircraft." As a well-trained professional pilot Steve did things correctly, even when in a hurry.

"Oh hell, the weather's great. Meet me in the lobby in five minutes!"

"Yes sir," replied the relieved pilot, already digging in a jacket pocket for a phone number. Good weather or not, local authority required that he get his weather briefing and file a flight plan.

Thirty minutes later Steve was ready and had filed a flight plan that called for an arrival in Florida just before dawn. With the professional pilot's aversion to carelessly stowed objects inside an airplane, Steve rearranged some of the luggage Monahan had thrown on board.

"C'mon kid, we gotta get a move on. I want every minute I can get in the office before those damn lawyers show up."

Another of the crises that seemed to fill Monahan's world. Though he was grateful for this one Steve knew that these apparent emergencies were all just part of Monahan's hyperactive way of doing business.

With Monahan strapped into the right seat of the aircraft and ready to go Steve took the left seat and soon had both engines running with healthy sounds coming from each. He taxied to the active runway and began his preflight checks of the fuel pumps and magnetos for both engines.

"Damn! Why now?" thought Steve as he found a problem. A few seconds earlier one engine had momentarily run just a little rough and a full power run-up had made Steve suspicious of either a bad fuel pump or plugged fuel injector. But now all appeared normal.

"Hey kid, you ready to fly this thing?" came Monahan's voice over the intercom.

"Sir, we may have a problem with the right hand engine." Steve pointed out Monahan's window toward the offending power plant. As he did so he noticed a momentary drop, just a twitch, in the number two engine tachometer. Then smooth performance again.

"Well, goose the thing," said Monahan as he peered out his window at the engine.

"Yeah, like you have any idea what an engine is", thought Steve as he eased a throttle forward. The engine roared appropriately and never missed a beat. After a few seconds Steve brought the throttle setting back to normal.

"Sounds fine to me; Ain't nothin' wrong with that puppy; lets go!"

Go is just what Steve wanted to do. He was thinking of his little boy and frightened wife out in the black night while his common sense, training, and federal regulations said get back to the ramp and have the engine checked out. Steve's thoughts became a mixture of hospital beds, engine parts, his wife's tears, and the cold, dark ocean.

"Mr. Monahan, that engine has an intermittent problem, it could give us trouble."

"C'mon son, you know this thing can fly on one engine if it has to. I wouldn't have bought the damn thing if it didn't have a spare. Get it rolling."

Yes, Steve knew the plane could fly, just barely, on one good engine in the unlikely event the rough one failed completely. But there was a lot of ocean to cross. And then Steve thought about Timmy, with tubes in his nose, and the frightening smells and noises that are part of any hospital. And Sue, sitting by Timmy's bed with tears in her eyes and fear in her heart. The engine seemed fine now and all the instruments said so too.

Using his radio, Steve reported to the tower that he was ready for takeoff.

The tower responded with "Zero Four Charlie, cleared for departure. Maintain runway heading until clear of the airport traffic area."

Noticing that Monahan was settled in for his customary nap on the trip home and himself feeling comforted by the familiar routine of the radio communications, Steve made his decision.

He eased the throttles forward and had the plane tracking right down the centerline of the wide, paved runway. In seconds the powerful aircraft reached flying speed and with a little backpressure on the yoke Steve lifted off. Soon he had the plane at crusing altitude and purring like a kitten through smooth air and a starlit sky over a black ocean. But with a feeling of guilt he paid even more than usual attention to the engine instruments, all of which read just as they should. With his passenger sleeping comfortably Steve's thoughts drifted even more toward his family somewhere in the darkness ahead.

Then, over an hour later during a routine scan of the instruments Steve was shocked to see a drop in oil pressure. A rising engine temperature confirmed his fears. That engine had lost its oil and would soon destroy itself, maybe even catch fire. With the practiced hands of a professional Steve smoothly performed the crucial tasks of feathering and shutting down the bad engine and retrimming all the controls for single engine flight. His passenger might not have even noticed except for the change in noise level.

"Hey, what's that?" questioned the corporate executive.

"We've just lost an engine," replied the pilot, with a bit of irritation, as though the man in the passenger seat had been responsible.

"Hey, this thing *will* fly on one fan won't it?"

"Yes sir, no sweat," replied Steve while thinking bitterly, "It had damn well better; we're 127 miles from the nearest land."

"Well, hang in there, son," said the executive as he relaxed a little in his seat as if to resume his nap. But he was keeping one eye on the aircraft's instrument panel.

With the loss of half its power and a tremendous increase in drag the airplane's flying performance was cut drastically. Steve eased back on the control yoke to maintain altitude as they lost airspeed. When the aircraft reached what Steve knew was its most efficient single engine cruse speed he retrimmed all the controls and waited to see if the plane could maintain altitude on its single functioning engine. He soon found that it could not, and that they were faced with a long, slow descent.

A mental calculation told Steve that in spite of his best efforts the aircraft was descending at a rate that would put them in the water before reaching land.

"Ah, how far are we from land?" asked Monahan.

"We are about an hour from landing sir."

"Ah, yeah. Well, in case you hadn't noticed we are going down!" Monahan's voice conveyed both concern and sarcasm as he jabbed his finger at the aircraft's altimeter.

"Yes sir, but as we descend the air will get more dense and our engine's power will increase." Then, to calm his passenger, he added, "I'll keep us flying at some lower altitude."

"OK, son, I guess that's why I pay you the big bucks. I ain't been swimmin' in about forty years and never was fond of ocean water at night!"

As the aircraft continued to descend Steve knew that his hope of maintaining normal flight on one engine was not to be. Concentrating with all his skill and experience, his hands and forehead wet with sweat, Steve watched the altimeter needle slowly creep down. His hope was the possibility of staying airborne in "ground effect," in the cushion of air that gives an airplane a little extra lift when it is flying just a few feet above a flat surface. Thankful for the calm sea and the fact that the runway at Key West is just a little above sea level, Steve prayed that he could make it all work out.

As the altimeter approached a sea level indication Steve turned on the landing lights to better judge their altitude. Looking out his window, Monahan saw gentle ocean waves just beneath the wing.

"My God, we're landing in the water!"

"No sir, we are in ground effect, we won't hit the water as long as nothing else goes wrong," said Steve.

"Jesus! How far is the damned airport?"

"About twenty miles."

"Hoo-ee!" muttered Monahan, cool headed enough to enjoy the excitement, but well aware of Steve's "as long as nothing else goes wrong" comment.

Minutes later Monahan, having realized they were indeed able to stay airborne just above the water, was enjoying the unusual flight. But noticing the clenched jaw, sweaty forehead, and intense concentration of his pilot, he began to suspect that there was more to flying on one engine than he had always supposed.

"Check that your seat belt and harness are really tight sir," said Steve. "In about two minutes we've got to climb a little to get over the beach and onto the runway.

With the airplane flying just above its stalling speed Steve watched the runway lights ahead. Just as the plane passed over the surf he eased back on the control yoke and traded some of his precious air speed for a few feet of altitude. Just seconds later, with too little speed to maintain flight, they stalled gently onto the runway and Steve was happy to hear the familiar "chirp" of tires on pavement just as he had prayed for.

The plane rolled straight down the centerline as it slowed to taxi speed. At the first turnout they left the runway.

Monahan, used to living in a high crisis environment and not knowledgeable enough about flying to know how serious their situation had been, took it all in stride.

"Nice landing son," said the executive, and at the same time he noticed that Steve wasn't displaying the casual coolness common to most corporate pilots. Monahan was looking at one nervous young man.

"Hey, cheer up fella. You said we had a bad engine but you could fly on one. Well, what the hell, we went, we lost one, and you flew it anyway. Nice work."

With a momentary glance at his boss, Steve braked the aircraft to a stop and pointed his flashlight out the left window toward the number one engine. When Monahan saw the motionless propeller he realized that it wasn't the bad engine that had quit.

A Kiss for Jack, A Pie for Little Petey[7]

It lies there in the afternoon sun, the center of attention but useless to anyone

Maria left the grocery store with her single purchase, a plastic bag containing six ripe peaches. For his fifth birthday party little Petey had asked for peach pie in place of a cake. Maria's happy dark eyes, her springy, almost dancing step, and cotton blossom yellow dress brightened everyone's day as she walked to her little red Volkswagen thinking of Petey and of her kitchen.

Just a few blocks away Willy was done frying hamburgers for the day. Glad that his work schedule gave him Friday evenings off, the teenager pulled his pickup onto Main Street and headed east to join his buddies at the mall, thinking of good times to come.

With thoughts of her little boy's happy face Maria drove out of the parking lot and turned onto a narrow street on her way to pick up Petey at a day care center. She knew she was lucky to have her little boy, one with an easy smile and permanent twinkle in his eye.

Not far away, Willy turned on his radio, loud, so he could feel the music. With his body swaying he'd caught the beat and was ready for a Friday night. Driving fast but skillfully as he thought he always did, Willy saw a traffic light ahead turn yellow. He continued on, knowing that if the light was yellow as he entered the intersection there would be no ticket. Not even if it turned red as he passed through.

As Maria approached the intersection where the little street crossed Main, she thought about Jack. She felt doubly blessed, for Jack was a fine husband. He would be on his way home too, ready to spend the weekend

---

[7] Published in *Desert Exposure*, June 2000

with his family. He would probably stop to pick up an inexpensive, but just right gift for his son Pete.

Maria saw her traffic light turn yellow and then red as she stopped. Knowing that the light was a long one and with thoughts of a kiss from Jack, she moved the rear view mirror to check her makeup. With her purse open on her lap Maria took out her lipstick.

Willy was enjoying the music when he saw another light turn yellow, further ahead. "Go for it," he said to himself and accelerated.

As Maria checked her handiwork with one more glance in the mirror she saw that her light had turned green. Feeling the pressure of traffic behind her she laid her lipstick on the seat and drove into the intersection.

Willy's increased speed was enough to get him there just as the light turned red—and green for Maria. Busy moving her purse and thinking of Jack and Petey, Maria only glanced to her left.

The screech of Willy's tires ending in a single loud crash masked the quieter sounds—cracking and squishing sounds—as Maria's chest was crushed.

The thing just lays there as strangers stand and stare.

Pale faces without smiles.

One officer measures tire marks on the pavement,

another writes in a notebook.

"So sudden—couldn't help it," says Willy. "I didn't mean; oh God I didn't—"

"Here son, you better sit down," says an officer as he takes Willy by the arm. Knowing the boy might faint, he lowers him to a seat on the curb.

The thing on the ground lays in the scattered contents of Maria's purse.

Its yellow dress is ripped; one shoeless leg is bare.

A stranger takes official photographs.

There is no dignity for the dead.

The lipstick for Jack's kiss is smeared now, on a purple face. An officer looks into the mangled wreckage of Maria's red Volkswagen and notices a ripened peach lying undamaged near a bent floor panel. Somewhere inside the dusty jumble of metal, plastic, and glass there is a single tube of lipstick.

Eventually a shiny truck takes the thing away.

But where have all the kisses gone? And the days Maria's family had ahead? They're just gone, like Petey's pie.

A PROMISE TO STEPHANIE

Some things are not meant to be—right away

In a village a few kilometers from the Czechoslovakian city of Prague is a park. It has lots of trees, a cinder covered path, a little brook, and in the summertime flowers provide eruptions of color everywhere. Near a grassy stream bank stands a fountain erected by the townsfolk to honor one of their own. Not far away is a concrete bench where one can enjoy the trickling water, the cotton puff clouds in the azure sky and the endlessly varied green hues of trees and shrubs. On one summer day in 1993 a middle-aged man from far away sat beside an elderly lady. Together they watched the fountain, each with quite different thoughts about the person whose name the fountain bears.

Wintertime, 1974
West Germany

I sat alone at a table covered with red-checkered oilcloth and located off to one side of the room, but I still had some view of the stage in the combination nightclub and restaurant. Being a foreigner I preferred to keep a low profile in that rough bar frequented mostly by soldiers from a nearby military training camp. Soldiers and local girls busily building the next morning's hangovers. I was happy to be back in the small German town I visited from time to time.

"Hello, Mr. Carsen, nice to see you again," said a waitress whom I knew only as Hanne—short for the German name Hannelore, a name that always sounds like poetry to me. Hanne had automatically brought me a glass of white wine.

I watched a comedian as he finished his act. Because German was a foreign language to me I couldn't catch much of his humor, but I enjoyed it all anyway.

Then several musicians took his place and began tuning their instruments. A violin, a base viol, several drums and a clarinet. As they began their first number they filled the room with a pleasant mix of sounds from their unlikely combination of instruments. I sat back to enjoy more of their talent; it blended well with the fine product of Germany's Mösel River Valley in my glass.

And then I saw her.

Like a springtime breeze through an open window she appeared at the back of the room and strode directly toward the stage, arms outstretched in greeting to the crowd. In her mid-twenties she was a truly beautiful girl. Her movements with the grace of an Olympic skater, her sky blue evening dress, and her waves of golden hair all demanded visual attention. With a charisma both overwhelming and indefinable she bowed to the audience, turned to the stage and took her place in the quartet of which she was a part.

And then she sang. Some might say that the German language is coarse, not so naturally pleasant as is French or Portuguese. But when spoken by a woman with the right accent German can be music to the ear. And if the speaker can sing—well, then it can be an experience never to be forgotten.

This lady could indeed sing, with a range of voice at one time reminiscent of Caterina Valente and at another with the lusty sexiness of the ballad "Lili Marleen." She did indeed deliver a rendition of that German World War I favorite, an appropriate choice for the mostly military audience. Stephanie Volodin was her name, stage name anyway.

After several more numbers in German I got yet another surprise. She sang a new song that was popular in Europe. It was "La Paloma Blanca," a favorite of mine. And Stephanie sang the English version with an accent that would make an American diction teacher proud. So, I presumed she was a German girl who had learned English well, very well indeed.

But I was not in Germany on vacation. I was an American scientist working on matters of interest to several European governments and to that of West Germany in particular. With work to do early the next day I finished my glass of wine and left.

I came back several times to that club, sometimes ordering a pizza and a *Weizenbier* as did many of the local people, or sometimes just a glass of white wine, but always alone and always at the same table. I sat through various comic routines, lesser musical groups, an occasional burlesque show, and a couple of drunken brawls just to be there when that particular quartet with its delightful vocalist took the stage. I was captivated by this creature who could attack my mind with the beauty of sights and sounds from all around, as though from deep inside my soul.

And yet I knew nothing of who or what she really was. Talent, charisma, and skill as a performer say nothing about character or intelligence, the things that matter. Still, I spent several pleasant evenings in that club alone and lost in Stephanie's magic.

One evening after completing her set Stephanie left the stage by gliding through the throng of enthusiastic, ogling soldiers and their various dates toward the back of the room and disappearing. With her voice echoing in my mind I felt that nothing bad could ever happen in a world that had someone like that nearby.

Moments later I felt a presence beside me. Looking up I saw a vision of loveliness like nothing I have seen before or since. Stephanie stood there, her clear blue eyes matching her evening dress and earrings, all in brilliant contrast to her sunset colored hair and those fine red lips that were about to speak to me. I knew I hadn't died and gone to heaven, but the thought crossed my mind.

"Good evening," she said, speaking in German. "Would you mind if I sat here with you for a while?"

Not waiting for an answer, she put a small golden handbag on the table.

Every bit as suave as Peter Sellers, I spilled some of my Zinfandel and nearly stumbled over my own chair as I stood to hold one out for this lovely creature who had just acknowledged my existence.

"You are not like these others," said the vision, waving a hand toward the room in general. "And you are alone. If I sit with you they will leave me alone long enough for me to have a glass of *Sekt*."

I ordered a glass of the bubbly wine called *Sekt* in Germany, but *spumanti*, sparkling wine, or Champagne in other parts of Europe. When her wine arrived Stephanie asked the waitress—Hanne again—for a straw. She was given one in its usual paper wrapper which Stephanie did not remove before placing the straw into the quietly bubbling glass.

Puzzled by her actions and being great with small talk I muttered, "Huh! That's interesting!"

"I like the wine," she said, "but there is too much carbonation. The straw takes some away and makes the wine softer."

Indeed, she was right. Thousands of tiny bubbles streamed up from the paper wrapper. After a few seconds she removed the straw.

"My name is Tom Carsen," I said, offering my hand. I almost blurted out the German equivalent of 'what's a nice girl like you doing in a place like this?' but caught myself in time.

"Pleased to meet you, Tom. I have not heard that name before. I think it is not German, no?"

"No, I am an American. Probably the only one in town."

"Ah, that is nice. I have never met a Westerner who is not German."

A peculiar comment I thought, remembering how well she sang English lyrics.

"Do you speak English?" I asked.

"No, only German, Russian, and my own language."

"Your own language? Where are you from?"

"Czechoslovakia. My home is near the city of Prague."

Stephanie explained that her quartet was a group of Czechoslovakian musicians who had managed to win a short visit to West Germany as part of a cultural exchange program. An impressive accomplishment at a time in the Cold War when for most Soviet citizens visiting "The West" was just a dream.

I thought again of her flawless rendition of the lyrics of "La Paloma Blanca."

"The song you sang in English, do you understand its words? You sing it so well and I like it very much."

"No, but I have listened to the radio and to phonograph records."

Like many good vocalists Stephanie could memorize foreign words with near perfect pronunciation. That evening I translated her memorized English lyrics into German for her, and pointed out that the title was not English at all, but Spanish for "The White Dove." She seemed happy to know these things about the meaningless words she had sung so many times.

Over the next few weeks Stephanie and I grew closer. Whenever she was on stage and I chanced to come in she would wave to me and not long after sing "La Paloma Blanca." I would just stand and listen as though nothing else existed.

But there was a war going on. A cold one, but a war that was quite real for its serious participants, of which I was one. Because of the secret nature of my work I was subject to special laws concerning contact with people from communist countries. And I was well aware that the Soviet Union used attractively innocent looking women in its espionage activities against the nations of The West. So, I had to wonder why Stephanie had singled me out as a friend. But my oh my, how that girl could sing!

She introduced me to the others in her group. They too were from Czechoslovakia, except one older man—the drummer. Who was it somewhere who said, "Drums are for people who can't make music"? Probably some concert violinist, or maybe a piano teacher I'd met long ago. Anyway, I watched this fellow carefully and could see that he was not there because of musical talent.

In spite of the Iron Curtain that separated us, Stephanie and I shared our thoughts on the little things that interest a man and woman who are happily discovering each other. But always at that little table and always with the knowledge that in just weeks she must go back inside the cage that the Soviet Union had imposed on half of Europe.

"Where is your favorite place in all the world?" Stephanie once asked me.

I described a remote canyon in my native state of Arizona. I told her of the giant saguaro cactus, the thorny chaparral, the yapping of coyotes, and the silent silhouette of a red-tailed hawk soaring high in the turquoise sky. And I told her of the special solitude that sometimes comes to the desert when the evening air gets ususually still just as the sun goes down.

"Ah, the American Southwest, cowboys and Indians," she said. She knew of these wonders from books and from the two American movies she had seen. But for Stephanie such things were as remote as the surface of the moon.

"I too have a favorite place," Stephanie told me. In a park near my home there is a place with lots of flowers of many colors, even some tiny violet ones. When I was a little girl there was magic there and I think there still is."

I pictured a lively little lass with shiny black shoes, her dress a bouquet of color, her blond hair in braids, kneeling in a green meadow picking flowers.

Stephanie smiled and said, "When I lay there on my back the scent of blossoms is a magic potion in the air. If you listen carefully the breeze through the trees makes a chorus with each leaf adding its own tiny voice. And there is the orchestra of bubbling water in the stream; it too adds to the music of my magical place. I think it is perhaps the same magic you feel in your Arizona."

Stephanie spoke to me with words that were not sung but sparkled in my mind. In her rhythm of speech I found the talent of a poet as well.

The music and the magic potion are there for a purpose she told me. "To help you see the 'cloud dancers' in the sky. Each cloud is a life that has gone before, one that was here only for a short time," Stephanie said. "The clouds dance to the music in the trees, in the water and in the breeze."

Almost forgetting to breathe as I listened to her voice, I inhaled sharply, and for just an instant I knew the scent of Stephanie's magic flowers. I was enchanted just being by her side.

Then Stephanie told me that "*The music is soft and quiet and the cloud dancers move ever so slowly because now they have all the time in the world.*" Many years were to pass before I would grasp the significance of those last few words.

For a long time I had been thinking of ways to spend some time with Stephanie away from the night club atmosphere. Maybe just a walk around town or lunch together. So, I decided to give it a shot.

"Stephanie, I know you live here in this club's hotel, all of your quartet does. And I know you always go in a group to restaurants for dinner. But perhaps just you and I could go somewhere together?"

I waited for an answer, my mind a turmoil of embarrassment, fear of rejection, and a hurried review of military security regulations regarding contact with communist nationals. Had I reached out for the treasure of a lifetime, or had I just taken Soviet bait? If Stephanie said yes I would have government paperwork to fill out.

Stephanie laid her right hand on mine and smiled in silence for a few moments. Her eyes, blue like tropical ocean waters I had known, conveyed to me her desire to say yes.

But she did not.

She raised the fingertips of her other hand to her lips and then laid that hand on mine as well. I felt at that instant all the wonders of being alive, healthy, and human, and yet I was in the middle of a quiet war—one that forced answers to be wrong.

"Do you see that man, the one who watches us?" She nodded ever so slightly toward a table occupied by, yes, by the drummer.

"He says what I can and cannot do, and he would say no, and I will never forgive him or my country for that."

I knew then that the drummer was the "keeper" for the little group of musicians who had won a temporary taste of The West. At international conferences I sometimes had contact with scientists from the Soviet Union. I was aware that when these people traveled outside the Soviet Union they were often accompanied by someone who was ostensibly a colleague, but seemed disinterested in science. "Keepers" is the term I used in my mind for these shadowy individuals. In the Soviet world everyone was being watched by someone.

I changed the subject. I asked Stephanie about her music, about what kind she liked best.

"Children's songs," she said. "I like to be with children and help them sing. Their hearts grow best when they all sing together."

That evening Stephanie asked me for a promise.

She started, "In two days we are leaving—"

"But you still have more time to be here in West Germany," I protested.

"Yes, but we are going to a new town, a fine club near Munich. And you must promise to come and see me there, at least once, if you can."

"Tell me where, and I'll be there," I said, and she told me the club's name. We spent what little time we had left that evening just sitting together, both aware of the minutes that were slipping away.

I had just one chance to visit Munich, my favorite city in all of Europe, during those days when Stephanie's quartet was there. On that evening I hurried to an up-scale nightclub and saw at the entrance photographs of Stephanie. Professional Hollywood style pictures advertised the establishment's main talent for the time being. Many times in the years since I wished that I had taken a picture away with me.

Inside I found a room awash with the sounds I had come to hear and on the stage was again the loveliest woman I had ever known. She saw me right away, smiled and pointed at me, and the next song she sang was "La Paloma Blanca." In minutes the rest of her quartet and some of the regular patrons knew I was there to see her.

I was seated at a table to one side as was my preference. The club manager provided a complimentary bottle of *Sekt* for his headline singer and her guest. Stephanie's talent gave her some pull around the place. At the end of her set she came to me.

We spent time together as alone as anyone can be in a room full of nightclub patrons. I had to tell her that I was leaving for America the next day. And we both knew that she would soon return to the land of confinement on her side of the Iron Curtain.

"You know of my village, you remember its name?" Stephanie asked.

"Yes, I do."

"And you know of my special place, my magic place. We only have one park, it is not hard to find."

"Yes, I know that too."

With candle light gleaming from the gold of her hair and her blue eyes reaching into my heart, she took both my hands in hers.

"You must make me another promise." She looked deep into my eyes and I was putty in her hands. "You must promise to come and see my special place. Not now, but some day."

Seeing a tiny flicker in my eye that she knew was because of the impossibility of her request Stephanie continued, crushing my hand tighter as she spoke.

"Someday, come when you can. Please tell me you will; I only need the promise—"

"I will Stephanie, someday I will." Tears came to her eyes and mine as well.

We spent what time we could together that evening, each aware of but not mentioning the Iron Curtain that was coming down between us on this, our very last hour. Then, as closing time neared, I knew I was watching Stephanie sing for the last time.

Minutes later, with my thoughts in sad confusion, I stood in a small anteroom getting my overcoat from a hatcheck girl who suddenly disappeared from behind her counter and Stephanie took her place. We were actually alone—for the moment.

Stephanie came to me, put her arms around my neck and kissed me, and I held in my arms all the best that life has to offer any man, anywhere, anytime. And then she was gone. Then I bumbled outside into the winter night barely aware of the fluffy snowflakes falling softly in my path.

The following week I sat on a sandstone ledge in a remote canyon watching a warm, quiet Arizona sunset. The little nightclub where I had spent so much time seemed like a dream or a soft memory from that old movie about "Shangri-La." But I knew that for a few more evenings an incredible voice would ring through a room in a faraway land singing "La Paloma Blanca," and that a lovely lady would be thinking of me.

Eighteen Years Later

We have all witnessed an event that may be unique in the affairs of nations. I know of no other time in history when one of the most powerful military structures in the world just rolled over and died without a shot being fired or a blow being struck. But the Soviet Union did this. It just stepped out of existence and the hated Iron Curtain came crumbling down.

Many times during the years since I met that extraordinary girl from a communist land I had thought of Stephanie. Throughout my life and considerable travels she was never far from my mind. Like a spinning carousel, memories of her eyes, her smile, her music, and her way of making all of life seem good had won a place in my heart that left no room for anyone else.

And now, after all these years, the Cold War was over. Retired and no longer restricted by European or American laws and no longer a target for Soviet espionage, I could now visit "the other side" if I chose to. More and more I thought of the promise I had made to Stephanie so many years earlier.

So, I found myself in a rented car in the newly unified Germany (no "East" or "West" designation now) approaching the Czechoslovakian border. It seemed strange to pass with ease through a border checkpoint where armed men would have stopped me for interrogation—or worse—years before. Now courteous customs officers pointed me on my way toward the city of Prague. It was awkward to deal with the unreadable road signs and an incomprehensible language, but German is a common second language in Eastern Europe so I knew I would get along fine.

I easily found the village I was looking for. Its name had stayed with me all through the years. I felt sure that I could find some trace of a girl as unusual as Stephanie.

As I drove into the village the street ahead was blocked by an approaching procession of some kind. A police officer, yelling and waving his arms, made it clear that I should either get out of the way or disappear. I drove onto a sidewalk as a throng of people began passing and then I worked my way into a small side street. Twice I asked what was going on, but the Czechoslovakian answers meant nothing to me.

I found a small hotel and got a room for the night. The clerk, whose name was Karel, spoke a little German so I asked him about Stephanie hoping that at least the family name might mean something to him.

"Yes, I know her, everyone knows her," he said, looking at me with an odd expression.

"Can you tell me where her home is?"

Karel stood in silence for a time, and then, with the deference one gives to small children and ignorant foreigners, he rummaged through some papers that looked like magazine pages and chose one in particular.

"This is her family's address." On a scrap of paper he scribbled some words that would have been no less recognizable to me if they had been upside down. I gave him my best expression of pleading confusion and he drew me a little map.

The next day I followed the mapped instructions. The streets were laid out well, but not paved, as they would have been in a West German town. I found the address and walked up a gravel path through a broken gate to the door of a small cottage. Standing there for a few moments I wondered about my folly. A total stranger from the other side of the planet, did I have any business being there?

Knowing that I had to sooner or later, I knocked on the door. It was answered by a teen-age boy who spoke no German. I repeated several times a name that Karel had taught me to pronounce. Hopefully, a relative of Stephanie's.

The boy nodded then ducked inside and a woman came to the door. I saw immediately blue eyes like I remembered from long ago, but now in a face surrounded by gray hair. The woman was much older than Stephanie would be.

"May I help you?" she asked in German, much to my relief. She had noticed the nationality marker on my rented car.

"Yes, ma'am. I hope so. I am looking for Stephanie Volodin."

This was a sturdy woman in spite of advanced years, but she trembled at my request. Again I felt that I did not belong there.

"Who are you?" she asked.

I gave her my name and told her that I was a friend of Stephanie's a long time ago, in Germany. She just watched me for a long, awkward moment.

"You are an American, yes?"

A perceptive lady, I thought. Anyone who speaks German well would know that I was not German, but I knew that I did not have the usual American accent. How did she know where I was from?

We stood in silence for a moment, and then with a slight slump of her shoulders she spoke again.

"Please wait here for a moment. I would like to talk to you. It is best that we walk, so I must get my wrap."

She returned with a green wool shawl wrapped around her shoulders and clutching an old cigar box tied with a sky blue ribbon. Soon we were strolling along a pleasant dirt road paralleling a small stream that was overgrown with weeds. Though she took my arm as we walked it was only a polite gesture. This lively, elderly woman set a brisk pace as we headed toward a city park.

Gathering her thoughts, the lady walked in silence. I thought of the promise I had made to visit Stephanie's magic place. Apparently I was about to keep it.

The park we came to was well kept with nicely mowed grass and a decorative stone fountain bubbling pleasantly. At a simple concrete bench the lady suggested that we sit. We talked for a while about how pleasant the sunny day was.

Finally, she said, "I am Stephanie's mother."

Two young boys and a rust colored cocker spaniel ran past, interrupting our thoughts.

"A nice place for kids to play," I ventured to get the conversation going again.

"That is what parks are for, Mr. Carsen. They are for people to forget other things and enjoy being alive." Stephanie's mother took a small tissue from a pocket and dabbed an eye.

Putting away the tissue, she asked, "Do you like children, Mr. Carsen? Do you have family—children—of your own?"

"No ma'am. I have never been married."

With her hand the lady touched my face and turned my head so that she could look straight into my eyes. She wanted to see my answers rather than just hear them.

"Why not, Mr. Carsen. Why don't you have children?"

Not knowing what to say, I just started talking.

"I believe that a man should have children only when he has found a woman who makes him want to be a family with her. I have traveled most of my life and have known many interesting people but I have never found a woman who was the right one for me."

Surprised and embarrassed by the little speech I had just made I tried to look away from the lady, but she wouldn't let me. Still with her hand on my face she peered into my eyes.

"Mr. Carsen, you knew my daughter, in Germany."

"Yes, I did."

The intensity of those honest blue eyes searching deep into my own made me feel exposed and vulnerable. This peasant woman in this land so far from my own was making me realize why I had never married. And we both knew that what I had just said was not true, not at all. As I thought of Stephanie I felt all hollow inside.

Aware that I was uncomfortable, she took her hand away and said, "I think you have suffered a great loss, Mr. Carsen." Then, with a slight tilt of her head and shrug of her shoulders she added, "Ah well, most men do not know what is good for them until it is too late."

I felt like a schoolboy chastised by his teacher.

The two little boys came by again, going back the way they had come, and as they passed the spaniel stopped to sniff my foot. I scratched behind his ear and ruffled his fur some and his stubby tail wagged appropriately. As he scampered away after his buddies I remembered Rags, a red cocker spaniel that I had known when I was a small child. And I thought of my mother and father and the solid, happy family that they had created together long ago.

When we were alone again the lady untied the bow around the worn cigar box in her lap.

"When my daughter was in Germany she wrote to me often. I want you to read something." She started to pass a handwritten page to me, and then realized that I could not read the language. "I will read it for you," she said, holding the small, light blue paper with both her hands.

"Mama, tonight I met a nice man. He comes into the club and he likes my singing. He is not like the soldiers or the others. He is quiet and really listens to me sing. Tonight I went to his table and we talked. I hope he comes back and I think he will."

Shuffling through the box she chose another letter and continued reading.

"He comes to see me often Mama. Each night I hope that he will come. When I sit with him the soldiers do not make rude comments about me or pester me. I feel safe when he is there; other men seem to respect him."

"You see, Mr. Carsen, from her letters I believed that my daughter was writing about a citizen of West Germany. I did not like that. I believed there could be no future for Stephanie and a man from The West."

Carried back to that distant time and place I thought of the Cold War and of the Iron Curtain that sliced Europe apart with dark forces that I had believed no man or woman could overcome.

Or could they have? Now, in a different time in history, a void in my heart said that I had been wrong about that too.

She started reading again from another page, this one pink colored.

"Mama, I am going to a new club! It is much nicer. I will ask Tom to come see me there. I want him to see me in a place without soldiers and bad women. Tonight I will make him promise to come and I will sing for him there. Mama, when we sit together and he holds my hand we talk about many things. His words take me away to other places and to his Arizona. Even when I say confusing things he understands. I know he likes people and I think he would like children too."

The lady brought out her tissue again, her eyes tearful as she clutched her daughter's written words to her breast. I sat beside her in a confusion of happiness and despair, flattered that a girl such as Stephanie had such thoughts of me, and at the same time feeling ashamed that I had not been man enough to deserve those words from long ago. I was becoming more lonely than I ever thought possible. We let some time pass in silence while I stared unseeing at the bubbling, little fountain.

The lady put away her tissue, turned her face straight toward me and said, "Mr. Carsen, there is one last part that I must read to you." Again she rummaged through the box.

"Mama, tonight he kissed me! He held me in his arms, strong and gentle all at the same time. He held me close and made me feel safe. Mama, I want to give him children. I want my children to feel this good man's strength. I remember how good it was to be in Papa's arms before he died. Tonight when Tom kissed me we were both very happy for that little time that this life gave us. In two weeks, Mama, I will come home, and that makes me happy. But I am sad too because I know that I will never see Tom again."

By this time the lady's scrap of tissue was done in so I gave her my handkerchief. A silly sight we made, a middle aged man and an elderly woman who had just met, sitting in the sunshine crying together about the contents of an old cigar box.

"Ma'am," I said, not confident that I could handle my voice, "Where is Stephanie now?" (Is she married? That's what I really wanted to know.)

"Oh Mr. Carsen! You don't know!" The lady clutched the handkerchief to her mouth.

"You came here yesterday; the man at your hotel sent his son to tell me so. Perhaps you noticed the procession in the village?"

"Yes, I saw it." It almost ran over me, I said to myself.

The lady's hand clutched my arm almost painfully hard as she said, "That was my daughter's funeral."

Like a bucket of ice water from behind, those words struck the depths of my very existence. Without coherent thought, I cried softly in the presence of this graceful woman who had undoubtedly seen far more sadness in her life than I ever would.

She put her hand on mine in a gesture that reminded me of Stephanie. Then, looking up at me she seemed smaller and older, with a soft and trusting expression that made me think of my own mother in the days just before she died.

The gentle, gray-haired lady laid her head on my shoulder for a time and then sat more upright. Again the sturdy European homemaker, unbowed by her years.

"Was Stephanie happy?" I asked a question that was at the heart of my journey. I had needed to know that the lovely creature I had discovered long ago was having a good life.

"Yes, always." Then after a pause, "Let me tell you about my daughter."

"When she came back from Germany she became very popular. She sang in restaurants, at weddings and at city celebrations. Mostly she sang in schools where she taught children. She was happiest when she could hear children sing."

"Did she get married; did she have children of her own?" I blurted out the questions. Over the years I had tried to imagine what sort of man could win the heart of a girl like Stephanie.

"Ah, she had many suitors, but she never married. That was a loss to me; I wanted to have grandchildren."

There was a hint of scorn in her voice and for a moment her eyes blamed me for her disappointment.

"Mr. Carsen, even as a child my daughter knew that she had a heart condition that would make her life short. Such a thing would make many children sad, but not Stephanie. She said it meant that she would just use up her full lifetime of happiness in a shorter time. It seemed to work that way too. She was always cheerful, always seeing the good side of life and sharing it with people around her.

"You see, even as a child everyone loved Stephanie. Our village helped send her to Germany because all of us were proud of her."

"I know that she liked this park very much," I ventured, as the lady dabbed at her eyes with my handkerchief.

"Yes, Mr. Carsen, she did. She came here to watch the 'cloud dancers' she said. When I asked my daughter what they were, she just said they were special friends. Most little girls have imaginary friends, not so, Mr. Carsen?"

"Yes ma'am, I guess so."

I thought of Stephanie, always knowing that her life would be cut short. And now I realized what her words from so long ago— *the cloud dancers move ever so slowly because now they have all the time in world*—really meant.

"I once told my daughter that she should marry so she would not be lonely, and she just said that she would never be lonely as long as she could teach children to sing."

Again Stephanie's mother put the handkerchief to an eye and her voice cracked as she continued.

"And then my daughter put her fingertips to her chest and said to me, 'Mama, I could never be lonely anyway because I have my American in my heart.' That remark will be with me all the rest of my life, Mr. Carsen."

A silence ensued, and I knew that those words would stay with me as well.

We sat there for several minutes in that pleasant little part of Eastern Europe, each with different thoughts. Stephanie's mother began telling me more about her daughter and the telling changed her somber mood to one of nostalgia, and then to cheerful parental pride.

It seemed that Stephanie had won considerable fame in her country among young people who flocked to hear her sing. She had worked most of her abbreviated life with a local orphanage and she was the pride of the whole village.

Finally, Stephanie's mother got to the final thing she wanted to tell me.

"Mr. Carsen, in the weeks before she died Stephanie said many times that you would come. She said that you had promised that you would come, and that when you did I should bring you here, to her special place. And that I should leave you here—alone."

Stephanie's voice was crystal clear in my memory as I thought of her words from that night in Munich. *"Some day, come when you can. Please tell me you will; I only need the promise—."*

"Mr. Carsen," whispered Stephanie's mother as she nodded toward the bubbling garden fountain, "over there is something for you to see. Years ago our town built it for my daughter and after she came back from Germany she had something added to it. I think that is what Stephanie wanted you to see." The lady motioned toward the fountain a short distance away as she stood up.

I offered her my arm, presuming we were to go where she had pointed.

"No, Mr. Carsen. I must go home now."

With the formal courtesy so common to elderly European women she offered me her right hand and bowed ever so slightly, saying, "It was nice to meet you Mr. Carsen. I have enjoyed our talk this afternoon."

I politely shook her hand and then she impulsively kissed me on the cheek, turned, and walked away.

Feeling curiously at home in that little Czechoslovakian park, I walked toward the memorial fountain. Built of stones set in concrete with water bubbling from its top, it bore Stephanie's name and some words I could not read. But I noticed a carved panel of white marble on one side, an image of a bird perched on a man's hand. Engraved below were the words "The White Dove," and those words were in English.

I laid my palm on the white stone and felt the cold water run over my hand. Then I walked to the bank of the little stream, free of weeds in this well cared for park, and sat down in waning sunlight near a rainbow-colored bed of tulips bordered by a profusion of tiny pink flowers.

There were cotton-puff clouds in the sky, a sky the same blue color as the dress Stephanie was wearing the moment I first saw her. Succumbing to the scent of the "magic potion" from the nearby blossoms, I lay back on the soft grass in that peaceful place and listened carefully, hopefully.

Yes! It was subtle, and faint, but I heard the chorus of voices that were the leaves in the trees, and the orchestral accompaniment of the nearby brook. And as I slipped further into memories of Stephanie the puffy little clouds, turning orange in the evening light and moving ever so slowly— with all the time in the world—danced for me.

As all the others faded away in the darkening blue sky, one small cloud took on the color of Stephanie's golden hair in the last light of that summer sunset. Then, as I lay there in her magic place watching that one special cloud dancer, I heard Stephanie's lovely voice sing "La Paloma Blanca" one more time, just for me.

ARTIE LOWELL'S FIRST SCOOP

Sometimes a lawman has had all he can take

Leaning with a two-hand grip on his broom handle Artie Lowell stood on the wooden sidewalk as he watched the motorcar pop and bang its way up Bozeman's main street. It wasn't the first one Artie had seen. Still, the little car slipping around in the mud of a recent Montana snowstorm with its driver wearing goggles and a tan duster was a sight worth watching. Especially for a boy deliberately cultivating the habit of being observant as he knew any good newspaperman should be.

As the car and its noise disappeared around a corner Artie glanced in the other direction where the street ran out of town. His attention was caught again by two men approaching single file on horseback and a scrawny dog that scurried across the street just ahead of the hooves.

Artie recognized the first rider. He was William Marshal, a sturdy man in his late fifties who occasionally visited the town. Looking uncomfortable, Bill was sitting his saddle slumped a little sideways. Artie noticed too that his blue cotton shirt was torn, apparently to provide cloth for the bandage around his left thigh. But there was enough shirt left to hold the badge of a Deputy United States Marshal right where it had been for the last twenty-two years.

The second man looked huge, even on the big appaloosa gelding that was being led by the marshal. Sitting backward in the saddle with no hat and a big bruise on the side of his face, this man had his hands tied to the saddle horn, behind his back.

Artie let go of his broom and scurried through the doorway.

"Mr. Greener! The marshal's in town and he has a prisoner!"

The owner and publisher of the Gallatin County Dispatch came to join Artie who was already back outside.

"Good morning Bill," said Mr. Greener as the two riders passed by. A friend of the lawman, he would have said more but didn't. The perfunctory nod he had received in response to his greeting let the newsman know that his friend was not in a good mood. The dusty clothes and dark stain from a knife wound in the marshal's thigh were explanation enough. The fractured left wrist didn't even show.

"Well Artie, it appears that those boys have scuffled around some."

"Yes sir, Mr. Greener, it sure does! There may be a story here."

The old man smiled, knowing how much Artie wanted to be a real reporter instead of an errand boy and helper around the printing room. "Well, son, maybe so. Why don't you go see what you can learn?"

"Yes sir, Mr. Greener, sir. I will!" Artie started off to follow the two riders.

"Wait a minute. Don't you think you might need to make some notes?"

"Oh. Yes sir." Artie ducked into the shop and came out with a pencil and a scrap sheet of newsprint and again started for the street. But his boss was not ready to let him go.

"Easy son, they're only going as far as the courthouse. I don't think you should leave your broom out here on the sidewalk; do you?"

Holding the reins of the horse he had been leading and grasping his own saddle horn with his right hand, the lawman kicked his left foot clear of its stirrup. Wincing from the pain in his left thigh, he swung his right leg over the back of his bay mare and let his body slide slowly to the ground. He then tied both animals to a steel hitching ring set in a marble post near the side door of the courthouse. As he glared up at the back of his prisoner he noticed the young man running toward him with a sheet of paper in his hand. Too sore to move much, Bill stood staring at the boy.

"Sir," said Artie. "Mr. Marshal—ah, Marshal Marshal—"

"Oh hell son, my name's William Marshal and I got this gov'ment star, true enough. You kin call me Bill, or Marshal if ya have to, but don't call me 'Marshal Marshal.' I had enough of that a long time ago."

"Yes sir, Mister Marshal, sir. I'm Arthur Lowell. I'm a reporter," said Artie with pride at his first use of the title.

"Yeah, I seen ya broomin' off the sidewalk at the newspaper office as I come into town. That's reporter work, I guess."

Artie blushed a little and said, "I just came here to ask what your prisoner has done. And when the trial will be."

"He's done plenty and there ain't gonna' be no trial. Just a hangin'."

"Hanging? No trial? You mean you're—"

"Bill," called out a heavy set man just coming out of the courthouse door. "What's that you got there?" The new man also wore a badge, one proclaiming him to be the Gallatin County Sheriff.

"Hey, Jeremiah, good to see ya," said the marshal. "How about helpin' me get this load off this helpless animal and into your jail."

"Sure. Hey, he's a big one." Then, noticing that Artie was walking over toward the prisoner to get a better look the sheriff added, "Don't get too close son. He'll likely kick or spit at ya." Then the lawman noticed the blue cloth that was tied around the prisoner's head and through his mouth.

"Jesus, Bill, you got this one wrapped up proper!"

"Yeah, well, I got tired of his talk durin' the little ride we took together."

The sheriff noticed the marshal's wounds and added, "Gave ya a tussle did he? Looks like you might could use some doctorin'."

As the two lawmen got the big fella off of his horse and disappeared with him into the courthouse Artie, thinking about what he'd seen and heard, decided to go back to the newspaper office.

"Well, Artie, did you get yourself a story?" asked Mr. Greener.

"I may have a real scoop here, sir," said Artie. "I found out that the marshal's going to hang that guy without a trial. I asked hm. He's gonna lynch—"

"Whoa, son, hold on. You may have a scoop all right," said Mr. Greener with a chuckle, "considering the fact that we are the only newspaper anywhere around here. But Bill Marshal is a fine lawman and he isn't going to lynch anyone. Sheriff Turner wouldn't put up with any of that nonsense anyway."

"But he said—"

"Now I can help you out some," continued the newsman. "That prisoner is a notorious fellow called 'Kid Lanteen.' He has been wreaking havoc of one kind or another for two years around the three forks country and Bill has been chasing him real hard all winter. Now a sharp reporter would not be standing here talking to his editor. He would be down at the sheriff's office finding out what really is going on, don't you think?"

"Yes sir," said Artie. Clutching his sheet of newsprint and pencil he dashed out the door.

At the courthouse Artie found an office door with the title "Gallatin County Sheriff" printed on its glass window. The name "Jeremiah Turner" was on a second line. Inside he found the sheriff himself behind his desk.

"Hello son, what can I do for ya?" asked the older man.

"Good afternoon, Sheriff Turner," said Artie, doing his best to show a professional air. "I am Arthur Lowell of the Gallatin County Dispatch. I want to see what you and the marshal can tell me about the prisoner he just brought in."

"Well, Bill has gone up stairs to talk t' Judge Bollard. Doin' some papers and all and—"

"OK, Jeremiah , here's the damn paperwork," said the marshal as he came into the room, strode over to the desk, and dropped a tattered arrest warrant along with a crisp, new document in front of the sheriff. With a glance at Artie he bent over and whispered into the sheriff's ear, then left the room.

Artie turned to follow. "Mr. Marshal—"

"Best stay stood were yer at son," said the sheriff. "Bill's a good natured man, but was I you I wouldn't go near 'im today. He's in a real bad frame of mind."

"But what is he going to do?" asked Artie.

"I expect he's gonna lick his wounds, have a beer, feed his face, and bunk out. Anyhow, that's what I'd do was I him."

"But what will happen to the prisoner?"

"Him? He's gonna stay right down in the basement where we put him till Bill hangs 'im in the mornin'."

"But a trial, there's no trial?"

"Nope, there ain't. Bill has said what he's gonna do, and the Judge has put it in writin' that he can do it." The sheriff nodded at the two papers lying on his desk.

Artie started to reach for the papers, but Sheriff Turner stopped him. "Just a minute ago the marshal said I ain't t' let nobody see them papers just yet. But they're legal."

In the spirit of being a reporter, Artie decided to get a little pushy.

"Sheriff," he said, trying to keep his voice from cracking, "Isn't it true that those are public papers, court stuff that anybody can see?"

"Yep, son, you're probably right. If you want to, you can argue that fine point of law with the marshal over to Doc Jenkins's place while he's gettin' his leg sewed up. But that's a plan of action I wouldn't recommend."

Noticing Artie's perplexed expression the sheriff softened up a little.

"Look son, I've known Bill for years, and he's just a decent man doin' his job. Usual thing is he just dumps his prisoners off on me, makes a report, then takes no further interest in 'em. True enough, he's a little out of sorts over that one down stairs, but you seen what the fella done to Bill. Seems clear the marshal's gonna hang this one personal."

"But Sheriff, without a trial? Is the Judge going to let him—can he do that?"

"Yep, he can. And here's why. Along with the other misdeeds Kid Lanteen has been perpetratin' on the countryside, he done one real bad thing. He's got a habit of gettin' drunked up and beatin' on anybody he can, and considerin' his size that includes just about anybody at all. Seems after a bender last spring he had a fight with his own ma. Just as she was fixin' his breakfast he went wild and punched her up side of the head, he did. Killed his own ma. Right by her own cook stove."

Artie just stood still, the blank newsprint and pencil in his hands at his side.

"Damn mother-killer, he is," said the sheriff as he tapped the tattered arrest warrant with his finger.

"Y'see son, he's already been tried for that stunt and sentenced to hang. But he escaped right off the gallows, he did. Big gorilla overpowered a guard, shot at another one and lit out." Pointing one finger at the ceiling the sheriff continued, "Judge Bollard upstairs says the Kid don't need no trial now. We can hang him. And it's clear that's what the marshal's gonna do."

"When will that be?" asked Artie.

"Tomorrow, right after breakfast. The law says we gotta feed 'im proper. Ain't that somethin'? We gotta fix 'im breakfast so's we can hang 'im."

"But there's no time to build a gallows—"

"Don't matter. There's a sturdy old cottonwood tree out back that's seen a rope or two. Reckon Bill's gonna use that."

"My god, I have to be there," said Artie. "What time of morning will that be?"

"Can't say for sure. Best way t' tell is go see Katey Mulgrew over at the diner. She's got the contract that feeds prisoners. Opens at six."

At about twenty minutes to six the next morning Artie saw lights on at Katey's diner and hurried over to find out what her feeding schedule would be. Surprised to find the door unlocked before opening time Artie entered and found Katey cleaning a counter with the pleasant smells of breakfast in the air.

"Good morning Mrs. Mulgrew, I see you're open early today."

"Hello Arthur, what brings you around so early yourself on a cold morning?"

"Mrs. Mulgrew, I need to know when you're going to fix breakfast for the prisoner in the jail."

"Shush," said Katey with a finger to her lips. Then she pointed into her kitchen.

Artie could smell and hear eggs and bacon frying and through the doorway he saw the back of a man standing at the stove. The man moved awkwardly, with his left hand in a cast, his left leg heavily bandaged and a flower covered apron around his waist.

"That's Marshal Marshal! He's got an apron—"

"Shush," said Katey again. "Nobody cooks in my kitchen without an apron."

"But I don't understand."

"Neither do I. Bill came in and said he was going to fix breakfast for a prisoner. With the look in his eye I wasn't going to argue. Then he said 'No woman is ever going to fix breakfast for that mother-killer again' and just took over my stove."

"Wow."

"I've known Bill Marshal a long time," said Katey. "He's a fine man. But I've never seen him like this."

An hour later Artie, Sheriff Turner, the marshal, and two curious citizens stood near the big cottonwood tree behind the court house. Kid Lanteen was sitting on his own bareback appaloosa. The rope around his neck was looped twice around a solid branch just above his head and tied off. Unceremoniously, Deputy U.S. Marshal William Marshal looked up at the hulking man, muttered "mother-killer," and laid a braided leather quirt across the horse's rump. That rid the world of Kid Lanteen.

The marshal handed the quirt to Sheriff Turner and said, "Jeremiah, I think I'll go over to the Madison River and see how the trout are doin.'"

"Sure Bill, sounds like a good idea."

With that the marshal mounted his own bay mare and rode away.

"Lordy," said Artie, his knees a little weak from what he had just seen. "I still don't understand why—"

"C'mon son," said the sheriff as he put his hand on Artie's shoulder to guide him toward the courthouse door. "Those papers you said was public. Well, they sure are, and now that Bill's gone, you kin see 'em."

As the two entered the office Sheriff Turner asked, "Well, what do you think of our marshal after the reportin' you been doin' lately?"

"Gee, I don't know. People say he's a good man but he seems kind of hard to me."

"Maybe so, but just so you don't misunderstand 'im I gotta ask you somethin'."

"Sure, what?"

"Well son, if you're gonna be a newspaper man you need to pay more attention t' the fine points. For example, Do you really think any woman is gonna birth a baby boy and then name him somethin' silly like 'Kid Lanteen'?"

"Well, no, probably not."

"Kid Lanteen," said the sheriff, almost spitting out the name. That's just a barroom monicker the mother-killer picked up amongst the lice he did his drinkin' with."

"What was his real name then?"

Sheriff Turner pointed at the two documents lying on his desk. "You don't think any judge is gonna write out hangin' papers on somebody without gettin' the name right do ya?"

Artie picked up the newer of the papers and there was the name of the man who had just been hanged.

"Oh Lordy," said Artie as he read aloud. "William Marshal, Junior!"

"I have to get to the office. I have a story to write, type to set, work—"

"Yep," said Sheriff Turner. "Reporter's work. Good luck to ya son."

SAVING CHARLIE

You never know what the future might bring

Sam drove his white pickup past the weather-beaten wood frame building and casually glanced at the sign proclaiming the business inside to be "Longstreet Aviation." He proceeded on toward his hangar near the far end of Oceanside Airport's single runway hardly noticing the pleasant sea breeze, salt air, and sounds of breakers on the nearby beach. Six months earlier he would have been smiling at the thought of flying his Cessna 185 on such a fine spring day.

But not now, never again. Sam just stopped his car and walked to his hangar with a slouch not consistent with his fifty year old but vigorously athletic build.

In the little two-room business office Susan Longstreet sat at her desk. She looked up from her paperwork as her husband Walt entered the building, back from one of the many chores that face anyone trying to make a living servicing the aviation community at a small airport.

"Walt, I just saw Sam go by heading for his hangar."

"Hey, how about that. Haven't seen him out here in a long time. Hardly at all since Jenna—"

"Yeah, I know," said Susan.

Jenna, whose striking blond hair and smiling blue eyes made her everyone's friend, had been Sam's wife. The two couples had been close for many years and Susan was still saddened by Jenna's death in a skiing accident the previous winter.

"Poor guy," said Walt as he took off his baseball cap and wiped his balding hairline with his sleeve. "They worked so hard to get that plane paid off, and they had it made. Then Sam's problems start and while they deal with that she—"

Walt didn't finish. He'd noticed a sadness in Susan's expression that made him wish he hadn't brought up the subject.

"Look, here he comes now with Charlie," said Susan.

She had noticed Sam's Cessna taxiing past the business's large window. Just as Jenna had always done, Susan referred to the airplane itself as "Charlie," using the aviator's designation for the last letter of the plane's registration number.

"Jenna sure was proud of that plane," added Susan. "Always polishing or fussing with it somehow."

"Yep. Their pride and joy," said Walt, "and we had some good times with it too." Then the conversation lapsed, with both Walt and Susan thinking of the trips the four friends had made flying together along Mexico's Baja Peninsula, camping on deserted beaches, and playing in the surf. Having once been an Olympic class competitive swimmer, Jenna had loved the water anywhere.

Sam taxied Charlie past the service ramp. He had thought of stopping to say good-bye to his two friends, but decided not to. The pain he was bearing, even with the medication, was too much. He knew that Susan would see in his face that he shouldn't be flying.

"Kind'a hoped he'd stop by and say hello," muttered Walt. "I'd like to know how he's doing, what his medical problem is. He wouldn't tell me anything about it, but last time I saw him he looked pretty bummed out."

"Jenna told me Sam was pretty sick" said Susan. "But she never told me why."

Sam reached the run-up pad at the departure end of the runway and got out his preflight checklist. Jenna had been a pilot too, and whenever they flew together the one not actually flying the plane always read the checklist to the other. But now, holding the plastic laminated card in his hand, Sam did it alone.

As he performed the engine run up and other checks Sam had a casual thought that the whole procedure was needless now. The constant pain in his head dominated much of his thought.

Susan could see Sam (well, Charlie actually) in the distance and was waiting for his radio call. Soon it came.

"Oceanside traffic, Cessna Four-Mike-Charlie rolling for take-off, runway one seven," came Sam's voice over the radio. A matter-of-fact voice, not like the Sam that Susan had known over the years.

Susan responded with "Hi Sam, good to hear from you. Have a nice flight." She waited, hoping for a reply, but none came.

Sam sat for a minute staring at Jenna's empty seat beside him. He thought of the dozens of flights they had made together and with Walt and Susan, camping on the beaches from La Paz to British Columbia. But the pleasant memories were being pushed aside by the pain in his head.

As Sam straightened up the cockpit, putting charts carefully in place, he noticed dust on the panel and that the windows weren't as clean as they should be. Jenna would not have allowed that. She was proud of that airplane, their Charlie, and lavished care on it in any way she could.

With eyes moist from thoughts of his lost wife, Sam eased the throttle open and picked up speed down the runway's white center line. Without the weight of Jenna, friends, or camping equipment Charlie lifted quickly into the air. A minute later they were following the coast line southward, a hundred feet up and just far enough off shore so that Sam could watch the beach go by.

Tracks. Sam felt that he should see Jenna's tracks in the sand, that he should catch up with her as she ran along the edge of the surf for her customary morning exercise. Sam always associated Jenna with the sea. Oh how that girl could swim! And how she loved to have Sam with her, sharing her world where sky, sea, and sand came together.

But for Sam there could be no world without Jenna. All there was now was a persistent pain in his head.

Admitting to himself that he would not find Jenna on the beach and realizing that he was approaching a metropolitan area with its high density of air traffic, Sam began to climb and made a smooth turn out to sea. Knowing that Charlie's fuel tanks were full, he noted the time and continued the climb.

Inoperable. Sam thought about the word as he and Charlie continued on their westward course. Of all the medical information about his headaches he had been given in the weeks since Jenna died that one word was the only one that mattered. His tumor was inoperable.

Later, still on course out to sea and almost 200 miles from land, Sam marveled at the sense of solitude he got from the clear blue sky and the darker blue ocean two miles below. He decided that he and Charlie should have some fun before the fuel ran out.

Sam dropped Charlie's nose to accelerate a little. Then, bringing back the control yoke till the g-forces shoving him down in his seat felt just right he began a climb that became steeper and steeper till the plane was over on its back. Cutting the power Sam let the plane fall through the rest of an inside loop. As Charlie reached level flight again Sam felt a burble of turbulence indicating that he had flown the loop perfectly and had hit his own wake, his "tracks in the sky," and was right back on his original course away from land.

Exhilarated in spite of the pain in his head Sam performed more aerobatic maneuvers: rolls, spins, lazy-eights, and even a Cuban eight. All maneuvers that were not legally approved in any Cessna 185, but Sam knew that the plane could handle them easily. He liked to think that Charlie enjoyed them too.

But the headache soon spoiled the experience for Sam, and he resumed level flight on his original seaward course. And as he did so he thought of the scorn such flying would have gotten him from Jenna. She would never have allowed such things, not with their Charlie.

The minutes ticked away and then Sam's attention was caught by a little notebook and pen tucked into a pocket on the door by Jenna's empty seat. The notebook she used in flight to make notes about any tiny problem with Charlie that might need maintenance attention. Sam began to feel guilty about his failure to keep things up to Jenna's standards.

As Charlie hummed along, running perfectly, Sam's guilt built up more. He began thinking about the "point of no return," the time when he would not have enough fuel to return to the mainland. After a quick calculation his pain-fogged mind knew that he was almost there.

Thinking of Jenna and her sacrifices in the household budget to make payments on their aircraft and the pride she always took in Charlie's appearance, Sam realized that the pain he was suffering was his, not Charlie's, and he turned back toward land.

Charlie was flying even better now that he was pointed toward the mainland, or so it seemed to Sam. He changed power settings and cruse altitude to use fuel more efficiently and recalculated. He could make it to land if he had not used so much fuel playing with aerobatics for that twenty minutes or so, but now there was no way to tell.

Sam flew on in a fog of guilt, heartache and pain, and brought the coastline into sight. A few minutes later, within gliding distance of a sandy beach, Sam knew he could at least keep Charlie out of the ocean.

Then it happened. Charlie's engine started missing, and then quit altogether.

Just as he had practiced in flight training with Walt instructing, Sam began to descend at "best angle of glide" speed and picked up the radio's microphone. He wouldn't be able to reach his home field, but he could talk to Walt or Susan and tell them where Charlie was going down.

"Oceanside Unicom, Four-Mike-Charlie," radioed Sam.

"Four-Mike-Charlie, Oceanside," came an immediate response. Then "Sam, that you?"

"Yeah, Walt, and I got a problem. I'm dead-stick and I'm going down on that stretch of beach where you make helpless student pilots practice soft field landings. Know where I mean?"

"You bet, Sam. About fifteen miles down the coast. We'll be there in a flash."

"Yeah, OK. And bring fuel, I'm dry tanks." With that Sam put the microphone back on its hook and concentrated on the extra quiet landing that was about two minutes away.

Walt loaded two five-gallon cans of aviation fuel into his pickup as Susan climbed into the cab. Minutes later they crossed some brushy land and reached the isolated beach where they could see Charlie sitting in the sand about fifty yards from the surf. But they could see no sign of Sam.

Walt opened Charlie's left side door. Inside were Sam's shoes sitting on the pilot's seat, covered by his blue jeans, a white T-shirt, and a neatly folded leather jacket that had been a Christmas present from Walt and Susan. Sticking out of a pocket was a white envelope. Walt picked it up and handed it to his wife.

As she opened the envelope Susan found two pieces of paper. One was a bill of sale giving Charlie's ownership to Longstreet Aviation. The second was just a simple note reading, "Take good care of Charlie for us. We miss you both."

"My God," said Susan as she looked at the papers. This is Jenna's handwriting!"

"Yeah, well, look here," said Walt, pointing at the sand. A single set of bare footprints, man sized, led away toward the surf.

Susan and Walt followed the tracks for a short distance until a second set of smaller footprints joined the larger ones. Further ahead both tracks disappeared into the water.

In silence Susan and Walt looked up and down the beach, each of them secretly hoping to see Jenna running along the wet sand, now with Sam at her side.

DOS BANDIDOS

The luck of the draw, in poker and in life

"Well son, that about wraps up the paperwork; looks like you just bought yourself a bar," said the frail little man with a rheumy left eye. His bartender's apron seemed inconsistent with a face and hands that made one think of well-worn leather. Bowed legs along with cowboy boots scuffed to the point where color no longer mattered marked Mike as a man who had spent much of his eighty-eight years as a working cowboy.

Seated on a stool on the customer side of the bar Jeffery Anderson finished signing his name with an elaborate flourish on a dotted line dated February 8, 1953. With a contented grin he said, "Yes, and now I'm a property owner and brand new citizen of the State of New Mexico." Jeff swiveled his stool around to gaze at the restaurant, bar, and dance hall with living quarters upstairs and smiled happily.

"You said our deal includes all the decorations in the place, right?"

"Shoot yes. Them old spurs and pieces of tack of one kind or another—some junk guns—lots'a bars around here has that kind of stuff haingin' in 'em. Don't amount to much."

"Good decor though. Hey, let me take a closer look at that old revolver."

"Sure," said Mike as he picked a relic off the back bar and handed it to Jeff. "Wish I could tell ya that it belonged to Billy the Kid or some such, but it didn't."

On closer inspection Jeff saw that it was a break top model in really bad shape and laid it on the bar.

"You told me that after we completed our deal you'd tell me how this place got its name."

"*Dos Bandidos?* Sure, you gotta know about the two bandits. That's part of that 'decor' stuff, ain't it? But first things first."

Mike pulled a bottle of *pulque* from under the bar, grabbed two glasses and said, "I don't rightly know whether at this point in the doin's I'm buyin' you a drink or vicey-versey, but we gotta finish up our bargain Mexican style." He poured two shots of the murky, fermented juice of the Mexican maguey plant, and pushed one toward Jeff.

After looking at the glass skeptically Jeff took a sip.

"Now, about the name. Years back this place was *Dos Ladrones* but I changed it to *Dos Bandidos* when I figgered out that most gringo tourists don't know that *ladron* is Mex talk for thief. I got the name from one of them treasure stories this part of the country is full of. We got a lost treasure in just about every bunch of mountains in the Southwest, ya know. Anyhow, you gotta know about the two thieves 'cause it's your bar now and you can use the story to dazzle some of them long legged blondie gals that comes in here in the winter time.

"Now you see way back before the Revolution in 1910 there was a fella name of Louis Terrazas who had him a cattle spread, a big one, south of the border. So big, why he owned most of western Chihuahua and some of Sonora too. Seemed like half the folks in Mexico was workin' for him back then." Mike paused to refill his glass.

"You ever seen them rock fences down in Chihuahua, them smooth rock walls that stretches out across the desert?"

"No, I've never been to Chihuahua."

"Well anyhow, they was mostly built by Terrazas's people. I guess it was cheaper to make fences out of rocks than with honest bob-wire what with the place bein' mostly rocks anyway. But one thing's for damn sure, it ain't *easier* to build 'em out of rocks. On a hot day ten, maybe twenty, feet of fence is all two men could put up between dawn and dark."

Looking at his glass, Mike said, "Whup, I see I'm gettin' off the track some. This *pulque* kinda does that to a fella."

"Anyhow, one day way back then a *vaquero* name of Martin Cordova Griego was workin' on such a fence with the help of a decent young fella named Miguel. Now this Marteen (Mike pronounced the name the Mexican way, and with a deliberate sneer) was generally bad news on account of he was big, quick, and mean as hell. Nobody liked him much and he would of been give his leave from the ranch long before except he was a shoestring relative of old Terrazas his own self. Once in a while Marteen would even get to hang around the main house down by Casas Grandes."

Mike coughed a little to clear his throat and daubed his bad eye using his wrist. "Now mind you, this is just a story I'm givin' you to dazzle folks with."

"Anyhow, like I said one fine summer afternoon Miguel and this Marteen was out stackin' rocks makin' one of them fences. Hotter than blazes it was, but the fence was runnin' kinda east west, which was good. That way the thing made some shade which come to think on it is somethin' a bob-wire fence can't do at all."

Mike paused to stare at his glass. "See, there's that *pulque* leadin' me off again."

"Well, sittin' in the shade of their handiwork them two fence-makers got to talkin' and Marteen mentioned a special wagon old Terrazas was gonna send up to Douglas, in Arizona. Seems the old buzzard had quit trustin' the banks in Chihuahua City and wanted some of his cash in a gringo bank.

"Well, them two fellas got to plannin' and a few days later they knocked off that wagon and lit out into the Sierra Madre Mountains with three sacks of *centenarios*."

"What's a *centenario?*," asked Jeff, as he poured himself more *pulque*. He had noticed that if you can stomach the first shot the next one isn't quite as bad.

"Oh yeah, I forgot you ain't from around here. It's one of them big Mexican coins, big as a silver dollar and got a ounce of gold in it. And them sacks was heavy, let me tell you," said the old man. Then, after a pause, he added, "Of course that's just how the story goes you understand."

"Anyhow, after them two retired rock stackers got a ways into the Sierra Madre they come across a bunch of turkeys down in a draw the best part of a hundred yards off. So Miguel, feelin' frisky what with his newly acquired wealth and all, hauled out his pistol and let fly. Now don't ya know as luck would have it one of them birds decided to drop dead on the spot!

" *'Ay Dios,'* yelled Marteen with a grin, 'we eat good tonight!' Then, sliding back into his normally rotten disposition, he looked at Miguel and muttered, 'Stupid to shoot at that distance; just dumb luck.'

"Now Miguel knew Marteen was right, but feelin' good anyhow he puffed up some and said, "This old .44 has always been lucky for me" and went to pick up his bird."

After a sip of *pulque* Mike continued. "Well, them two fellas had greasewood smoked turkey that evenin' and while the cookin' was goin' on Marteen had been workin' on a bottle of tequila he had liberated from the wagon along with the gold. Bein' stuffed full of turkey and booze, the fella just natural got sleepy.

"Now Miguel, not bein' much partial to tequila, was still interested in the turkey. So, with the toad sticker he had took out of his boot to eat with, Miguel reached across old Marteen, who was sprawled out half drunk, to cut hisself another piece of bird. Now mind you, that is just exactly what Miguel was plannin' to do, just get hisself some more turkey," said Mike while squinting his rheumy eye. "Course it's just a story y'unnerstan'."

"Well now Marteen was no dummy, and he had been keepin' one eye sober durin' his drinkin' and it saw the knife. Marteen figgered that, like hisself, Miguel knew them *centenarios* would spread around better if there wasn't so many ex-fence builders involved. So, quick as a cat Marteen grabbed the pistol that Miguel carried stuck in his belt and shoved it hard into the completely innocent turkey eater's belly. Next thing happened was Marteen yells 'it's all mine!' and pulls the trigger," said Mike, managing a pious look as he recounted this part of his story.

"Yech!" exclaimed Jeff. "Then what?"

Mike coughed a little and cleared his throat. "Y' have to excuse me some, this is more talkin' than I've done all week; voice ain't what it used to be." The old man paused to admire the *pulque* remaining in the bottle, then continued.

"Well, two seconds later there was Miguel lookin' at his knife stickin' in Marteen's neck and wonderin' why his own personal plumbing wasn't splattered over the countryside behind him. It seems that Miguel's lucky gun just hadn't fired in spite of Marteen's best efforts on the trigger."

Mike sort of stretched and then decided to wrap up his story so he could focus more properly on the *pulque* bottle.

"Well, there was Miguel, night comin' on, sittin' in the Sierra Madre with two horses, them bags of gold coins, some turkey leftovers, half a bottle of tequila, and one used up *vaquero*. Bein' smarter than the average bear, Miguel decided to carry the gold off and hide it for a time, then hightail it into Arizona till Terrazas's people quit wonderin' what happened to the wagon and why two fine, upstandin' fence makers had also disappeared."

After another shot of *pulque* Mike said, "There, now you have it, your story about the two thieves I named this place after. People hunted for years for that gold. Never found it. Of course it's all just a yarn for the tourists, mind you."

As the old bar keeper looked wistfully at his nearly empty bottle, Jeff picked up the worn out revolver again and examined it with more of an eye for detail.

"An old .44 Schofield, serial number 22777," said Jeff. "Lucky number; make a good poker hand."

Then, moving the hammer, Jeff noticed something else.

"Huh—the main spring on this thing is broken."

"Yep," replied the tired old man in the barkeeper's apron. "22777, that's a good number." Then, with a grin he added, "That old .44 has always been lucky for me."

THE DA'S DILEMMA

Sometimes the law needs a helping hand

Leslie Newman opened the glass office door bearing the words "Frank Warren, District Attorney," walked right in and unceremoniously sat down in a chair facing her boss's desk. Her blond hair, set off by a well-tailored light blue business suit and her confident body language marked her as a well-established member of Frank's staff of assistant district attorneys.

"Well good morning, Les," said Frank. "Jesus, ten after eight and already you're going to dump one on me; I just know it." Just back from a four day fishing vacation Frank was not yet into the swing of things.

"Lemme get some coffee, huh?" Then he noticed the mug Leslie was carrying and, knowing that she didn't drink coffee, realized that it was for him.

"Here boss, now you can listen to my sad story."

"Umm, OK." Just the steaming vapor from the hot drink had perked Frank up already.

"It's the Waterston homicide."

"I was afraid of that. I caught the tail end of something about it on the radio this morning; what's got the press into it anyway?"

"OK, here it comes, the good news and the bad." Leslie opened a folder she held on her lap.

"We have a clear homicide, the smoking gun, with prints, an arrest, three reputable witnesses who know the suspect personally, and we have a great motive. A prosecutor's dream, right?"

"Yeah, sounds like. But that wouldn't put it on the morning news now, would it?"

"Nope, it wouldn't. Now comes the bad part." Leslie stalled just a little, teasing her boss. When he frowned and with his free hand gestured for her to get on with it, she continued.

"In a nut shell, we don't have a prayer of getting an indictment, and a first year law student could beat us in court even if we did."

"Yeah, that's about all I got out of the radio blurb. Now, gimme a bigger nut shell, OK?"

"OK. Last Thursday a handsome blond lad, age twenty-five, dressed in designer jeans and an expensive white blazer, walks into the offices of Waterston Enterprises, Inc., and says, 'Jack Waterston to see my old man.' Sally, the receptionist knows him and says go right on in. He does, politely saying 'good morning' to an office boy as he passes. Then he walks up to the old man's desk, pulls out a revolver and pops Pop right between the eyes. Then he saunters out, nods at the postman who is there delivering the day's mail, hops into a red Audi convertible and drives off."

Finishing a sip of coffee Frank said, "I've heard of the deceased—Bill Waterston. Richer than a ten-term congressman, right?"

"Right. Oodles of bucks. And therein lies our terrific motive. Seems old Bill had two sons, Jack and Jesse. Both adopted very young. Apparently Mrs. Waterston died long ago, and the boys have grown up as quick-tempered kids spoiled by a less than attentive but filthy rich father. Now Pop realizes, from a series of arrests for public brawling and DWI, that his only heirs are not model citizens. So, he issues an ultimatum. They each must graduate from some accredited university with a degree in something other than basket weaving and then hold a professional job for one year. Otherwise, all those oodles go to the Society for Something Silly, or whatever."

"Come on Les. Am I gonna have to get some more coffee before you get to where the rub is?"

"Almost there, boss." Leslie was enjoying Frank's impatience. She didn't often have the upper hand in the good natured bantering the two had developed in seven years of work together.

"As you can imagine, two uniforms oozing with probable cause went 10-33 out to the Waterston Estate looking for Jack. What they found was both Jack and Jesse, and each one was pointing the finger at the other. So, the uniforms arrested both."

"Ouch," said Frank.

"Yeah, well here's why. It seems that Jack and Jesse are identical twins. They were even dressed identically. Jesse says Jack did the deed, and Jack claims Jesse did it while impersonating him. Now you are going to ask me about paraffin tests aren't you?"

"It does come to mind," said Frank. "With an arrest that quick, it's easy to know which one had fired a gun recently."

"Yeah, well, we didn't even run the test."

"Heh?"

"It seems that the Waterston Estate is pretty snazzy, enough to have an indoor pistol range in the basement where the boys were found. And, unfortunately, both were shooting paper targets at the time the uniforms showed up. Using two identical Smith & Wesson K-38 target revolvers with identical ammo yet. We have both guns, and lab tests have established one as the murder weapon. Both boys' prints are on both weapons."

"Hoo boy. You said you have somebody in custody?"

"Well, I fudged a little there. Two Armani suits lookin' like Richard Gere and John Travolta in tandem had them out in two hours. All the usual noises about false arrest."

"Any defense attorney would see the built in reasonable doubt in a flash, and so would a jury," said Leslie, with a slump of her shoulders.

"All too smoothly done," said Frank. "Gotta be conspiracy."

"Sure, but how in the hell can I prove that? Our investigation shows that the two boys are notorious for squabbling between themselves and have never shared or cooperated on much of anything."

"They shoot targets in the basement together," said Frank a little sarcastically. "Anyhow Les, keep me up to date. I'm gonna get some phone calls on this—Jeesh, there the thing goes already." Frank had noticed a flashing red light on his desk phone which he picked up himself, knowing that his secretary was out of the office.

Leslie gathered her papers, nodded at Frank and left. A few minutes later Frank stopped by her office with a message.

"That was maybe a nut call I just got. Some guy says he's a forensic technician from the state police labs in the capitol, saw our twins on the TV this morning. Claims he can help us out. I referred him to you, Les, and he said he'd see you tomorrow afternoon to 'save your bacon for ya.' Probably just a smart-ass."

The next afternoon Leslie was busily pursuing her caseload, having forgotten about her expected visitor. Then she heard a polite knock on the glass of her open office door and saw a young man dressed in faded jeans and a denim jacket. Holding a black motorcycle helmet bearing a Harley-Davidson logo under his arm, he stepped right up to her desk.

"Ms. Newman? I'm Eric Johnson, here to make things all better for you."

Leslie looked up, and stared at the visitor whose long hair and scruffy appearance put her in mind of clients she used to deal with during her two years with the public defender's office. Surprised at the casual appearance, she inspected the smiling young man for a few seconds.

"Eric Johnson, the forensics expert, bacon saver supreme?"

"Yep, that's me. But I've been hustlin' that hog outside all day, you know, bug stains in the teeth and all. So, you're gonna have to spring for a clean up for my services, OK?"

Leslie looked the charismatic visitor over carefully, then smiled and sat back in her swivel chair with her hands behind her head.

"All right, Mr. Johnson, we'll see. Now, have a seat and tell me what you have in mind."

Eric sat down and crossed his legs, enjoying the comfortable visitor's chair. Remembering that he had a hole in his prominently displayed Tony Lama boot, he put both feet flat on the floor.

Leslie smiled at this and became even more comfortable with the oddly charming young man.

"You see, ma'am, I did the ballistics work on the .38 slug and those two Smiths you sent us. I didn't think much about it at the time, but when I saw the TV stuff I knew I could help you out."

"And how would that be?"

"Those two fellas you arrested. I knew their mother real well back before she died—"

"Ms. Newman, sorry to interrupt," said Frank Warren's secretary as she stepped into the doorway. "Two attorneys are here to see you about the Waterston case."

"Oh, yeah, the Brooks Brothers again. Mr. Johnson, could you please give me a few minutes? Then we can talk."

"Sure, I'm set up to hang around a few days."

"Great." Leslie left the office, her spirits considerably improved.

The next day Leslie arranged separate meetings in her office, first one with Jack Waterston and counsel, and then another with Jesse Waterston, and his counsel.

In each meeting she stated that she believed that both boys were guilty and that based on expected new information from the state police labs she was considering charging them jointly with first degree murder and with conspiracy before the fact. However, she suggested, the trial would be highly complex, drawn out, and frankly, there was a slight possibility that a jury might not grasp her entire argument. Thus, she was willing to plea-bargain with either of the suspects. Whichever one would come clean first could expect a reduced sentence rather than risk being found guilty of capital murder.

Leslie was not surprised when both meetings had the same result— Righteous indignation about how ridiculous conspiracy was and how impossible it would be for her to prove anything against either client. In each of the two meetings the attorney left, his client in tow, threatening to add prosecutorial harassment to the charges of false arrest.

On the following day, however, Jesse Waterston and distinguished counsel were asked to stop by to speak with Frank Warren himself.

Access to Frank's office necessitated that the pair walk by Leslie's glassed in fish bowl style office where she and a man sat with the door closed. Jesse stopped and stared at the visitor who, wearing the same kind of designer jeans and blazer that both boys had worn when arrested, sat chatting with Leslie. Jesse saw Leslie reach across her desk and the two shook hands. Then both sat back in their chairs, as though in agreement on some subject.

Grabbing his attorney's arm, Jesse shouted, "What the shit is that?" and lunged toward the office. Immediately a uniformed officer appeared and ushered the confused attorney and his irate client into a nearby interrogation room, promising that the district attorney would be with them shortly. As the officer left an animated conversation ensued between client and counsel.

Minutes later Jack Waterston and counsel, also at the request of the DA, passed down the same hallway and were treated to an identical performance occurring in Leslie Newman's office. Another uniformed officer ushered Jack Waterston, as irate as Jesse had been, along with his own confused attorney into a second interrogation room where Frank Warren and a legal stenographer waited. Minutes later the fuming Jesse Waterston with his attorney whose mental wheels were spinning at full tilt, were escorted into this second room.

Jack jumped up as his brother entered the room and shouted, "You gutless bastard! Couldn't keep your fuckin' mouth shut!"

Jesse then lunged at Jack shouting "Me? You sold out, you stupid prick!"

Uniformed officers separated and handcuffed both boys who, in spite of the best efforts on the part of their respective attorneys, continued to yell all the accusatory evidence of conspiracy that any prosecutor could hope for.

A few minutes later as everyone's adrenaline began to ease away both Jack and Jesse were charged with capital murder and conspiracy before the fact to commit murder in the first degree. They were read their rights and shackled under the careful eyes of two officers. Then Leslie Newman and her visitor, entered the room.

"All right, who the hell is this?" shouted one attorney.

"Allow me to introduce State Police Forensic Technician Eric Johnson, the man who has the additional information I mentioned to you when I made plea bargain offers two days ago. Offers that are no longer on the table."

"Oh shit," came from Jesse, and "Jesus," from his brother, "This is a setup," from one attorney, and "What the hell is going on?" from the other.

"Let me explain," said Eric Johnson. "It's quite simple really. All these years you two fellas have been thinking that you were adopted twins. Well, I gotta tell you, that ain't quite so."

"See, when a woman from the wrong side of the tracks finds herself giving birth to more kids than she can handle and the father is long gone, she has to make some tough economic decisions. That means put 'em up for adoption, at least some of 'em. And then she does her very best to raise the first-born triplet herself. A fellow who turned out to be a pretty good armature actor."

No Gold Star for Ma

Sometimes it's nice to have a big brother

In the little Minnesota town of Davidston Mike Greenberg, finished with his work day at the lumber yard, watched his brother Larry step off the bus from the airport.

"Hey Lar," said Mike. "How'd it go today; did you get to fly?"

All through high school Larry had been working at odd jobs at the local airport in exchange for flying lessons, one way for a young man to learn to fly in the early days of World War II. In three more weeks he would reach an eagerly awaited birthday and be eligible to join the Army Air Corps.

"Yeah, little brother, I got in two whole hours! Mr. Barns let me take his Taylorcraft over to Martinsberg and back, solo. I've got enough time logged now to take my"—Larry's enthusiasm was interrupted by a fit of coughing—"my CAA flight exam, maybe even next week."

"I think flying's not good for your cough Lar; maybe it's the cold air up there in the wild blue yonder." Mike pointed a finger up as he spoke and made circling motions. Then he slapped his older brother on the back, and both started toward home a few blocks away.

Sparring around with each other, Mike and Larry traded good-natured blows as they walked. Larry grabbed Mike's hat and scuffled his little brother's blond hair. Ducking down, Mike grabbed a pair of fur-lined gloves out of the pocket of Larry's leather jacket.

"Hey, Hey, Mikey, give 'em back!"

"Wow, neat! Where'd you get these?"

"Those are aviator's gloves, not to be defiled by nonfliers like you, little brother. Mr. Barnes said I'd need 'em more than he would. He's too old to join up."

"Gotta catch me if you want 'em back," yelled Mike as he took off running down the pleasantly treelined sidewalk.

Larry ran after him but was not able to keep up and watched Mike turn the corner at the end of the block. Seconds later Larry, breathing heavily, turned the corner too only to find his younger brother standing still and facing the front of a small, white frame house. The gloves were in Mike's hand at his side.

"Hey, Mikey, What's up?"

Mike pointed toward the house where a silk flag about the size of a sheet of letter paper was hanging inside the front window. Trimmed with gold tassels, the red-bordered flag had a white field with a single star in the center. With World War II in full swing many homes had such flags proudly displaying a blue star for each member of the household who was serving in the armed forces.

But this flag was different. Very different. Its single star was not blue, it was gold.

"Oh Jesus," said Larry. Mr. Bensonhurst, he's—"

Larry, coughing from the exertion of their run, spat toward the street and continued. "He's been killed in the war."

"I wonder what happened," said Mike as the two brothers turned toward home. "Somebody said he was in the Pacific."

Neither spoke for some time, then Larry said, "You know, when I sign up mom will have a flag with a blue star."

"Two blue stars, man. I'm joining up too next year." Mike still had a year of high school to finish.

Larry put his arm around his younger brother's shoulders, turned his head to the off side, coughed again, and said, "And those two stars are gonna stay blue, right Mikey?."

"Yeah, you bet, man."

Mike handed the gloves back as the two walked home together.

Over the English Channel
Two Years Later

Second Lieutenant Mike Greenberg felt nauseated as he glanced at the blood soaking the calfskin glove on his right hand. The hand felt weak and Mike was barely able to maintain control of his powerful fighter plane, a Republic P-47 Thunderbolt. Irrationally, Mike felt angry because the blood was obliterating the barley legible letters "L G" scratched into the leather with black indelible ink. Mike's older brother had put his own initials there just before he got really sick. Sick enough to die of pneumonia complicated by tuberculosis. Now the leather gloves were all Mike had left to feel that Larry was still with him.

But the bloody glove was only one of Mike's problems. His battle damaged airplane was barely flyable since the German twenty-millimeter explosive slug had destroyed the instrument panel in front of him and damaged his right wing.

His oil pressure gauge and engine temperature gauges were working and all said that his engine was too. But Mike had no artificial horizon, no altimeter, and no air speed indicator. Mike wasn't even sure of the direction he was flying. The blast of cold air from his wrecked canopy made it nearly impossible to see his compass. But from the sun position Mike knew he was headed west, and probably nearing the English coastline.

From the mission briefing that morning Mike knew that the top of the solid white deck of clouds beneath him was at 11,000 feet. And below that was a ceiling of about 800 feet. Almost two miles of zero visibility between the hapless pilot and enough clear air in which to look for a decent place to try a crash landing. But he knew that without his flight instruments he had no hope of flying the airplane through that cloud deck.

Mike had one chance. When he was sure he was over England, he could bail out. That is, if he could be sure he was over land. But with his radio destroyed he had little more than a guess about how far west he was.

Finally, deciding that he must be over England by now, Mike made up his mind to get out. He tried to open his damaged cockpit canopy and felt the Plexiglas and aluminum structure slide on its rails for a few inches then come to a stop. It would not open further. Mike couldn't see well, but with his good hand he felt around and found enough jagged aluminum to know that the canopy was jammed. He couldn't get out.

With rage in his heart and tears in his eyes Mike slumped back in his seat in frustration. He listened to the smooth sounds from his engine which almost seemed to be mocking him by running so well. Choking with frustration, Mike looked again at his blood soaked glove on the control stick.

Larry's glove. An aviator's glove. Mike relaxed some and, resigned to his fate, though of giving up. But as he slumped more into his seat he thought of the blue star of the red, white and blue flag he knew was in his mother's window at home in Minnesota. Just one single blue star instead of the two that would have been there if Larry had reached his Army Air Corps dream. A dream that Mike was completing in his older brother's place.

Still staring at the bloody control stick Mike realized that, like his engine and throttle, the control surfaces were working fine too. So he reduced the power some and began a slow descent toward the white deck below that spread to the horizon in all directions.

Mike had never felt more alone. He knew that in a matter of minutes his plane would have to enter that world of zero visibility fog. And he knew that without his flight instruments he would soon lose all reference to the horizon, to the sky, and to the simple concept of up and down. He would probably enter a spin with no time to recover when he saw the English countryside coming up in what would be the last few seconds of his life.

Mike reached the cloud tops and wispy tendrils of fog started streaming past his canopy. He raised his good hand, the one where Larry's initials weren't soaked with blood, and tried to wipe moisture from the damaged windscreen. The glove reminded him of Larry, and he thought again about his mother's blue star. Not blue for long, he muttered aloud as the Thunderbolt flew into the darkening gray fog.

Mike held the controls steady, hoping he would just descend straight ahead till he got below the overcast. But he knew he would never make it. Already he felt like he was in a steep turn to the right. But as a trained instrument pilot he knew that his senses would be wrong; the plane could be going almost anywhere.

"I'm sorry, Ma," he muttered again as panic welled up.

But then somehow Mike felt he should lower his right wing, just a bit. So he did, and was immediately startled by a voice in his head saying *That's right, just hold her steady now.*

The confused and frightened pilot felt that he had done right, that a voice in his head had told him so. Mike shook his head and continued on, muttering "The blue star, Ma; I'm sorry."

Get your ass in gear, Mikey. Pay attention. Ease your nose up a little, you're too fast.

Again, the voice from nowhere. With his bloody hand Mike eased back on the stick till he heard the voice say, *OK man, that's better. Now, a little left rudder and lower your left wing some, just a tad.*

Mike felt as if he wasn't even moving. Outside there was nothing but dull grayness, inside, just cold wind on his half frozen face. In a near trance Mike thought of a dark blue star embroidered on white silk as he continued to make small corrections to his stick, rudder, and throttle in response to the voice from nowhere. Without instruments the crippled fighter plane descended smoothly through instrument flying conditions.

Nose up just a little, OK, a little more, now pick up your right wing some.

Mike followed the faint voice in his own mind till he noticed the fog was getting lighter outside his canopy and becoming blotchy; he was dropping out of the clouds!

Suddenly Mike saw open green grass just a few hundred feet below and ahead of his aircraft. Now able to see his surroundings he felt in control as he cut the throttle, shut off his electrical system and stalled the damaged Thunderbolt onto the wet grass in as smooth a belly landing as anyone could ask for.

For the next minute Mike sat listening to the hissing and crackling sounds of his cooling engine. He still couldn't get out of the damaged canopy, and thought about the possibility of fire.

But then came the voice one more time.

No gold star for Ma, Mikey; no gold star for Ma.

Mike Greenberg knew then that there would be no fire, and that soon someone would be along to help open the canopy.

THE ASSASSIN

Fate can intervene in peculiar ways

"Pa, where you gone to?" muttered ten year old Susan Yancy as she sat alone looking out of the front window of the rooming house where she and her father had been staying for the last few nights. She had been watching the gas streetlights brightening up the entrance to the flag decorated building across the street and down the block. She was watching the people coming and going like moths around a kerosene lamp flame. The laborer's young daughter was fascinated by the fine clothes the people were wearing as horse drawn carriages brought them to the "party house" as she thought of the fancy building entrance.

Susan tried to imagine the wonders she knew would be inside that rich people's party place she was watching in the fading light. But then she caught a movement near some freight crates and bales that had been delivered that day at the front of the house next door. She recognized the movement as a man, her father, and she knew from long experience that he was drunk.

Christopher Yancy, with his heavy overcoat collar scrunched up around his neck in a silly effort to conceal his face, was huddled amongst the crates. Nearby, as out of sight as he could get it, was a fine Kentucky rifle. Chris knew, when he was sober anyway, that he could hit a fly in the eye at fifty yards with that rifle and he had proved his marksmanship skills both in contests and on the battlefield more than once. Chris's attention was focused through an alcoholic fog on the same building down the street that had attracted little Susan's interest, until he was startled by a child's hand tugging at the sleeve of his ragged overcoat.

"Suzie," he whispered as he pulled his daughter into his crude hiding place hoping to keep anyone from noticing. "What the hell you doin' here; told you to stay in the house didn't I?"

"Pa, it's cold out; what are you doing here? Oh, oh no." She had noticed the rifle.

"You git back t' the house! I got work to—"

"Pa, what're you doing?"

Looking at Susan's frightened face, the father softened his tone, for he truly loved his little girl.

"Y'see them lights down there," Chris whispered. "Well, he's gonna show up pretty soon and when I see him I'm—"

"Who Pa? Who's coming?"

"The man what killed my brother, that's who!" Chris's voice rose, then remembering his need to stay hidden he went back to a whisper.

"Oh Pa, Uncle George died in the war, you know that"

"Yeah, he did, and I know 'zactly the man what killed him."

"No Pa, come on, lets go in the house." Susan's couldn't take her eyes off that long Kentucky rifle she knew her father could use so well.

"No. I promised George I'd get the man what —"

"Pa, no, they'll kill you for doing that. Pa, don't—"

With his left hand Chris pulled Susan up close to his face as he belched a little, and said, "Suzie darlin' you just do as yer old dad says and jist walk up them steps into the house and stay put."

Frightened by her father's rough treatment and repulsed by his vile breath that was like that of an old dog, Susan stood up and backed away, out of the man's vision and thoughts.

"Won't be long now George. That bastard is gonna die just like I promised ya," muttered Chris as he waited for the telltale cloppity-clopp of shod hooves on the street's paving stones.

After three more carriages arrived, dropped off their passengers and drove way, a finely appointed carriage stopped in front of the "party house." Pulled by a pair of white stallions, it seated four people—a driver, a uniformed army officer of obviously high rank, a civilian man, and a finely dressed middle aged woman. A second vehicle just behind it carried four more passengers, all soldiers.

"That's him; there's the man what killed ya George," muttered Chris, his attention on one of the carriages. He felt the same adrenaline surge he had experienced many times in combat. "And I swear he's gonna' die this very night."

Chris moved the rifle into position, hoping no one would notice it, and began to prime the pan using a powder flask he had ready at his side. Then, just as he cocked the hammer he felt the blow of a wooden nightstick against his head as the rifle was jerked from his hands.

"Get some shackles on this sot now will ya Bert?" yelled a city policeman to the younger officer at his side.

"Sure Sarg, I sure will!" And he promptly put handcuffs and leg irons on Chris who was trying to wobble to a standing position.

"Don't hurt him; you promised you wouldn't hurt him," squealed little Susan Yancy as she tugged at one policeman's pant leg.

Moments later, without noticing the events down the street, the passengers dismounted from both carriages and started walking up the steps of the building's well lit entrance.

"Eyeing the second carriage and its four male passengers, the younger police officer said, "Sarge, ya think we ought to let them fellas know what just happened here? Jesus, maybe he was tryin' to assassinate—"

"Naw, The chief kin send word over in the mornin' about this little ruckus. For now let's just let old Abe and the Missus enjoy their evening at the theater, hey?"

LUCKY

I'm old and a little beat up, but I still get the job done

My name, well, what I call myself anyhow, is Lucky. I'm just real good to have around, 'cause I can help a fella out just by bein' handy when things get messy. And right about now my boss is gonna find out just how lucky he is to have me with him. Just about any minute now.

But before we get to that I figure I gotta tell you some about myself, 'cause there's more to me than you might realize. When the chips are down I'm not just a good friend; I take a real active part in the goin's on. And part of why I can tell you about all this is 'cause I get to know things a little in advance. I got a feel for coming events that would be near impossible for you to understand.

Whups! Gotta keep an eye on the boss's troubles; rough times comin' for him and he hasn't got any inklin' of it at all.

Anyhow, back to tellin' you about myself. If you was to get a look at me first thing you'd say is whoa, that's an old one. And to look at me you'd be right. I first come into this world back in 1883, in a town name of Hartford, back east. But don't hold bein' an Easterner against me. I been out here in the Northtwest near all my life. What with—

Hup! My boss's problem just got a might closer. Wish he'd quit payin' so much attention to those tracks he's followin' and look around more. But the real trouble ain't started yet.

Anyhow, what with it bein' the year 2007 right now that makes me right around 124 years old. Well, durn near anyways, what with me comin' to the light of day in the winter and all. If you was t' see me you'd notice that I got a bum complexion, but hell, who wouldn't what with my age and all.

Ah, Boss, he's found that stove up steer he was lookin' for. He seen it cross the road in front of our pickup as we drove onto the ranch headin' home. Seen it limpin' bad from a real bunged up foreleg. I expect him an' me is gonna have to put the thing out'a its misery when we catch up to it.

Trouble is, that steer just run off into this brushy canyon full of pines and junipers, and the boss is so fixed on following the tracks he ain't payin' good attention to who else is around here.

But I am. Like I said, I get to know things you folks don't. That kinda makes up for me only bein' able to handle a few simple things in this world, not near all the stuff you can deal with.

Y'see, Boss he's real good at followin' animal tracks; no doubt we'll chatch up to that steer soon enough. But I wish he'd realize that steer tracks and his own tracks ain't the only footprints around here.

Anyhow, back to tellin' you some about who I am. Y'see, back in the '80s, and I mean 1880s, I was one sharp lookin' dude. But I was haingin' out with a fella who was not what you'd call a savory type of guy. Matter of fact he was a deputy sheriff, but one who liked the bottle a little more than he liked doin' his job. But I gotta hand it to 'im, when he got us into a jam he could really deal with them rustlers and such we come across. Four times he and I fought it out together and came out on top.

But it bothered me some the way he acted when we got done. Hell, each'a them four times he real deliberate like got out a foldin' knife and put a little scar right on my own personal butt! Can ya Imagine such a thing? Didn't do no harm though; they wasn't deep scars and they been near worn away by the years now anyhow. They ain't no big deal to me. Still, seemed kinda needless. . . .

But ya know, in a sort of poetic sense I was a "hard case" in them days myself. Well, I had a steely complexion that was "case hardened in colors" as the folks that built me would say. Made me real distinctive, easy to recognize by anybody who knows my kind.

Whup! Better get back to my boss; he's closer yet to the trouble he's got comin'. Them extra tracks that been followin' us as we been followin' that bummed up steer ain't following' no more. Nope. Y'see, that damn cat is watchin' us from up on the side of this draw. He knows we're gonna catch that steer and he's real interested in what comes of that.

Ah, the boss, he done found the steer. Seems the critter is down, probably bled to death. That's good, means less work for me. But the boss, he's messin' around to see what bunged up the steer's neck. Real quick he's gonna see that a cat had somethin' to do with it.

Now like I was sayin', I can't do all the stuff you folks do. I gotta mostly do just what my boss says. Just exactly. I'm a real mechanical sort of guy.

Like way back when that deputy sherrff and me got inta our fifth scrap. We didn't come out so good on that one. I did my part best as I could, but I needed some cooperation from that deputy, real fast, and he just didn't make it. Our reationship was over, and like I said I'm a mechanical sort of guy and all I thought about was "well, this time he ain't gonna carve on my butt!"

After that I spent a lotta years just stuck away in the sheriff's office, not doin' any work, not with anybody at all. Was OK with me though; nobody was wearin' me out, and my blued finish stayed in reasonable condition along with the varnish on my walnut butt. I kinda wished that deputy hadn't of took my ejector parts off from just under my barrel. He used to tell folks that gave me better balance and made me quicker to use. Maybe so; he ought'a know. Fast shootin' is what he knew most about, 'cept maybe for how to empty a bottle. Still, I sometimes feel a little naked without my ejector assembly bein' there where it oughta be.

But then hoo boy, I had no idea how hard I was gonna work in the comin' years. Seems the sheriff give me off to his cousin who was a workin' ranch hand on the Circle J down in that sagebrush country. They ran cattle, lots of 'em, and that meant they had—

Oh Jesus, Boss he better get ready; that damn cat is comin down off the hill. He wants that steer, probably figgers it's his since he's what bunged up the critters leg and cut up his neck some, makin' him bleed faster. Pretty soon the chips is gonna be down as they say, and Boss he'd better get his act together. I expect he will. Him and me has been through some times and he generally does all right.

Anyhow, back to that cousin I had to hang out with for a lot of years. One thing about him, he kept me right with him all the time. Wore off all my fine finish, even gave me a few rust pits here and there. But the worst thing was that ranch, the Circle J. Like I said, it was a really big spread. And that meant a lot of fences. And the job cousin had was to mend them damn fences, month after month, through the years.

Now that wouldn't a been so bad if the guy didn't forget some of his tools now and again, and when he needed a spare hammer, well, I was it.

He'd grab me by the barrel and use the steel part of my butt t' drive them damn fence staples. Put a lot of dents down by my serial number, and loosened me up a lot. Hell, a couple of my screws came out at one time or another, and one of 'em he replaced with an old wood screw! Can you imagine? Me, a genuine product of old Sam Colt, and there I was with a flat head wood screw holdin' my base pin in place. Humiliatin', to say the least.

Anyhow, I knew it was bound to happen one day. We was out one cold winter mornin' an' he was usin' me to pound horseshoe nails that was loose on that old Appaloosa gelding he had. And sure enough, my walnut butt stock split, broke near clean in half!

Hey! I think Boss, he's heard that cat. Them damn cougars can be quiet as a star in the sky, but this one was about to get nasty, and I think Boss is getting some caution up. Me, I'm ready all the time, five Pyrodex loads in my chambers, ready to go. (Boss, he don't like usin' black powder in me and I'm too old to handle smokeless powder.) I'm all set with full power behind all five 255 grain .45 caliber slugs.

Heh, looks like Boss's standin' up and lookin' around has made that ole cat get some caution up his own self. He ain't come out of the brush yet and Boss can't see him, but Boss, he's lookin' hard.

Gives me some time to tell you more about that cousin of the sheriff back about a hunderd years or so. You'd think he'd get me a new walnut stock to replace the one he broke, but no, no, the jerk; he just drilled some holes and put *more* wood screws in my butt. Cripes, that fine piece of Colt carved walnut, looked like a drunked up carpenter fixed it. Only good thing is all the use that cousin put me to, them four notches the deputy put on my butt so long ago is about wore down so's they don't show so much.

I gotta keep thinkin' about that cat some. Gotta be ready when Boss needs me. I know that cat; he's sneakin, just inches at a time, down on his belly where he knows he's hard to see and waitin' for a time to make his play.

Anyhow, a few years after he bunged up my butt that cousin guy he lost me to a sheepherder in a poker game. And that fella he carried me day in and day out for another twenty-two years up in the Northwest, in the sagebrush country of Washington State.

We got along fine; he took good care of me and had sense enough to know I wasn't meant to be a hammer. So, the edge of one of them wood screws in my butt got wore down flat with time, that sheep herder handled me so often. We did a lot of shootin' in them days, mostly at rabbits and coyotes and such. We got along good too. I guess you noticed them worn old screws in my butt. I've kinda got used to 'em over the years; they kinda give me character, y' know?

Anyhow, one day that sheepherder ups and dies, and the fella that owned the outfit he was workin' for didn't even know that I was bein' kept in an old box of stuff in the bunk house. So I just stayed there for another thirty years or so till a young fella workin' there as a ranch hand come across me.

Whup! That cat's about to make trouble. Gotta stay alert. To make a long story short that young fella showed me to the ranch's foreman, and the foreman just said, "Huh, just a beat up old Colt junker. You want the thing you can have it."

Well, you can imagine bein' called a name like that kinda ticked me off some, but what could I do? Like I said I'm just a mechanical kind of guy and can't do much of anythin' Sam Colt didn't intend I should.

But that young fella, well, he had never owned a Colt, and bein' dirt poor he was sure glad to get me. Him and me we been haing'n out together ever since. I'm haingin right now in a holster he made his own self from a piece of tanned cowhide and a saddle latigo. Suits me fine. And he took that durn wood screw out'a where my base pin screw shoulda been and put in a proper one. Didn't mess with them worn wood screws in my walnut grip though. I kinda think he figured they give me character too, just like I said a while back.

Oh, I oughta mention, that young fella is a lot older now. And things are about to get hot for him and me what with that dead steer and that cat. But I'm not too worried; Boss, he knows what's goin' on; he's seen the cat get all hunkered up, ready to jump.

Right about now you gotta excuse me for a time. I gotta go to work. Y' see, that cat could rip my boss apart if it wasn't for me bein' handy. All by hisself Boss ain't no match for the thing. But I'm here to even things up by providin' some extra luck. Just like folks used to say, I'm what you call an equalizer. That's what I do best, in my mechanical way. And as luck would have it, I'm very good at my job. I guess that's why they call me Lucky. Now that cat is—

Whooie! That was excitin' for a few seconds. Me and Boss, we let loose two of my loads and that cat turned into a pile of fur jerkin' around on the crick bed in the bottom of the draw. Boss decided we should put another load in the cat's head to convince the critter that he was really dead. Now me and Boss, we can go t' the house. He'll give me a good cleanin' with Hoppie's #9 and a rubdown with light oil, reload me so's I'll be ready to go, then get hisself some chow.

I like haingin' out with this fella; he takes better care of me than them others did. And he wouldn't think of carvin' on my butt or usin' me to pound fence staples!

THE KING'S PROBLEM

An old joke told in a new way

Once upon a time there was a European kingdom so small that hardly anyone remembers its name. Nevertheless, it was run by a real king who was a good looking guy with wavy blond hair, an easy smile, and not a mean bone in his body. An all-around nice fella.

King didn't really have the education or inclination to earn a living in any conventional manner. Fortunately though, his father and those before him had all been kings and this qualified him for his job. He liked being king and figured he was reasonably good at it since nobody complained and the realm pretty much ran itself anyway.

Now King had a wife named Queenie. Fond of the royal social scene, Queenie was always ready for a party. Definitely a member of the European fast carriage set, she flitted about the land at will never missing a ball, coronation, or blast of any kind.

Queenie was always readily accepted at social events because she made any of them more interesting by being something to either gossip about or gaze at, depending on your disposition, and gender. Her charm, beauty, and friendly manner made her a big draw, at least among the royal men folk, at any event she chose to grace with her presence.

The tendency for Queenie to be a bit casual with her favors here and there didn't bother King at all, because she was discreet and treated her husband just fine too. There was plenty of Queenie to go around. Thus King, without a jealous thought, could bop along and retain his happy go lucky countenance that pleased his subjects so much.

Now King did make an effort to keep up to date in his line of work. Traveling by fast carriage, he always attended the KKED (Kings, Kaisers, Emperors, and Despots) convention held each year in Vienna.

Being a serious professional, King always tried to put to use what he had learned, for he wanted to be a good ruler for his little realm. So, a few days after a recent convention King made a decision. Having done so he called in his most trusted advisor and best friend to discuss the situation.

"Yo, Best Buddy," said King. "How are things going out there in the realm?" King liked the word "yo" that he had been hearing around town lately.

"Hey, not bad, King," said Best Buddy. "We got that dead horse out'a the moat, and harvest is about over. That always gets the peasants excited."

"Yes, a good crop I hear. For the last week Queenie has been asking me about the harvest festivities calendar. She seems anxious to get the guest list mailed out."

"She's been on my back too," said Best Buddy, "about the new peacock pens."

"Peacock pens?"

"Yeah, peacock pens. You got any idea how fast that wife of yours goes through feathers? We decided it would be better to grow our own."

King smiled a little and said, "Yes, she likes to keep her appearance up, and peacock and ostrich feathers do give her a special charm."

"Oh cripes, King. Don't complement her on the ostrich feathers. We ain't got room to grow them things too. And then we'd have to bleach and dye 'em—"

"OK, OK, you and Queenie can work all that out. I have something more important, one of those matters of state things, to talk to you about."

"Sure King, shoot!"

"Well, at the KKED convention there was a lot of talk. Nothing big, but I got the feeling that behind my back some of the guys were making remarks."

"Hey man, what about?"

"Well, you know, the Crusades and all that."

"Oh yeah, that Kaiser guy. He buggin' you again?"

"Well, yes. In Session Three, on Foreign Entanglements, he pointedly brought up the fact that I have never been on a crusade. It was embarrassing."

"Oh man, I know what you're thinking; you wanna go off crusadin'."

"Well, it does appear that I should do my part."

"Jees, King. You know you don't know nothin' about that crusadin' stuff. Remember the last time you tried to ride a horse—"

"You mean I can't take my carriage?"

"Course not, King. Them crusaders, they get all decked out in armor on big-assed horses and do that army stuff."

"Well, that will be inconvenient. Nevertheless, I have made up my mind. I'm off to the Crusades."

"Oh boy. I suppose you figger you gotta have soldiers."

"Yes, I propose to take half the Royal Army with me. I will leave the other half here to defend the realm."

"Look King, we been friends a long time and I gotta' level with ya. I think you're lettin' peer pressure from your colleagues in the king business get to ya. Besides, the Royal Army's only got twelve guys."

"And three cooks," added King.

"Oh Jees, how many cooks you plan to take?"

"Well, I thought I would take Ferd. Nobody can peel potatoes and cook them up as fast as Ferd can."

"That's true," said Best Buddy thoughtfully. "He really makes them spuds fly."

"And Andre," added King.

"Andre! You can't take him! Who's gonna build Queenie's orange crepes and eggs Benedict!"

"It's a noble cause and we will all have to make sacrifices," replied King. "You can find some way to keep her happy. Upgrade a peasant or somebody."

"OK, but she's gonna be pissed!"

"Tell ya what," continued Best Buddy. "You take Andre, and leave me the other two. Jaque can handle Peach Melba, and Ferd is getting pretty good at making peacock stew."

"Well, I suppose I can rough it with just one cook. After all, this is a military expedition."

Then King was about to bring up a more important subject, but Best Buddy interrupted.

"Hey, about Andre. While you got him off t' the Holy Land have him pick up some new recipes. Get him checked out on falafel. You know, the garbanzo beans and pita bread thing. That way I can tell Queenie he's off to expand his professional skills."

"Yes, good idea, I will do that."

"Now, Best Buddy, I have another subject to discuss, one of great importance and considerable delicacy. It's personal."

"Sure King, shoot."

"Well, you know that I trust you completely with all my affairs of state and my personal life. We have been buddies for as long as I can remember."

"That's true, King. We been wine brothers since we was twelve."

Best Buddy was referring to a time when he and King had planned to cut their fingers and become blood brothers. Unfortunately, neither could do the cutting, so they drank a bottle of Bordeaux and handled the ceremony that way.

"Well," continued King, "It's about Queenie."

"Queenie?"

"Yes, Queenie. This is a little hard to say, but Queenie is what you might call a needful lady. Actually, she needs her man lots, if you know what I mean."

King added a knowing tilt of his head, to help get his point across.

"Yeah, well, she's real center-fold material, we can all see that," said Best Buddy.

Afraid that he might have been overheard, Best Buddy had second thoughts about his comment as he noticed Queenie entering the room. The place was brightened by her bubbling charisma as well as by the world-class jiggle of the bust of her low cut gown.

"Good morning Sire, good morning Court Advisor Buddy, how are we all today?" Queenie always used formal greetings. She wanted to stay in practice at making good impressions during formal occasions.

"Hello, hello," said King with a smile. Happy to see her as always, he held out his arm so Queenie could stand close beside him.

"G' mornin' ma'am," said Best Buddy.

"How's your world today gorgeous?" continued King, always interested in his wife's well-being. Then he added, "Great gown. The blue matches your eyes, and the red and gold flowers are nice."

"Fine thank you Kingey-poo, but I do have just a teensy weensy problem," said Queenie with a beaming smile at the main man in her life. "It has to do with the new Plumage Production Facility."

"The what?" said King.

"Those birds. They're very aromatic, so to speak, and they interfere with the fragrance of the rose garden outside my chamber window."

"Oh boy," muttered Best Buddy, quietly.

"Couldn't we have the facility moved farther away?" asked Queenie. "Perhaps down by the Ham and Boar Production Unit?"

King turned to Best Buddy and said, "You put peacock pens right by the rose garden? Why not down by the hog wallow in the first place?"

"Well Jees, King; the realm's only so big, and I thought—"

"Never mind now, you two," interrupted Queenie. I know you boys can work things out. I have an engagement."

With a loving wink at King and a hand covering her mouth she whispered to Best Buddy, "Glad you finally got rid of that horse!" Then, with a practiced flounce Queenie turned toward the door. After a step she stopped and turned to Best Buddy. Her full skirt needed another half second to catch up with her maneuvering. "Oh hey, what's a center fold, anyway?"

Best Buddy looked helplessly at King who said, "Never mind honey, I'll explain later."

With a slight shrug to indicate the question's lack of importance, Queenie and her blaze of colors floated out the door leaving the room at a loss for the lack of her presence.

"Well, where were we?" said King, knowing exactly where they had been in their earlier conversation. "Ah yes, now here's my problem. I know that crusading does involve an element of danger, and since I've never done anything else particularly well, and this is soldiering and all, well..."

King started to choke up.

"Oh hell, King, with Andre bein' the cook he is the other guys will want to keep you all in the rear area, real safe. Nobody wants to lose a good cook."

"Yes, well, here's my problem. I plan to be gone for one year. But if worse comes to worse and I don't get the hang of crusading too well I might not make it back." That could be tough on Queenie, what with her needs and all."

"Oh boy," exclaimed Best Buddy again.

"And while I'm gone, well, Queenie is pretty friendly and I don't want her to have problems with local fellows, if you know what I mean."

"Yeah, like the new blacksmith," muttered Best Buddy without thinking. He raised his hand to his mouth.

"Blacksmith?" said King.

"Oh nothin'. Just talkin' to myself. Now, about the peacocks," said Best Buddy, eager to change the subject.

"Never mind the birds; I'm not done yet. I'm coming to the embarrassing part of my problem."

"Hoo boy, what now?" thought Best Buddy.

"I have been considering Queenie's situation, so, at the New Technology Exhibition at the conference I bought a device that seems appropriate for the occasion."

"Eh, what's that?"

"Well," said King, looking down at his feet as he poked his toe at the floor. "I bought her a chastity belt. The latest gold and silver model, jewel encrusted. Incidentally, I must tell the royal accountant about that."

"A chastity belt? Oh boy! Queenie, she ain't gonna' like that."

"Oh it's OK. I installed it last night. I've got the key right here around my neck. She wasn't too upset, especially when I reminded her that my ancestors were kings but her father was just a used carriage salesman. And I think she especially liked the tiny ermine tassels on the sides."

"Uh huh," muttered Best Buddy.

"So, since you are my best and truest friend I plan to leave the key with you. If I do not make it back within one year, well, then—and only then—you have my permission to unlock Queenie and handle the situation as you see fit. Keep the old realm in good shape, that's all I ask."

The following morning King, six of the realm's finest, Andre, and a cart loaded with pans and provisions gathered in the courtyard ready to go.

"Now, Best Buddy, I know I can rely on you to guard this key until I return." With that, King took the key from around his neck and handed it to Best Buddy, saying to him, "Remember, one year!"

"Sure King, you can count on me. We're wine brothers, ain't we? Come back safe and sound covered with glory for the realm and all that. Then we can have a big peacock roast and all."

With a regal wave of his hand King started his white horse down the cobblestone street and, ka-clopata klop, ka-clopata klop, rode off toward the Crusades.

That afternoon King, Andre, and the rest of the expeditionary force were following an old road and watching for signposts pointing toward the Crusades. King was a little concerned about getting lost, but Andre had been to a cooking school in France and was used to traveling. One of the captains (all six soldiers were captains, a point they had negotiated before they left) was normally a carriage driver and knew something about navigation, so King wasn't too worried. Besides, the route they were following was well paved. Those Romans built fine roads, although the signs being in Latin was a nuisance.

Presently one captain at the end of the expeditionary force noticed a rider coming up on them from behind.

"Hey King, somebody's catchin' up to us. Maybe he knows where the hell the Crusades are."

So, the soldiers came to a stop, and ka-clopata klop, ka-clopata klIp klip klop, King stopped his white steed too.

Soon all could see Best Buddy bouncing along in the saddle on his own horse—galloop, galloop, galloop—obviously in a hurry.

Catching up with the group—galloop, galloop, gloop, gloop—Best Buddy brought his horse to a stop beside King's white charger.

"Hey man, 'fraid I wouldn't catch up to you guys."

"Yo, Best Buddy," it's good to see you. But you can't come with us. You've got to run the realm while I'm away."

"Yeah, King, I ain't goin' along. I just come to tell ya you gave me the wrong key!"

WILLY WRONG WAR

Can a man get even with himself?

English Channel, 1943

Alone and leaving a pale trail of smoke the green and brown Boeing B-17 bomber lumbered westward across the grungy gray of the nearly freezing water below. The famous white cliffs of Dover were just a hazy dark shoreline in the distance ahead, but the sight of land made Captain Homer Wilson feel better. With his three remaining engines running well, the pilot felt confident that he would be able to bring his battle damaged craft to a decent landing.

The sooner the better. They had one casualty. Willy Dunn, the top turret gunner, was passing in and out of consciousness because of a concussion he had suffered from the cannon shell that had wrecked their number three engine.

On the intercom Homer said one more time to his nearly worn out crew, "Hey guys, eyes sharp. Hollystone radio says there sending a plane out to follow us in."

"I see something Cap'n," said the right waist gunner. "He's at four o'clock, a little high, just moving in abeam of us."

"I got it too, Boss," from the copilot. "Can't make out what type he is though. He's painted bright red."

"OK guys, get on him and watch him close till we get a positive ID." Then, thinking of his injured gunner, Homer added, "Willy, how ya doin' buddy. What do you see? Willy! You still with—"

The captain's call was answered by the chatter of fifty caliber machine guns, followed by the copilot's surprised reaction.

"Jesus! Willy's shootin' at 'im."

"Christ, it disappeared," from the waist gunner.

"Report! Waist, what do you see?" yelled Homer, reestablishing discipline among his crew.

"I seen Willy's tracers go at 'im, then he split s'ed out'a here! He's long gone now."

"Willy! You with us up there? Somebody check him; see what the fuck is goin' on."

"He's a little woozy, Boss," said Bill Carlton, the navigator, who had already climbed to the top turret. "He's kinda out of it; says there was a biplane comin' at us and he just shot 'im!"

"Damn! If that was our escort . . ." said Homer. "We'll be over land in two minutes. Everybody eyeball everywhere; tell me if you see anything."

Twenty-two minutes later Homer shut down his three engines, blew out a full breath of air through pooched cheeks, pushed his earphones and hat off his head and slumped in his seat to watch an ambulance crew help Willy down from the top gun turret

Three weeks later, fully recovered and ready to rejoin his crew, Willy Dunn had become the brunt of good-natured joking. Nobody ever reported a damaged or lost red biplane, but through the rest of his combat tour Willy Dunn was known as "Willy Wrong War, the man who shot the Red Baron—again."

Anderson County Airport, Kansas, 1976

Glad that his white flight helmet was keeping the summer sun off the bald spot in his graying hair, William Dunn strode up to the Great Lakes biplane on the ramp in front of the main hangar of Wilson and Dunn Aviation. Already feeling a little warm in his Nomex flight suit, Willy was anxious to get airborne and up into the cooler air. As he did a careful preflight inspection of the freshly repainted candy apple red aircraft he grinned with pride at the words "Willy Wrong War" lettered in gold just below the rim of the plane's open cockpit. A touch Homer Wilson had added when he finished the eye catching paint job. The words reminded Willy of the missions he and Homer had flown together in World War II before the brass found out that they were half-brothers and separated them. "Family members can't crew together," the rule said.

Forty-five minutes later, having just finished an aerobatic flying practice session in the finely tuned Great Lakes, Willy Dunn was feeling good. He knew he was going to take top honors in the limited aerobatic tournament he would be competing in soon.

As Willy scanned the air space below him in preparation for one more maneuver, he got a surprise. A little below him and off to his left he saw a four-engine airplane flying normally except for a thin trail of smoke from its number three engine.

Curious and recognizing the old bomber as the antique that it was, Willy moved closer, thinking that the B-17 had to be one of those the Forest Service used to use for fighting forest fires. But as he got nearer Willy saw that the plane was painted correctly for wartime service in Europe. "Probably somebody making a movie," Willy thought, and then wondered what it was doing in the middle of Kansas.

Willy's radio antennas had not yet been reinstalled after the painting, so all he could do was rock his wings and wave at the plane, hoping a crewman would see him and acknowledge his greeting.

Nostalgic about the B-17 he and his brother had flown long ago in Europe, Willy continued to note details of the plane. "Man, that thing even has all its turrets and with dummy guns mounted in 'em," thought Willy.

Moments later Willy was surprised to see the top turret rotate to bring its twin .50 caliber guns to bear in his direction. Guns that began to twinkle with little flashes of fire.

In an instant Willy slammed the Great Lake's stick to the left and back and rammed the throttle full open. Diving straight down was the fastest way to get away from the strange bomber.

Seconds later as Willy recovered from the dive oily smoke and orange flame billowing from his engine blocked his forward vision. With flames in the cockpit Willy released both of his harnesses, rolled the Great Lakes inverted, and let himself fall free of the burning airplane. Suddenly blue sky and green land were spinning around his head.

Minutes later Willy felt the slapping of coarse leaves against his body as wind in his parachute dragged him through a cultivated field. He came to a stop in a heap of white nylon and green leaved stalks, with his face shoved into clean Kansas soil. Disoriented, Willy thought about how good the ripened cornhusks smelled and how odd his boot looked all covered with blood.

The next day Willy's brother and business partner visited the injured pilot in his hospital room.

"How ya doin' bro?" asked Homer Wilson.

"OK. Foot hurts some, head's a little fuzzy from something they gave me, I guess."

"Yeah, I came by yesterday and you were too doped up to make any sense. Doc says you're gonna be OK though, even with what they think is a bullet hole in your foot. Jesus Willy. How the hell did you do that?"

Willy winced a little as he scrunched to a more comfortable position and said, "You remember when we flew together in the war?"

"Sure. Willy Wrong War, terror of the Red Baron," laughed Homer, kidding about his brother's old nickname. "You were the best—well, most amusing top gunner I ever had."

"Yeah, that's what I mean." Willy scrunched around some more, still not comfortable. "Homer, you're not gonna believe this, but I was shot down!"

"Heh?"

"Yeah—how about my plane? They haven't found it yet have they? They're never gonna find it Homer."

"No, not yet. But they will soon. You can't lose a plane crash in the middle of Kansas for Christ sake."

"It's on the bottom of the English Channel and—"

"Oh man, what'd the doc give you anyhow?" Homer laughed at his brother's words, then added, "Hey, you owe the folks that invented Nomex a thanks. Without that fire retardant flight suit you'd have been a crispy critter by now."

"I guess I shot myself in the foot, man," said Willy, shaking his head.

"Hey, what do you mean? The engine caught fire; you jumped, just like you should. Not your fault."

"No, man. I mean I *really* shot myself in the foot," said Willy, trying to make his brother understand.

FEAR OF THE OPEN SKY

We don't always know why we feel uncomfortable

Comfort. And peace of mind. That's what the little fellow had felt for the past few hours. Curled into a fuzzy gray ball in his nest, he had slept. But as time passed a new sensation built up making comfort go away. He was growing hungry at the start of a new day. So he scurried toward the mouth of one of several tunnels that led from his nest.

At the end of the passageway hunger went away and in its place came uneasiness. So he stopped and his tiny pink nose went to work. His ears got busy too. At the edge of the safety of his nest in the rocky stand of sagebrush, the mouse studied the hostile outside world. Several noises and smells came to mind. He didn't know what many of them were and didn't care. They were all safe and didn't cause alarm. So the uneasiness went away and the hunger became important again.

For somebody who is only an inch tall, whose breakfast might be seeds the size of a pinhead, foraging is the main activity of life. From one bush to the next the mouse went, searching the ground. Several times he scurried across an occasional open spot to get to another bush.

He tried to avoid the open places. Having nothing between the sky and his soft, gray back made him uncomfortable. He scooted across such places quickly, with the fear of the open sky riding on his tiny shoulders until branches and leaves overhead made things better. But crossing to a spot under a new bush always required that he listen and test the air until he was satisfied that all was well in this new place.

Later in the day in just such a situation he found an odor that was wrong. It couldn't be ignored like all the others; it caused fear for the little fellow. He had found the acrid scent of a rattlesnake. All he knew was panic as he ran from the bush back into the open. The ominous feel of the open sky then added to the bad smell and put extra speed into his feet. In a few seconds he was far away, under a new sage bush. There the smells and sounds were safe so his heart slowed down and fear faded away. Life got better again, but the hunger was back.

Under the new bush he found grass seeds. So he tore the hulls apart with sharp little teeth and ate the seeds that gave him life. And life was good as the little guy foraged under the protective sage bush.

Then, a noise! There were always noises, but this one was unusual enough that fear flooded his mind another time. Yes! There it was again, and a bad scent too! Instantly he was running, and the sensation on his back was there again, for he had run out onto open ground. Now life was bad, all bad. And the sound was getting worse; it would not go away! The scent and noise were those of a coyote who also knew about hunger. But seeds were not enough to satisfy him.

The mouse ducked under a slab of rock in an ancient lava flow with his heart thumping and all thoughts of hunger gone. Only the terror of the bad scents and sounds, and the relief of being closely surrounded by rock and sand occupied his busy little mind.

The coyote's sniffing nose, digging paws, and panting, hungry jaws were trying to get at the little fellow. The nose alone, black and wet, was as big as the gray fluff of fur that was nestled securely in the deepest, darkest part of the rocks. The darkness made the terror bearable for the little mouse.

Slowly the fear died away because the coyote had decided to search for a better deal elsewhere. Now that the smells and sounds were good again the comfort of the rocks seemed less important than the hunger that had come back.

Looking for seeds, with all fears forgotten, the mouse ventured away from the rocks. But not under the open sky. Life was not good there. He didn't know why, or understand, and he didn't care. He didn't even know that every mouse who ever lived had felt the same way.

Then searching the dry land to satisfy his hunger he found a new, strange place where the bushes were tall and close together, almost blotting out the sky. And there were seeds on the ground. Big, fat grains, bigger than the grass seeds he usually found. Now life was very good indeed!

Eat a grain, hurry to the next and eat again. The mouse was on the edge of a vast sea of ripened wheat. After a time he was twenty feet into this fine place. A place where food was plentiful and there were no open spaces to cross! The little guy was happy, as happy as a mouse can get.

Then his ears found a sound, one he had never heard before. New meant bad, so hunger disappeared as his ears and nose went to work. He could not know that the strange noise was caused by machinery. A farmer's combine was making its first pass around the edge of the field of wheat, for late summer is harvest time.

The noise got louder—squeaks and hums, banging and a roar—all sounds that nature never prepared a mouse to deal with. But these sounds caused fear, and fear was something his mind could handle. He scurried quickly away from the sounds, deeper into the haven of tall, dry grain. The combine passed him by as it mowed a swath of grain along the edge of the field where the wheat bordered the rocks and sagebrush. The mouse didn't mind; the sounds had grown weaker so hunger could replace the fear. And the fine field of grain could take away the hunger. Life was getting good again.

But then the sounds came back and were getting stronger! The tiny brain could not know that the combine had gone completely around the field and was cutting its second swath of grain. Scooting quickly away from the noise the little fellow ran through the wheat stalks. Suddenly he bounced to a stop. Ahead was open space! Just dirt and stubble where the wheat had been cut away by the combine on its first pass.

Confused, and with the noise growing louder at his side and open space in front of him the mouse ran away from the combine and the open stubble, deeper into the field of grain.

The security of the tall grain made the noise easier to bear as he rested with his heart pounding. Slowly the sounds grew weaker and faded away. Soon their memory and the fear were gone too.

But as the combine passed around and around the field cutting away more of the tall grain it drove the mouse toward the center of the field. Finally the mouse found that the noise never really went away. The nervous fellow wanted to go away himself. He had eaten well that day in the fine field, and he wanted the safety of his own little nest in a nearby stand of sagebrush.

When he tried to leave he came to the vast open space where the combine had cut away the grain. To cross, he would have to bear the fear of the open sky. The thought of it made his back feel cold and exposed. With his stomach full and the noise of the machine loud in his ears all he wanted was the safety of his little home.

But the noise got louder; the crashing and roaring were worse than ever. The field of wheat was no longer a haven because the combine was finishing its work. The last of the grain was about to be mowed away.

Finally the mouse burst out into the open, his mind screaming with all the fears it could hold. He now had the awful sensation caused by the open sky to add to his troubles. With his little heart pounding and his four tiny feet buzzing along the ground the gray ball of fur bounced and stumbled in his dash to get through the open stubble and into the sagebrush. He was trying to save his life with a long desperate race across open ground. And it was working because the sound of the machine was getting weaker. Just a few seconds to go! Then he would be into the sheltering rocks and sagebrush not far from his nest.

But then a quiet shadow swept across his soft, gray back and for just a moment the talons of a red tailed hawk showed the little mouse why he should fear the open sky. Life became nothing but painful terror. And then the little life was gone.

ED AND MRS. RUTHIE

A man hadn't ought to get all twitterpated

"Well folks, did you enjoy your stay here"? asked Sam McCandless as he headed the air conditioned Mercury station wagon away from the ranch house and toward town forty-two miles away. His two passengers, Mr. and Mrs. Marvin Collins, from Dayton, Ohio, had completed their visit to the guest ranch where Sam was employed.

"Oh yes, yes indeed. I have never seen a ranch before and it was wonderful to visit a real one," said Lillian Collins.

"I'll second that," said her husband who was as happy with their week of vacation as was his wife.

"Well thank you kindly," said Sam.

"It will be a little hard to adjust back to city life," added Marvin. "But it's always good to get home."

"I expect that's true," said Sam, as he braked a little to avoid a cottontail rabbit on the gravel road.

As they reached the paved county highway they passed a large sign reading "Ed & Mrs. Ruthie's Bed, Breakfast, & Cattle Company" which prompted a question from Marvin.

"You know, I've been wanting to ask about the name of this place. I know the lady who runs it is called 'Mrs. Ruthie.' Is that really her last name and who's Ed, anyway"?

"Lott'a folks ask about that," said Sam, with a grin. "It ain't her first *or* last name—neither one. Actually, the lady you are referrin' to is Svetlana Katerina Badrinovich McCandless. Ain't no Ruthie in that."

"Your wife?" asked Marvin, remembering that Sam's last name was also McCandless.

"Nope! I've never been that lucky. Never had a wife, probably 'cause I never come across one anywhere near like Mrs. Ruthie," said Sam, enjoying his passengers confusion.

"Y' see, she is Mrs. Ed McCandless, my sis-in-law. Now that brings us to the Ed part of your question. He's my brother, lot older than me. Or, least he was till two years ago when too much tobacco caught up with him and his heart decided he should quit smoking."

After a short pause for everyone to be politely somber, Sam continued.

"Now, about your question, there's still the name Ruthie haingin' around, right?"

"Yes," said Lillian, "I would like to know why you all call her Mrs. Ruthie."

"Well," said Sam, enjoying the couple's curiosity and using a polished speech he'd developed over many trips hauling visitors to town, "therein lies a story, and you got just time enough to hear it betwixt here and the airport."

"Y' see, I got a nephew, my brother Ed's boy, Charlie. Ed was a widower back then. We always call the boy Chuck but town folk called him Charlie. Anyhow, back in '54 Chuck was graduating from high school and so was a young lady name of Ruthie.

"Now Chuck, he was really taken with little Ruthie; she was cuter than a pup in a little red wagon. Anyhow, Chuck had brought Ruthie to the ranch once or twice, back when all we did was run cattle, and he wanted to impress her some by invitin' her out to the branding."

Sam paused for a moment to raise his head and one hand a little in response to a similar greeting from a pickup approaching in the other lane.

Then Sam continued. "Now what with you folks bein' experienced with ranch life now, you've probably heard about the branding each year."

"Oh yes," said Lillian from the back seat. "You do it to mark the new calves. We learned about that."

"Yep. Sure enough," said Sam. "Back then we ran a lot more cows than we do now, and each spring we had maybe a hundred calves to deal with. So, we'd bring in all the cows and calves nearby to the corral and collect the calves in holding pens, leavin' the cows outside. The cows just stood there chewin' and lookin' silly like cows most always does. Then we'd bring calves a few at a time into the corral and do the job on 'em— rope 'em, throw 'em, and such, like used to be done.

"Y' see, nowadays, and even back then, most ranches use a squeeze chute for the branding cause it's a whole lot easier. But Ed, he still stuck with the old way cause he just liked it better.

"Now branding that many calves was a lot of work for the hands at one ranch, so the custom was that neighbor folks would come t' help. The men worked the calves and the ladies brought chow of all sorts. Late afternoon, when the work was done we'd have a party. That's what Ed liked and so did everybody else. That's why Chuck invited little Ruthie out.

"Anyhow, on that morning we had the irons hot in a sage wood fire, a bunch of calves in the corral, a few hands present, and things goin' along. Then Ed saw one of them little German beetle cars, a pure white convertible, comin' up the road.

"About then Ed muttered, 'Who do ya expect that is?'

"'That's Ruthie, Pa,' said Chuck who had been keeping an eye out for her all morning. 'You remember, she was here a few weeks ago.'

"'Oh yeah, yer little cutie with the name I can't pronounce.'

"'Ruthie?'

"'No, no, her hind name! I can say 'Ruthie' just fine,' said Ed, with a smile. Both he and Chuck had kidded around about his earlier attempts to pronounce the name Badrinovich.

"'Well anyhow, you'd best wipe yer nose an straighten yer tie, then go welcome our guest.'

"'Sure Pa, sure will,' said Chuck as he pulled off his gloves and laid them on a fence rail where one promptly fell to the ground.

"Noting this and Chuck's excitement, Ed said, 'Hold up a minute son. Yer lookin' like a love-struck pup 'cept yer tongue ain't haingin' out quite as far. Remember, a full growed man hadn't oughta get all "twitterpated" over one of them sweet young things no matter how charmin' she might be.' Ed had got that word from the old movin' picture Bambi we had all gone to see when Chuck was just a little tyke. Probably the only one Ed had ever seen.

"'Yeah Pa,' said Chuck.'"

"Well," continued Sam, "Chuck he gave each boot a wipe on the back of the opposite leg of his jeans and stuffed in his shirt tail. I could tell he noticed that the armpits were all sweaty with grime from the corral dirt. He pulled off his hat, ran his fingers through his hair once, then set his hat back on his head to an angle he thought Clark Gable might have picked—he'd been to the movies the night before—and started toward the bug car. That thing sure looked white out there on the ranch.

"'Charles, is that you?' said the lady in the driver's seat. 'I hardly recognized you. You appear much differently when you come to town.'

"'Yes ma'am, it is. Good morning Mrs. Badrinovich, I'm glad you could make it out here too.' And then, 'Hi Ruthie. I'm sure glad to see you.'

"Chuck helped the two out of the car and I could tell he felt embarrassed some when he saw how spiffy clean and fresh they were, him bein' all sweaty like he was.

"Both Ruthie and her mother was real blonds, with the same hair styles and the same figure that would turn a man's head anywhere. Both wore crisp, starched white blouses that looked the same. Ruthie had them red slacks they used to call 'pedal pushers.' You know, the ones with the cuffs just below the knees, leaving the lower leg nicely bare. Her mother had some light blue slacks that went all the way to the ankle.

"About then Chuck brought the ladies over to meet me and Ed. We was standing by the fire, it being my job to keep the irons hot and all.

"'Pa, this is Ruthie Badrinovich, and her ma, Svetlana Katerina Badrinovich,' said Chuck, easily pronouncing the names correctly and grinning at Ed.

"Ed just stood there, with his head down a little, like a school boy at his first dance. For a minute there I thought he might put his hands behind his back, poke a toe in the dirt, and mumble 'pleased ta meet ya ma'am.'

"Anyhow, Ed didn't. Instead he just said 'Good morning, Mrs. Ruthie.' He'd been wrestling with the names and just gave it his best shot.

"Then, pointin' at me, Chuck says 'And this is my Uncle Sam, he's my pa's brother.' Chuck was blushing enough to show even through the grime on his face, and Ruthie's ma was enjoying everybody's embarrassment. My oh my, them two gals looked like shiny new dimes in a mud hole standing by that holding pen with sage smoke blowing everywhere. Especially the older one. She was just oozing charm all over the place as she looked at Ed and said, 'I am so pleased to meet Charles's family.' I tell you that woman's voice could really make a feller smell the roses.

"Anyhow, after a little polite chit-chat Ed suggested to Chuck that there was calves to brand and that maybe he ought to find a nice place for his guests to watch the proceedings and get hisself back to work. So Chuck took his lady collection over to the corral where they could perch on the top rail and see real fine. This suited the other fellas good too. Them two ladies surely could decorate a fence.

"Then Ed said to me, 'Lordy Sam, y' ever seen a gal like that?'

"'They're something,' I said. 'Mother and daughter, heck they look like twin sisters, except one of 'em has a little more mileage on her.'

"Ed frowned some at my comment. That's when it dawned on me that in spite of his little speech to Chuck about not falling for some gal just because she's a charmer, my brother Ed was about as 'twitterpated' as a feller could get. Mrs. Ruthie, as he had called her, had done him in.

"After a few minutes Ed got up nerve enough to wander, real casual and all, over to the fence a ways down from where those gals was sittin'. Next thing you know, Mrs. Ruthie came down the fence to sit on the top rail by where Ed was standin'. Little Ruthie, having noticed that Chuck was over in that part of the corral about t' grovel in the dirt with a particularly large bull calf, followed her ma.

"Chuck had got a loop on the bull's head and had pulled him in, throwed and hog tied 'im in real quick time. I expect he was hopin' little Ruthie was watchin'. So there's the bull-calf layin' on his right side in the dirt with his front hooves and his right rear one tied together with a piggin' string. Chuck was on his butt in the dirt with both hands stretchin' the critter's left rear leg out straight behind to clear the way for—ah—for what comes next.

"Another ranch hand comes up to give a shot of Black Leg serum, and another plants a hot brandin' iron on the calf's rump. Lots'a smoke and all, and since the calf had the scoures it let fly right up Chuck's leg. Got him good."

"The scoures, Mr. McCandless. What is that?" asked Lillian Collins as Sam expertly guided the station wagon around a tight curve in the road.

"Oh, well, that spring we'd had a lot of rain and the grass was real good. Sometimes calves get too much rich grazin' and it gives 'em some diarrhea, what we call the scoures. That tends to make brandin' a less pleasant experience than it might otherwise be if ya get my drift."

"Anyhow," continued Sam, "Chuck finished with that calf and walked over to the fence to see how little Ruthie was doin'. This was just as my brother Ed was tryin' to start up a little conversation with Mrs. Ruthie, him lookin' silly as any teen-ager.

"Mrs. Ruthie looked at Chuck standin' there smellin' like burnin' cow hair and too much rich grass an all, and said, 'Charles, is that you?'

"About then Ed got in the conversation and said, 'Yes ma'am, that there's my boy. He smells a lot better if ya hose him off some.'

"'Yes,' Mrs. Ruthie said, 'it does appear that he has stepped in something.'

"About then the fellas in the corral had noticed Chuck talkin' to the ladies. They'd all been watchin' them two gals doin' about as fine a job of sittin' pretty as they had ever seen.

"'C'mon Chuck, the ladies can hold up the fence without your help,' yelled one of the hands. Then another fella who's got a critter down and needs a little help yells, 'Hey Chuck, get yer butt over here, we got some other heifers that need your attention.'

"Chuck made some offhand remark to the crowd in general and went back to work. A few moments of polite embarrassment passed between Ed and the two gals who had blushed properly at the remarks and gestures the ranch hands were usin' to tease Chuck. Ed didn't know what to say next.

"Mrs. Ruthie did though. She just looked up at Ed with her big blue eyes and asked, 'My my, just what are those gentlemen doing to those cows?'

"I'd figured out by then that Mrs. Ruthie was a lot more interested in my brother Ed than she was in the cattle business, but Ed sure didn't know that.

"'Well,' says Ed, 'first off, ma'am, they ain't cows. They's all calves.'

"'Calves?,' says Mrs. Ruthie. 'They look too big to be baby cows.'

"'They're near to bein' yearlings. We should'a branded 'em sooner. The heifers ain't too bad, but some of the bulls are hard to handle.'

"'Bulls?' says Mrs. Ruthie. 'You said they are all calves.'

"'Well, yeah,' says Ed, not knowin' how to go about explaining the birds and the bees, cow style, to strangers. So he says, 'They's two kind of calves. They's bull calves and heifers. A heifer's a female that ain't been, ah, that hasn't had a calf yet,' said Ed with only a glance at young Ruthie. The bull calves, they's self-explanatory if you take a look at the back end of one.'"

Sam paused to wave at another approaching pickup, then continued his story.

"About that time one cowboy stuck a quart sized bottle of liquid into a hog tied calf's crotch and swished it around some."

"A bottle? What is that all about?" interrupted Lillian, ever eager to learn more about ranch life.

"Oh, that's disinfectant for after the, ah, the operation," said Sam, trying to avoid embarrassing his two passengers.

"Operation?"

"Yes ma'am, the operation that ah, that converts a bull calf into a steer, so to speak."

"Oh, the castration," said Lillian, not the least bit shy.

"Yes ma'am," said Sam.

"Well," said Sam to his passengers, "just like you just did Mrs. Ruthie asks, 'What is that man with the bottle doing?'

"Then Ed says 'Ah, well, these bull calves has come to a milestone in their biological careers, if you get my meanin'.'

"I'd figured she was teasing Ed, but she looked puzzled enough that little Ruthie said 'Oh Ma,' and leaned over and whispered something in her mother's ear.

"'Lordy!' said Mrs. Ruthie to Ed. 'You mean they cut off their chikie-chikies?'

"'Heh? Their what?' says Ed.

"'Oh Ma,' said little Ruthie again, then everybody blushed some and laughed.

"Just then one of the hands opened a gate and let some of the animals they were finished with back out with the cows. Noticing that most of them just went back to grazing, Mrs. Ruthie commented, Those creatures do not seem to have been hurt much.'

"'Nope,' said Ed. 'Y' take that big fella over there, he's just had a dose of black leg serum shot inta his shoulder, he's bleedin' from both his crotch and his new ear mark and his butt's still smokin' from the iron, and looky there. He just walks out t' pasture looking for somethin' to eat. Tells ya somethin' about the mental activity of cows.'

"'Cows?' I thought you told me that he wasn't a cow,' said Mrs. Ruthie. She clearly enjoyed making Ed talk about his cattle.

"'You're right ma'am,' said Ed. 'He's a shiny new steer. I was just now speakin' as a generalization.'"

About then the station wagon with Sam McCandless and his guests pulled into the airport entrance. "Well, we're almost there," said Sam.

"And now you've probably figured out that the lady finally married my brother. She wrapped him up in a ball and married the socks off him. They had twenty-six years of the best marriage anyone could ask for." Then Sam, a little misty eyed, added, "But Ed's gone now."

"As for the name of the place," continued Sam, "Ed had christened the lady 'Mrs. Ruthie' on the day they met, not bein' good at European names, and it stuck. She's always gonna' be Mrs. Ruthie."

"What about Chuck and little Ruthie," asked Lillian.

"Oh they never lasted long," said Sam. "Little Ruthie ran off with a football player and Chuck, he went to the University of Arizona. He's down in Tucson married to a pretty little dark eyed gal name of Victoria. Chuck, he never took too well to ranchin'—steppin in the scoures and such."

"Anyhow," continued Sam. "Turns out Mrs. Ruthie grew up on a farm in Poland where they raised horses for circuses and parades and such. Probably knew more about farm animals than Ed did. A fine horsewoman too—she could work cattle with the best of 'em. Old Ed—heh—he was married before he figured out that Mrs. Ruthie found love at first sight, and was just settin' the hook to reel him in that day at the brandin'."

Misty eyed again, Sam added, "Ain't life grand?"

Having reached the terminal Sam dropped off his happy passengers and headed back to the ranch.

THE LINEUP

Sometimes the system works; sometimes it doesn't

As usual the intruder picked his victim carefully. This time it was a real estate saleswoman he had noticed a week earlier. He always chose a young woman whose physical appearance and body language were just right. And always one of those modern professional types who didn't stay at home with her kids where she belonged.

A little snow had accumulated on the shoulders of his dark overcoat as he waited in the shadows with his collar up to ward off the winter night. Soon Gladys Benson came home and entered her front door, right on time. The house was set back from the pleasant residential street and separated by a low hedge from an almost identical home next door.

His hand in the right front pocket of his coat was wrapped around the metal object he kept there for these occasions. It gave him a sense of power as he walked toward the front door. After looking around to see that no one was watching, he knocked.

As the door opened in answer the intruder shoved through the doorway, then stepped into the room, closed the door behind him, and shoved his right hand forward. Surprised, Gladys looked at the cold metal the intruder was holding and then into his eyes. She would have screamed if his left fist hadn't crashed into her jaw.

Less than fifteen minutes later Mrs. Rebecca Morgenstern, an elderly widow who lived alone in the house next door, remembered that she had not let Muffin in. Old and lazy, the hungry tabby cat would be waiting by the back door.

A cautious woman, Rebecca flipped on her bright back porch light and pushed back a lace curtain before opening the door. There, caught in the sudden illumination, was a man in heavy, dark clothes crossing Rebecca's yard from her neighbor's back porch. He quickly turned his head away and ran down the alley. Moving to a different window Rebecca saw that her neighbor's back door was standing wide open, with no lights on inside. Forgetting about Muffin, Rebecca dialed 911.

Minutes later a police car arrived. The two officers could get no response by knocking at either the front of Gladys's house or in back at the open doorway, so they entered, searched, and found the young woman in her bedroom.

After an hour of flashing lights from other police cars, an ambulance, the fire truck that also answered the 911 call, and the confusion of a dozen people coming and going, Rebecca was told that her neighbor Gladys was dead. Even though a uniformed policeman had done so earlier two detectives, taking notes, had Rebecca describe again the man she had seen cross her back yard.

"It's dark outside, ma'am. Are you sure you saw the man's face clearly?" asked one detective.

"It is not dark in my yard with my porch light on young man. Like I told the other policeman earlier, I saw things just fine, thank you!"

"Yes ma'am," said the detective, as he wrote in his notebook.

The next afternoon Janet Winslow, a recent law school graduate, met with her supervisor, Denise Stevens, who was head of the county public defender's office.

"OK Jan, you get this one. The city cops had a rape/homicide last night and they think they have the perp in the tank right now." Denise handed a thin folder to Jan.

Jan looked at the arrest report and muttered, "Christ, old Bert again."

"Bert? Bert who? Oh, you mean the arresting officer."

"Yeah, I saw him on a case two weeks ago. Some of those guys, they just arrest the nearest homeless type whenever they need to make a collar."

"Looks like a good bust, Jan. They've got a good eyewitness and they found the guy walking along the sidewalk a block from the crime scene. Fits the description and he's got a record—been picked up twice for vagrancy."

"See, I told you. A homeless guy."

"Aw c'mon Jan," said Denise. "We've got a pretty good police force here. You just haven't had your coffee yet, right?"

"OK, OK. I better go see my client."

"Yep, and you better hurry. The DA's office wants a lineup this afternoon to give their witness a chance to identify the guy. You can go down there, sword held high, and defend the helpless underdog one more time," said Denise with a grin.

Like a lot of new public defenders Jan thought that the police tended to pick on the lower income people. But Denise knew that as Jan got more experience with criminal law she would come to realize that society's lower economic class has far more than its share of both criminals and victims.

Late that afternoon Jan met with Assistant District Attorney Joe Hernandez who she knew would take the matter to a grand jury if he felt his case was strong enough. Both attorneys were ushered into a somewhat darkened room by a detective. Through a large one-way window they could see five men in the brightly lit adjoining room standing side by side. All five men were of the same general build, height, and age, and all were dressed in dark clothing, each with a heavy overcoat.

"OK, what do we have?" asked Jan.

"There's two cops, a guy from the motor pool, one civilian volunteer, and, of course, our suspect," replied the ADA. "All match the witness's description; everything kosher with you?"

"Yes, looks all right to me," said Jan.

"OK, bring in Mrs. Morgenstern," said Joe as he drew a curtain over the window.

The detective opened the door and a uniformed officer came in with an elderly lady, wearing light framed spectacles, who walked with a cane. Joe introduced Rebecca Morgenstern to Jan and explained what would happen and asked if Rebecca had any questions.

"Nope sonny, I understand completely. I've seen this done on TV."

Jan rolled her eyes at the remark, and the detective smiled.

"All right Rebecca," said Joe. "You just take a look and see if the man you saw in your back yard last night is here. OK?" Then Joe pushed the cutain aside.

Rebecca stared for a moment, then walked closer to the glass, nodding her head affirmatively. "Yep, that's him. The second one from the left."

"Are you very sure, Mrs. Morgenstern. It was dark last night; think carefully," said Jan.

"It was not dark in my yard last night Missey. My porch light is bright, just like in that room there. Second man from the left."

Joe closed the curtain and said. "OK Mrs. Morgenstern, lets wait a mnute or so, then take another look. They look a lot alike."

Jan looked at Joe and saw that the ADA was not happy with Mrs. Morgenstern's choice.

"All right Mr. Hernandez, the lady made her choice," said Jan.

Joe swept the curtain open again, and said. "OK, ma'am, which—"

"Still the same fella, sonny. Second one from the left; that's him."

"OK, Mrs. Morgenstern. Thanks for your help." Disappointed, Joe nodded at the uniformed officer who escorted Rebecca out of the room.

"Well, not your suspect, right?" asked Jan.

"Fraid not. Second from the left is a cop. Sergeant Robert Jackson."

"Gonna be kinda hard for your goons to hold my guy then, isn't it?" said Jan. The ADA glared at her and didn't answer as both left the identification room.

"Your boy's not out of the woods yet lady. According to the police reports when the crime went down that witness wasn't using her glasses. We screwed up the lineup. May have to do it again."

"Not a chance, fella. She's already seen your suspect. Another lineup won't hold water," replied Jan with a satisfied grin. "Let the poor guy go."

Then, noticing that Sergeant Jackson was watching her as the other police officer kidded him about the identification, Jan waved and left the station.

Three weeks later the intruder was standing in the shadows again with his hand clenching the comforting object in the right front pocket of his overcoat. This time it wasn't snowing, but a cold wind was making him uncomfortable.

He didn't have to wait long. His chosen victim had already come home to her doublewide mobile home as expected. Inconspicuous in the dark neighborhood, he stepped the two steps to the door and rang the bell.

Expecting the pizza she had ordered on her way home, Jan Winslow carelessly opened the door and saw an arm reach through the widening gap in the doorway. And clutched in the intruder's right hand was a detective sergeant's badge.

"Sergeant Jackson, what are—"

His left fist smashing into the side of Jan's head stopped her questions, forever.

THE FLIGHT OF THE OLD VETERANS

Eventually, every pilot wonders about getting too old to fly

Jake McClusky stood by the door watching the other man fumble with his keys trying to open the big Master padlock. Bill something or other he had said his name was. Jake was impatient because inside could be the culmination of a life long dream.

Having worked hard for the last few decades, Jake was now able to buy himself a "warbird," a World War II fighter airplane. And only one model would do. A North American P51-D Mustang.

Bill rolled the hangar door open on its steel rails.

"Well, there she is," said Bill. "Since it ain't my airplane, I can't tell ya much 'cept I know it did fly in the war. It's log books—they're in the cockpit—show stuff about battle damage and repairs."

The two men walked around the machine once with Bill pointing out superficial details here and there.

"Hey, go ahead and check the cockpit if ya want. I got lots'a time."

"Thanks, I'd like to."

"Ya gotta climb up the front of the wing—"

"Yes, I'm familiar with that."

Jake stepped one foot on the left front tire, climbed over the leading edge of the wing and stood beside the cockpit. A pain in his leg reminded him that the simple climb had been easier last time he'd done it more than forty years earlier.

The canopy opened effortlessly, a sign that the plane had been well cared for. Jake stood for a few moments looking over the wing surfaces and the upper fuselage of the Mustang.

On the seat was a tattered brown accordion folder tied with a black cord. The aircraft records. Jake climbed into the seat and held the folder on his lap. With his hand on the control stick he sat in the familiar cockpit growing more attached to the machine by the second.

"The guy said there was battle damage" thought Jake as he sorted through the paperwork. He found the entry; someone had put a yellow mark in the margin knowing that proof that the airplane was a "purple heart combat veteran" would significantly increase its sales appeal.

Jake began reading.

"Patched 20mm hole rt. wing, station—" The writing was faded, hard to read. Something more about repairing some control cable damage.

"Number seven cylinder destroyed by twenty-millimeter hit, replaced—" Jake jumped ahead and another entry caught his eye. The front windscreen had been broken too.

Jake felt a queasy sensation as he realized that the damage had a familiar pattern to it. He looked at his own reflection in the small rear vision mirror and was startled to see an old man's face and thinning gray hair where the familiar image of a tanned young aviator would have been last time he had sat in such a cockpit. He reached up to the right front of the small, but two-inch thick glass windscreen, and ran his fingers along the aluminum frame at the edge. The glass was smooth and clean, but the aluminum showed evidence of having been reworked.

Realizing that he had read the logbook's words before, Jake skipped to the signature at the end.

Mst. Sgt. Scott Holloman, USAAC #2938 . . .

Scotty. Jake's own crew chief in Belgium.

Jake knew then that he was going to own that airplane, the same one he had flown over Europe nearly forty years earlier.

Emms River Valley, 1943

"Blue Leader to Blue Flight. Move in tight and sound off."

"Blue two," responded Jake, trying to keep his voice from sounding like that of a 12 year old.

"Here they come," said Blue Leader. "Remember, no chasin' strays, just keep 'em off the bombers."

Jake looked at the approaching German Me-109 and FW-190 fighters and wondered if his stomach would hold. Too much adrenaline, pulse rate too high, eyes trying to see everything and not seeing anything, Jake had all the symptoms of a first combat flight. Fortunately, he was sitting in the best fighter aircraft ever designed, and his Mustang was performing perfectly. But Jake was wondering how many butterflies one stomach could hold.

"McClusky. Stay with me, no matter what! Got that?" Jake heard the voice of his flight leader.

Jake keyed his mike and said "Yeah."

Embarrassed by his not so professional response, Jake added, "Blue 2 with you, Boss."

As a new man on his first combat mission Jake had been assigned to fly wingman for the group leader. He was expected to stay fixed in position relative to the lead aircraft and otherwise avoid getting himself, or anybody else, in trouble.

Watching the right wing of the lead aircraft, Jake saw the aileron drop as lead began a diving turn to the left. Jake responded instantly and stayed right in position off lead's right wing, slightly higher, slightly aft. His task now was to keep his aircraft in the same position relative to Blue 1 and provide cover. The lead aircraft would make the decisions, choose the targets, choose the turns. Jake was damn well not to get out of position.

That lasted for about thirty seconds.

Suddenly the sky was filled with careening aircraft, so many that Jake could not identify half of them. He found he had a new worry, the possibility of a midair collision.

Then as often happens in such a "fur ball," of confusion, Jake found himself almost alone. No group leader to stick to, in fact no group. Jake couldn't see any friendly fighters nearby and the main action seemed to have drifted away from him. Trying to collect his wits, the green fighter pilot headed toward the bomber formation where he could be of most use. He hoped that American B-17 gunners were good at recognizing Mustangs.

Jake was learning quickly. His head never quit moving as he scanned all the sky he could see. So, he saw the Me-109 that turned in behind him from eight o'clock low, almost in position to shoot. Jake shoved the stick hard left till he had a ninety degree bank then back to the center, with all the back pressure he dared hold. As tight a one eighty turn as he could make.

Not the best thing to do, apparently. Jake felt and heard a cannon round pass through his right wing. No serious damage, but Jake knew his combat career would span little more than the past five minutes if he didn't think faster.

Rolling back level, Jake looked around for his tormentor. Knowing he should never be straight and level for any time at all, Jake started another tight turn just as the right side of his canopy exploded and he could see nothing but brilliant yellow, then red. He smelled both smoke and blood, felt a blast of cold air, and noticed a sudden change in the sound of his engine.

Flying more by instinct than by visual cues, Jake tried to get his act together. Through a red haze he could see his instruments well enough to stay in level flight and to know he was heading almost west. His engine was leaking coolant into the slipstream leaving a noticeable trail of white vapor advertising the presence of his crippled aircraft. Unable to bail out because of the jammed canopy, Jake knew he was as good as dead. With little other choice he made a gentle turn toward his base in Belgium, an airfield that seemed a thousand miles away.

As Jake's vision improved he evaluated the condition of his aircraft. He had reduced the power some because of the sounds from the damaged Merlin engine and discovered that he had serious control system troubles as well. He was lucky to still be flying.

As he limped toward home Jake's worst fears materialized. An FW-190, attracted to Jake's vapor trail like a coyote who's found a crippled cottontail, was overtaking the damaged Mustang. With its speed advantage the German would soon be in position to fire.

As he beat his hand against the damaged canopy release Jake had a fleeting, irrational thought. It wasn't fair. He was a combat fighter pilot, but would never have a chance to pen a combat mission into his logbook.

Then, in his rear vision mirror, Jake saw the German aircraft drop its nose and with its speed advantage take a course that would cause it to pass directly under Jake's own crippled plane. And the reason for this maneuver was clear. The German was avoiding a near collision with another Mustang that had appeared from nowhere and was making a ridiculous diving pass from behind over the top of the German plane.

The other Mustang pilot had flown out of a perfect position to fire on the FW-190 that was about to destroy Jake, and had instead made himself a target!

Jake knew that because of their low altitude in a few seconds the two planes, the American in front and vulnerable to the German, would pass right up in front of his own crippled machine.

As he saw the two planes come up into view he mashed the firing button and unleashed a barrage from his six .50 caliber guns. He had been able to align his craft somewhat in spite of his damaged controls and did his best to destroy the German. Jake hardly realized that his machine gun fire was endangering the American P-51 almost as much as it was the German aircraft.

With a resounding explosion the German plane burst into an orange fireball through which Jake's own plane had to pass. Again Jake's vision was flooded with brilliant orange. He felt the searing heat and smelled gasoline. Fragments of debris hit his aircraft as he was tossed about by the turbulence. Jake had flown into the fireball, but his Mustang didn't like it there and flew right back out again.

Seconds later, with his ears ringing, his eyes stinging, his neck warm with his own blood, and his crotch wet where his bladder had let go, Jake was again flying straight and level toward Belgium.

Squadron Briefing Room
Near Turnhout, Belgium, 1943

Second Lieutenant Jake McClusky sat in a steel folding chair in the Quonset hut with his bandaged head aching. He was listening halfheartedly to conversation about the gun camera film the four men in the room had just viewed—film from Jake's own aircraft.

"OK, Sergeant, what did you see?" The captain's voice was more than a little exasperated.

"I seen McClusky shoot the shit out of that 190—sir."

"What else?"

"I seen 'im fly right through the fuckin' fireball. Jesus. Like divin' inta hell—"

"Damn it! Before that, Sergeant."

"OK Captain, there was this other Mustang too. He'd a been dead meat if McClusky hadn't got that Kraut."

"Awright Sergeant. Did you recognize that Mustang?"

"Ah, kinda' hard to tell, sir. Only there for a few frames."

"A few very clear frames, Sergeant. F' Christ's sake the squadron markings, look at the damn tail numbers. Who was it, Sergeant."

"Ah, sorta looked like McClusky's plane, sir."

"Damn right it was. Now Sergeant, look at the numbers on the leader of this reel we just watched."

"Sir, that's McClusky's tail number. That's the film I took out of his plane after he brought the wreck back here."

"Jesus Sergeant. You've screwed up again. You got the damn gun camera film reels mixed up! One of the other jocks will be pissed when he finds your screw up gave his kill to some new guy! Unless, of course, you are prepared to explain how McClusky, here, managed to shoot this little snapshot of himself!"

The captain turned to Jake.

"McClusky! What the hell you got to say anyhow?"

Jake looked up, the ache in his head momentarily increasing as he moved, and said, "Cap'n, I don't know no plane—shot the right one."

"Christ," said the captain. "Medic's got him so doped up he can't think."

The fourth man, the squadron intelligence officer who had debriefed the returning pilots, finally spoke.

"Ease off Sam. Nobody else claimed a 190 kill, and nobody but the lieutenant here thinks he flew through a fireball."

In his own defense the beleaguered photo operations sergeant added, "Capt'n, I checked all the other films. They all match aircraft numbers just fine. Ain't none missin'."

"And they match their respective pilot's debriefings too, Captain," added the intelligence officer. Then, after a short pause, "We have another mission tomorrow; the sergeant has work to do. We all do."

Taking the hint from the more senior officer, the irritated captain dismissed the sergeant who scurried out of the room. Then he muttered, "I gotta get some blowups of that damn Mustang. I'd swear it's McClusky's plane."

Jake wondered if he was going to be allowed a couple of beers since he wouldn't be flying for a while.

Arizona, 1995

Jake's hard and fast decision to own that one particular airplane didn't help him much when he bargained price with the Mustang's owner, but it did make reaching a deal quick. Six weeks later the aircraft had a fresh annual inspection, a few minor repairs, and was ready to fly. During the same time Jake had also added some cosmetic improvements. One of these was a new paint job that matched the colors the Mustang had sported when Jake had last flown it over Germany, forty-two years earlier. Details included the correct squadron markings and tail number, and a single, small, black swastika below the canopy on the left side of the fuselage that marked his one singe victory in aerial combat.

Jake had also used the time to get himself a private pilot's license. This was not difficult because of his military flying experience. However, the FAA flight examiner who tested Jake's ability in the air expressed concern for Jake's advanced age and his plan to fly a P-51. Knowing that military fighter aircraft can be physically demanding of even a young man, the inspector signed off the paperwork grudgingly, admonishing Jake not to fly stressful aerobatic maneuvers.

After spending time in the cockpit practicing emergency procedures, Jake was ready for his first Mustang flight since World War II. He taxied to the departure end of the field's single runway and performed each task on his takeoff checklist. Jake let the engine warm up thoroughly before unleashing the full sixteen hundred plus horsepower the Merlin could develop on this cool, winter morning. He would need it all for the relatively short runway.

As he sat waiting Jake thought of the medical examiner who had signed his medical certificate. This man too had cautioned Jake to take it easy, pointing out the frailties of old age. "Both your heart and your brain are not as tough as they used to be," the physician had said.

It had taken Jake most of a lifetime to save enough money to own a Mustang, and he brushed aside thoughts of failing health. He wanted to fly and he felt as comfortable in the cockpit as if he had flown the plane yesterday.

Though most won't admit it, lots of good pilots talk to their airplanes. Jake made a point of it. He felt that it was good for the pilot-airplane relationship. It encouraged the machine to tell its pilot more about things that might be bothering it as it bores through the sky.

The cockpit was good now, familiar, like an old friend. "You and I got our first combat flight together," thought Jake, "back when we were a shiny new airplane and a freshly minted pilot."

"A hell of a day for both of us," he thought as he remembered that flight. The terrifying experience had haunted the recesses of Jake's mind for years afterward.

"Well, now we've both been around some. We're just a pair of old veterans who have a chance to enjoy the sky without being shot at anymore."

Thinking of the risks of flying the high performance warbird without recent experience, Jake added out loud, "OK, let's be good to each other," and began his take off roll.

With the stick all the way back Jake slowly opened the throttle and the plane gathered speed. After a couple of minor swerves the Mustang was well under control, and he moved the stick forward just enough to lift the tail wheel off the runway. As the Mustang reached flying speed Jake eased back on the stick a bit and the warbird lifted into the air.

Jake always loved this moment in any takeoff. The time when his Mustang changed from an awkward ground vehicle into a thing of power and beauty, with a grace of its own that rivaled anything nature ever built.

Just a few feet in the air, Jake retracted the landing gear and as he climbed he soaked up the familiar vibrations and sounds the plane was giving him. "All is well" said the Mustang, speaking to Jake in its own special language.

Thirty minutes later Jake had completed all of the aircraft checks and practice maneuvers he had planned on for this first flight. His old skills were coming back fast and he felt as if he had been flying the Mustang all his life. So he decided it was time to have some fun. Jake took the plane to an altitude of 10,000 feet in an area well away from any of Arizona's controlled airspace. And he forgot all about what the stress of flying a high performance aircraft might do to a man of his age.

Noting his northerly compass heading, Jake dipped the mustang's nose into a shallow descent and opened the throttle. Then, bringing the stick back, He brought the Mustang into the first half of an inside loop. He felt the familiar heavy G-forces pushing him down into the seat and draining blood from his head. As he approached the top of the loop Jake rolled the inverted mustang into straight and level flight. Now heading south he had executed a nearly perfect Immelman turn.

Yelling with excitement for the whole state of Arizona to hear and grinning like a kid at Christmas, Jake looked out of the cockpit to clear the space below him in preparation for another maneuver. What he saw took his grin away.

Confused and a little frightened by what he thought he had seen Jake shook his head, stretched a little and tried to lose the light headed sensation from the maneuver he had just completed. He thought about what the medical examiner had said about old age and blood pressure.

Again the old pilot looked at the land below and what he saw made his legs feel weak. None of the tan color of the Arizona desert. Instead, he saw lush green pasture and farmland mixed with patches of timber and a small river passing down a pleasant valley. Again Jake felt the knotted stomach, the adrenaline, and fear he had known long ago. He knew exactly where he was.

The feel of the Mustang was a bit different too. Subtle differences, as though the airplane also recognized the scene from the nightmares that had plagued Jake for years after the war. Below and ahead another Mustang flying near the ground was leaking a thin, white trail of engine coolant.

Jake never knew whether he chose to turn toward the stricken aircraft or if his plane itself made the choice but soon they were diving toward the airplane below. And then he saw the German fighter that was moving in behind the crippled plane making the vapor trail.

Jake reached for his mustang's arming switch and found it wasn't there. With a sick feeling he glanced at the leading edge of his left wing, smooth where the muzzles of three .50 caliber machine guns once had been.

Jake had an altitude advantage on the attacking craft, and even though the German was approaching his target at his maximum rate of speed, Jake was overtaking him. He could easily nail the German before he got too close to the crippled Mustang, but not with an unarmed aircraft.

Jake tried to believe that he was looking at another warbird, or maybe someone making a movie. But Jake and his Mustang knew it wasn't a movie. And, as in his nightmares, Jake could not control his actions.

Jake approached the German from a little to one side, so the German would be sure to see him, if he had his act together. The man did, and dropped his nose slightly. At the same time Jake passed directly over the slower craft, hoping his turbulence would upset the German's shot. This caused both aircraft to pass under the damaged Mustang, and, being close to the ground, both had to climb back up.

Passing up in front of the crippled Mustang, and in spite of the high G-loading he was experiencing, Jake thought he felt or heard banging noises and an explosion behind him. He continued the high-speed maneuver into a steep climb, and then, executing his second Immelman of the day, found himself well above the action, looking for the German.

Jake didn't search long. Outside his aircraft all he could see was dry chaparral and the saguaro cactus of the Arizona desert. Feeling nausea from the adrenalin surge he had experienced, the tired old pilot tried to find reality.

Since only about three minutes had elapsed since his first high stress aerobatic maneuver, Jake thought of the medical examiner's comments, and wondered about hallucinations from G-loading.

Confused and feeling a little dizzy, Jake banged his fist on his leg in frustration. After a lifetime of saving and planning the infirmities of old age were cheating him out of his dream.

Badly shaken, Jake knew he had better get his nerves sorted out and get on the ground. With a heavy heart the old pilot turned toward his airfield.

Knowing that he might be making his last landing as a Mustang pilot, Jake wanted it to be perfect. Concentrating hard he gently set the heavy warbird down without a swerve or bounce of any kind. Pilot and machine, one smooth team.

Jake taxied to his hangar, completed his engine shutdown checklist, and leaned back in his seat as the Merlin's twelve cylinders and the huge four bladed prop came to a stop. Savoring the smells and inevitable noises of the cooling engine, he listened to the airplane tell him it had enjoyed the exercise. Jake tried to forget about his hallucination, but the bitter thoughts wouldn't go away. He was thinking about the probable loss of his medical certificate and the end of his flying days.

With a heavy heart the old pilot climbed down and walked around the fine old airplane, touching a wing section here, a prop blade there, sharing the moment with an old friend.

But when Jake reached the tail of the aircraft his legs turned rubbery and he grabbed the vertical fin for support. He stood there a long time staring at the single fresh .50 caliber bullet hole in the Mustang's polished aluminum tail.

BUSTED DOLLAR GRADE

Just a little history lesson

Sean McIntyre, a brakeman for the Northwestern & Pacific Railway, stepped out of the red, wooden caboose at the end of the short freight train and deftly hopped onto the station's concrete platform. With vapor blowing from his every breath and slapping his gloved hands together because of the cold, Sean walked through the six inches of new Montana snowfall to the freight office.

"Cold out there, hey?" said the elderly man behind the counter. Dressed in a white shirt, dark vest, and a green plastic visor to shield his eyes from the single, bare overhead light bulb, Orin McKenzie was clearly a man who worked indoors.

"Damn right it is," grumbled Sean. "Some of us are not blessed with a fine hot stove like you be." Sean headed to the potbellied stove and stood with his back to it, close enough to nearly scorch his wool pants and mackinaw.

Then, glaring at Orin, he said, "And what in thunder is that thing you've put in my caboose might I ask?" Sean's wet wool gloves were steaming from being held close to the cast iron stove.

"Just a box, Sean. Just a box."

"Hah, a box he says. It's a damn *buryin'* box it is! Not supposed to be in my caboose. Should be in the freight car."

"Only got one freight car and it's full. Then we got the coal tender, three tank cars, and just the one passenger car."

"Put the vile thing in the passenger car then."

"Sure Sean, I could do that. Put a dead convict in with those two nuns and those seven little girls from the church school over in Bozeman. Just the thing to cheer up their trip to Spokane."

"Yeah, well, I got a passenger too I'm telling you. Henry Ridel is engineer this trip and his twelve year old is riding with us. The boy Mikey gets space in my caboose if anybody does."

"Sure Sean. And you have another passenger too." Orin nodded toward a man Sean hadn't even noticed sitting alone on a bench across the room. "This fella came in just a minute ago and paid a caboose fair."

"Oh, hell," grumbled Sean scowling at the man. "I hope you don't mind sharing passage with corpses now do ya?" Then Sean took a last wistful look at the warm stove and headed back out into the winter night.

The man sitting on the bench didn't speak or smile. His heavy black beard and sweat stained Stetson hat scrunched down low in front hid any possible expression on his face as his dark eyes followed Sean to the door. After a few seconds he stood, nodded at Orin, and followed the brakeman into the cold.

The freight manager was glad to see the stranger leave. Something he couldn't quite put his finger on about the man's manner had made Orin uncomfortable. And it seemed odd that the man's worn cowboy boots were dry in spite of the snow outside.

Twenty minutes later the train was heading west toward the mountains of the Idaho panhandle. A young coal stoker named Bill had a good fire going in the iron stove and the caboose was warming up nicely. Bill, Sean, and an elderly freight handler named Martin were sitting in the front of the cramped caboose while young Mikey sat to the rear with the quiet stranger. Thinking about maybe getting a poker game going Sean looked for playing space in the crowded car. Remembering the stranger and thinking of his own senior role on the crew Sean felt introductions were in order.

"I'm Sean McIntyre," he said. "This be my caboose." He then told the stranger his co-workers' names and said, "And what do we call you might I ask?"

The stranger looked up and said, "You can call me Buck."

"Ah, the name's Buck, is it?" said Sean, angling for more information from the passenger.

"No, it ain't. I just said you can call me Buck."

After a few quiet seconds, Sean said, "Well, that's how things will be, hey?"

Uncomfortable with Buck's demeanor, Sean turned to Bill and said, "Help me move this accursed box down to the floor. Make a table for a wee game it will."

"Hey, it sure is light," said Bill after the two men had moved it to the floor. "Who's in it anyhow? Letterin' on the side says 'Property of the U.S. Government, Department of Prisons'."

"Bill reached for a canvass pouch nailed to the top of the simple pine box, opened the flap and took out some paperwork. "Let's see what the papers says." Bill read the paperwork soundlessly, moving his lips as he dealt with each word.

"Heh, just some dead convict named Spencer J. Peabody. Died at the age of ninty-six. Family wants him buried in Spokane. Looks like old Spence here just finished up a life sentence; that'd be my guess."

As the other men chuckled a little, Buck didn't even smile.

Uncomfortable, Sean took the papers from Bill's hand and put them back. "OK, laddies, who's got a deck, hey?" Turning his back on the stranger, Sean made it clear that Buck was not invited to join in.

As the game got underway Martin scratched at his gray beard and muttered, "Peabody, Spencer Peabody. Sounds kinda familiar. Wonder what he did?"

Meanwhile, Mikey had been sitting near the stranger. "My name's Mikey Ridel, Mr. Buck." The boy held out his hand.

The stranger looked at the boy for a few moments. Then, with a pleasant smile, he took Mikey's hand and said, "Pleased to meet you, son."

"I'm going to Spokane." said Mikey. "That's all the way over in Washington, you know. I'm going to visit my cousins for Christmas. Hope it's not as cold there like it's been here in Montana."

"Probably will be. Winter's cold everywhere," said Buck, his voice quiet enough that no one else noticed.

As the two sat listening to the klick-klack of the steel wheels passing rail junctions, Mikey fiddled with a box he was holding in his lap. Finally, he said, "You want to see my money collection Mr. Buck?"

"Money collection? Sure, son, why not?"

Mikey proudly displayed a couple dozen pennies, four three-cent pieces, two dimes and a quarter dollar. Several of the pennies were older large cent size and the rest were more recent Indian head pennies. "See here," said Mikey indicating a particularly shiny specimen. "I've even got one of the new 1909 pennies with Mr. Lincoln's picture on it."

"Well, son, you're a coin collector, looks like," said Buck. Then he looked out the window and said, "Long time ago when I was about your age I wanted to collect old stamps. Folks said it would be silly though, so I didn't."

As more track klick-klacked away the two talked about things of interest to a twelve year old boy.

At the poker game Martin, stopping in mid play, said, "Hey, I just figgered it out. I know who's in this here card table we been playin' on."

"C'mon, old man, your ante," said Bill.

"Oh yeah. I'll pass." Martin tossed his cards down and asked, "You boys know where we are?"

"You think I don't know where I be on track I have been riding these fourteen years?" said Sean. Starting up 'The Grade' is where we be."

"Yep, you're right. The Grade. Four miles of uphill, *steep* up hill, headin' into the—"

"You gonna play, or gab?," said Bill. "And anyhow, what's that got to do with this box?"

"Ya know what's right at the top of this grade? Trestle Number 1042, that's what," said Martin. "Highest one in the panhandle by gosh. Goes right across Tamarack Gorge."

His turn to deal, Bill slapped out the cards forcefully, indicating that the game was in progress.

"Well, y' see," continued Martin, "You whippersnappers is too young to know what this grade used t' be called. Back about fifty odd years ago when I wasn't much older'n Mikey there, they called this the 'Busted Dollar Grade'."

"You in or out?" muttered Bill.

"Y' see, westbound, with them old locomotives we had then this grade was a real boiler-buster. Engines crawled up no faster'n a man could walk."

Bill slapped down his cards in disgust. "OK, old man, lets get the history lesson over with so's we can play."

"What has that to do with this box we've all been blessed with, I'm askin' ya?" added Sean.

"Well, purely for the education of the young, I'm gonna tell y'all about your own line's colorful past. And about Johnny Peabody." As he spoke Martin pointed down at the pine box with one index finger.

"This here is Spencer Jonathan Peabody, at your service—well, present and accounted for anyway. It seems that back then this line hauled a military strongbox on its way to Alaska. And the train bein' slow right here on the grade made easy pickin's for old Johnny Peabody. He and two buddies used to stop the train and bust open the strongbox lookin' for payroll money. They done it three, four times till one train had some soldiers on it along with the box."

The three men sat looking at the cards and a few silver coins lying on the pine box. Then Sean spoke. "How did the name Busted Dollar Grade come to pass then?"

"Well, Old Johnny, he was a colorful fella, and damn good with a rifle. Seems he would intimidate the train crew with a little shootin' demonstration. He would make somebody throw a silver dollar up in the air and slicker'n greased lightnin' he'd put a bullet on that dollar. Then somebody would pick it up, all bent t' hell by a .25 caliber slug from Johnny's little Stevens rifle. Johnny carried it just for that purpose, folks said. Course I never seen it, but train crews talked a lot about Johnny in them days. Called this the 'Busted Dollar Grade' back then."

As the men spoke Buck watched quietly, his clear eyes peering out from under his hat.

"Wow," exclaimed Mikey who had been hanging on Martin's every word. "Ya think he's been in jail ever since?"

"Sure has. Accordin' to a newspaper I seen a few years back Johnny got to repentin' his wicked ways and became a model prisoner. Learned to read and write in the pen and then wrote what he called his memoirs— that means memories ya know. Bunch of stuff about how he regretted his evil doin's and how he wished he had been a better citizen."

"Heh, never knew you could read," said Bill.

"Better'n you, probably," continued Martin. "That's why I remembered about Johnny Peabody. Lots of folks claimed he wrote stuff tryin' to get his self a parole so's he could get back up here and pick up gold he'd stashed somewhere."

"Wow," said Mikey. "There's buried treasure up here?"

Martin smiled at the boy and said, "Nope. Army said that the strongboxes Johnny busted into didn't have much but some military script and some papers—dispatches—they called 'em. Seems like old Johnny was a lot better at shootin' dollars than he was at stealin' 'em."

"Awright now," said Bill. "In an hour I gotta go take my turn passin' coal t' the firebox. But first I'm gonna finish cleanin' you fellas out. So come on old timer, play cards!"

As the game got back into action, Mikey and Buck sat together.

"Wow, Mr. Buck. Train robbers right here! I bet Mr. Peabody's two friends got away. Maybe they had some high times robbing other trains, huh Mr. Buck?"

"Or maybe they went to prison too, or maybe didn't live long enough to get there," said Buck.

"Oh, I hadn't thought of that."

"Let me tell you somethin' son, somethin' real important. When you're a young man the outlaw way of life can look exciting, even tempting. But it ain't good, not at all."

As he spoke Buck opened his sheepskin coat and took a small leather pouch from an inside pocket. While the coat was open Mikey noticed a revolver stuck inside Buck's belt.

"Here, I have a little souvenir for you."

"A souvenir?" Mikey took the pouch in his hand.

"Yep, but you can't look at it right now." Buck took the pouch from Mikey's hand and stuffed it into a pocket of the boy's red and black wool coat.

"Now, if you ever get to thinkin' you'd like to try some of them 'high times' you mentioned, well, let what I gave you remind you of how the outlaw way of life worked out for Spencer J. Peabody." Buck nodded toward the pine box.

"Yes sir, Mr. Buck, I will. And thank you Mr. Buck, but—"

"Thanks for showing me your coin collection, Mikey. Now I need to talk to those fellas over there."

Abandoning his quiet voice, Buck said, "Mr. McIntyre, might I have a word with you?"

Sean turned to face the younger man and said, "Sure, and what might you be interested in, Mr. Buck, or whoever you might be?"

"I want you to signal your engineer to stop the train."

"Hey, stop the train, he says."

"Yes, I want to speak with your engineer."

"I think we will leave the business of running the train to us lads who work the line, Mr. Buck. Barring emergencies, this train doesn't stop unless the engineer says so."

Buck looked hard into Sean's eyes for a few moments, then stood up. His tall frame seemed huge in the cramped caboose, and the card game was forgotten.

"I thought I might have trouble convincing you with words," said Buck as he drew his revolver. "So, now you have an emergency."

Sean signaled the engineer. A few minutes later, just short of the top of the grade, Buck had the train's crew bunched together just below the cab of the motionless locomotive. Clouds of vapor drifted everywhere in the cold air and the sound of live steam hissing from various valves mixed with the low roar of the firebox.

All eyes were on Buck as he spoke, holding his little Hopkins & Allen revolver.

"All right boys, I know one or two of ya likely has a pistol hidden away somewhere. But right now is not the time to use one. Mr. McIntyre here and I are going to take a walk up the grade a little way. Now if one of you was to do something foolish, why I could get all excited and start shooting. Now I'm a bum shot with a revolver and somebody like say Mr. McIntyre here might get hurt."

With that Buck jabbed the revolver into Sean's back and the two started up the track through the fresh snowfall.

As they disappeared around a bend in the rail bed, Bill, Martin, and the others said nothing, each waiting for somebody else to do something. Then Henry Ridel, Mikey's pa, climbed back into the huge locomotive's cab and jumped back down with a big Colt Peacemaker .45 in his hand.

"Nobody does this to my tra—"

"Hey, wait Henry. Looky there," said Bill.

And there was Sean walking back down the rail bed through the ankle deep snow.

"Sean! Where's that fella Buck?"

"Right behind me, he is," said Sean as he glanced over his shoulder. "Hey, not a minute ago he was right there!"

"What happened? Where'd he go?"

"Blessed if I know," said Sean. "But the lad was right about an emergency. It seems we have a broken track, we do. Big rock has fallen, knocked a rail right out of line."

"Where?" demanded the engineer.

"Just a bit this side of the trestle, Henry. We would have gone right into the gorge were it not for that fellow Buck and his pistol now. And the sisters and their wee lassies with us!"

"Let's take a look—"

"'Tis not a bad break," said Sean. "We'll have her fixed in—"

"Looky, Pa," said Mikey, tugging on his father's coat and with his other hand pointing toward the tracks in the fresh snow.

"Look at what, son?" said the engineer as he put the Colt inside his heavy, wool mackinaw.

"The foot prints. There's one set for Mr. McIntyre going up the line and one coming back. But there's no tracks for Mr. Buck."

In silence the men stared at the snow in the moonlight, and then at each other.

"All right," said Sean. "Let's be getting out the tools now laddies."

An hour later the misaligned rail was repaired. The locomotive had a good head of steam and with Bill at the firebox it was crossing Tamarack Gorge.

In the caboose no one spoke for try as they might they had not been able to find any sign, not even a track in the snow, to say where Buck had gone.

Finally, Sean, who had been sitting on the end of the pine box, stood up and said, "C'mon laddies, lets be getting this box off the floor—not at all a proper place for such."

The three men hefted the box back onto the seats where it had been earlier in the journey.

"Whoof!" grunted Sean. This box, she's certainly heavy enough now."

"Hey, look, the nails has been pulled up!" Bill pointed to the lid of the pine box. It had obviously been opened.

The three men looked at each other as Sean opened the lid further. The white haired body inside was that of a tall, thin man with a pale face covered with the brown liver spots of old age. He was dressed in the light blue cotton shirt and pants of prison attire. Spencer J. Peabody's feet had on a simple pair of worn prison issue canvass shoes—wet canvass shoes. In spite of his advanced years, the deceased's withered features resembled the stranger, Buck.

"Jesus, that's—"

"Close the lid," demanded Martin.

Sean closed the box, and Martin fetched a hammer from a nearby toolbox.

Meanwhile, Mikey, sitting on one of the rear seats holding his boxed money collection just as he had earlier, remembered the souvenir Mr. Buck had given him. He took the soft, deerskin pouch from the pocket where Buck had put it, loosened the leather thong, and shook out the contents. Slowly he turned the object over in his fingers and hefted it in the palm of his hand. With a happy smile Mikey put the big silver dollar, somewhat bent from the strike of a rifle bullet, into the box with the rest of his coins.